I0629559

CATCH FIRE 2

TINA BROOKS MCKINNEY

Taboo Publishing

www.taboopublishing.com

TABOO PUBLISHING

Taboo Publishing
Catch Fire 2 Copyright © 2014
Tina Brooks McKinney

ISBN: 0982108931
ISBN-13: 9780982108932

DEDICATION

This book is for the readers that continue to support me during my literary endeavors. Without your support, I would have given up the ghost a long time ago. I cannot tell you how much you mean to me.

I thank my heavenly creator for being able to express my thoughts through words. I hope through my words I can inspire and invoke thoughtful conversations.

ACKNOWLEDGMENTS

This is always the hardest part of writing a book for me. I'm shouting out the special people who have impacted my life. A lot of the names stay the same. I have been blessed with an amazing group of friends and family who love me in spite of me. Starting with my husband, William McKinney. I don't know what I did to deserve such a loving husband. I live and breathe for this man who has shown me what love really is! My children Shannan and Estrell who have forgiven me for all the things I didn't know about being a parent and loved me in spite of my faults. My wonderful parents, Ivor and Judy Brooks who showed me the meaning of unconditional love. I am blessed to be your child. My sister Theresa Brooks for her loving support, I can't thank you enough for all that you do for me.

I have the usual suspects to thank for their love and support through this writing journey. My longtime girlfriend, Andrea Tanner, (thanks for allowing me to be a part of your beautiful wedding! It made my year.), Angela Simpson and Valerie Nixon. I've known all three of these ladies for most of my life! Theresa Gonsalves, my sister from another mother. She has become more than just a friend. She's my rock and I can't tell you how much I love her. Sharon Jordan, my other sister and road dog. I love you boo. Joyce Dickerson, the hardest working woman in the business, thanks for all the love you send my way. Barbara Morgan I love your spirit and the way you embraced me! Antoinette Gates, my literary princess, your continued support means the world to me!

I've got to cut this short, if I've neglected to mention your name it's not because you mean any less in my heart. Ricardo Mosby, Sharon Richardson (god bless you both and the baby), Launa Harcum and the Keough crew, Sharon Russ, Muriel Broomfield-Murray, Marvin Meadows, Sabrina Meadows, Candice Mumford, Detris Hamm, Kimberly Moss-Floyd and Patrice Harlson, (my other two sisters!), Shelly Halima, Sandy Coleman, Mia of Hair Therapy. A special hello to Brodie Crowder, keep on making my girl happy!

CHAPTER ONE
JORDAN BREE

I was sitting in the dining room, sipping coffee, when Lacy came in from her morning run. I had to give it to her, she was completely dedicated when it came to staying in shape. While I, on the other hand, would rather pluck out my eyes than exercise.

As roommates, we complimented each other perfectly. Where she would love to exist solely on fast food, I forced her to eat healthy by cooking most of our meals. When I went on a chocolate binge, she'd worry the shit out of me to walk or run with her.

Temperamentally, we were equally yoked as well. Lacy understood my need to be alone sometimes. She didn't press me when I needed my space, nor did I have to make up a thousand excuses why it was necessary. That was my biggest fear when I first asked her to move in with me.

If I had one complaint, it would be Lacy's habit of leaving a trail around our apartment. You could visually mark every move she made in the mornings. From the open water bottle in the sink, the empty breakfast bar wrapper on the counter and the towel she almost always left something behind. When she comes home, it's the running shoes by the door, her sports bra on the sofa, her iPod and keys on the counter and the paper towel she used when she wiped her face. It wasn't that she was a slob. It was more like a ritual for her. The first few months, it drove me nuts. Now, I looked the other way until she cleaned it up.

"How was your run?"

"It's hot as hell out there."

"You knew that before you went out there. How was the run?" I tried to hide my smile behind my cup.

"It was good. You should try it. It does the body good."

"That's milk you idiot. Milk does your body good. Running fucks up your knees. Just wait until you're older. You'll know what I mean."

"You are only a year or so older than I am. Get out of here with that mess." Lacy picked up her towel from the sofa arm and blotted her neck and back.

"Okay. You don't have to believe me. When you can't stand to wear those fuck-me pumps anymore, you'll say, I should have listened to Jordan." I could not hold back my laughter any longer.

"First of all, I don't wear fuck-me pumps. That's all you. My heels rarely get over four inches. Second of all, running has nothing to do with my being able to wear heels."

"Are you sure?" Joking with Lacy was fun. She took everything I said so seriously and I was cracking up on the inside. One time, I told her exercise was going to kill her. For a solid week, she didn't think about running. Then one day she came right out and called me a liar. She's been running like Forest Gump ever since.

"I'm not paying you any mind Jordan. You play too much. When you get all fat and shit, don't ask me to help you off the couch."

I felt the smile slip off my face as my old insecurities resurfaced. I was close to tears just thinking about it. I used to be fat. It was my mantra. I was a card carrying member of the chubby girls' club. But this was not my reality anymore. My despair must have been written on my face because Lacy came over to me and placed her arm around my shoulders.

"Oh, damn, I'm sorry. I can be so dumb sometimes." Lacy wore this tormented look on her face. She actually looked worse than I felt.

"Girl stop. You know how I get. Don't pay me any mind."

"You know I would never let you get that way right?"

Lacy pulled me by the hand over to the floor length mirror by the front door. "Do you see this beautiful girl staring back at you? She is fucking gorgeous! You make tongues fall out when you walk in the room."

"Tongues? Seriously?" I said giggling, feeling slightly better.

"Yes tongues. You could make a man slap his momma."

I turned and gave Lacy a big hug. I just loved this girl. It was so hard to believe that I hated her ass when I first met her. We had gone through so much negative stuff and now we were the best of friends. I would do anything for her and I honestly believed she would do the same for me.

"Shut up, fool. Ain't nobody gonna slap their momma 'cause of me."

"Hmm…How you going to find out if you never go anywhere? You live like a damn hermit. We're young. We are supposed to be out jumping up and down in the clubs, being seen, not holed up in this apartment like we have some curfew or something."

Lacy actually made a good point about my staying home all the time. The sad part was, I didn't even realize I was doing it. When I first met Lacy, we lived in a group home and we actually had a seven o'clock curfew. Since moving to the apartment, I could count on one hand, how many times I'd been out past that time. It wasn't a conscious decision on my part. It's just the way it was. "You know good and damn well we couldn't get in any club. We would be carded and embarrassed at the front door."

Lacy's smile slipped a little. "I know, right. We would be told to go home and take a nap."

"I don't know about all that. I might be able to pass. I have never been carded. You on the other hand, look very young. Especially when you wear your hair in that ponytail."

"This hair-do is just for running. Give me twenty hot minutes and I can whip it up big girl style. Don't act like you don't know."

"Calm down boo-boo. I know you know how to make it work!"

"That's right. I'm glad you recognize. I'm about to put some water on this body. Maybe we can get out the house and do something. These walls are starting to get to me."

"You know, these walls are getting to me too. I'm gonna go get cute."

"Don't get too cute! I might try to choke a bit—" Lacy's face turned bright red. Her chagrin was written all over her face. I wanted to laugh. Lacy knew how I felt about the word bitch. Joking or not, I didn't think it was cute. I only used it when I was mad.

"Damn girl, you know I didn't mean no harm. It's hard to change something I've been doing for years."

"I know. I'm getting better about hearing it since I've been hanging around your crazy butt. I really do appreciate your willingness to curtail your usage of it; especially as it relates to me. It brings back so many bad memories to me."

"I know, that's why I try so hard not to say it around you period."

My mother used to call me a bitch on a daily basis. She called everybody bitch. It didn't matter if you were a male or a female. My siblings didn't seem to mind, but for some reason, it cut through me like a knife. It was so negative and I hated it. I frowned as my mood instantly soured. I no longer wanted to get cute. I wanted to hide out in my room until my dark cloud passed.

"Oh, no you don't." Lacy frowned.

"What?" I asked feigning ignorance.

"That look on your face. I can tell you are about to go to the dark side. I'm not going to let you shut down on me. Not this time. You can have your pity party later. We are about to get out and do something fun for a change."

Lacy could be a hard task master at times. Unfortunately, bipolar disorder doesn't work that way. I couldn't turn off my feelings on demand. My anxieties tended to take over and the only thing I could do was ride it out.

"I'm sorry, girl. I can't right now. If I go out, I'm liable to fuck up your day too."

"The only way you could fuck up my day, would be for you to go in your room and shut that door. Hiding out in there is not going to change a damn thing. Feeling sorry for yourself won't help either. Now move that ass. We are about to do something."

As much as I wanted to give into depression, today, I felt like fighting it. When I hid from my truths, they never went away. Survival for me meant, living through my truths. I turned my smile upside down. "Where do you want to go?"

Lacy clapped her hands together like a child. "That's my girl! We could go to the movies or maybe even dinner and a movie." Lacy's smile could have lit up the entire room.

I frowned again. "A movie? Why do I have to get all fine for a movie? If we are just going to watch a flick, we can rent one from Netflix and call it a day."

"Wait, hear me out. There is this new place in Buckhead where you can go to the movies, have dinner and even get your drink on, all at the same time. I hear a lot of people our age go there. It should be fun."

"First of all, neither one of us are supposed to drink. Second, I still don't want to get dressed up to sit in the dark."

Undaunted, Lacy said, "We could go see The Butler."

"You want me to get dressed up to go see a movie to remind me that our ancestors used to be slaves? How is that supposed to cheer me up?"

"It's a story of our determination and perseverance!"

"Are you out your rabbit-ass mind? Do you seriously want to be in a theater with a bunch of half-drunk angry black folks? You know that movie ain't going to do nothing but piss folks off."

"Dag. I really want to see it. I don't care if it makes me mad."

"Don't get me wrong, I want to see it too. But when I get pissed off about it, I don't want any white people near me."

"Well damn. I guess you do have a point. I am not trying to catch no case either."

"Exactly. We can do that shit all by ourselves."

"If the movies are out, where do you want to go?"

"I don't know."

Lacy threw her hands up in the air. "What about skating? Do you skate?"

"Hell no. I'm not trying to bust my ass or break any of these bones by putting wheels on my shoes. It's difficult enough walking in heels."

Lacy obviously saw through my subterfuge. "I'm taking it you didn't learn how to skate when you were a kid?"

I hung my head. This was another reminder of how fucked up my childhood was. Every other kid in the hood knew how to skate but me! My mother wouldn't waste her money on something she couldn't eat, drink or smoke. I was beginning to think I would never out run those haunted memories of my past. "No. We didn't get skates as kids. Besides, if we had of gotten them, we probably wouldn't have been able to keep them. The kids in our neighborhood stole everything. They would take the shoes off your feet and the clothes off your back and would think nothing about it. Then they would have the nerve to say what's up the next day like nothing happened."

"Don't feel bad, I can't skate either. But the difference between me and you is, I don't mind busting my ass trying it. Long as I don't break anything, I'm good. I'll try just about anything once."

"The only way you will get me to do that, is if we rented out the entire skating rink. That way, if we fell, no one would be there to laugh at us."

"Girl, bye. I am not wasting my money on some dumb shit like that. I don't care about falling. If I fall, I'll be the first one to laugh. Who cares if someone else laughs too? As long as a motherfucker is laughing with me and not at me, we cool."

"How you gonna tell the difference? I ain't nobody's joke."

"Just because someone laughs at you, it doesn't mean they are making fun of you. You just need to learn the difference. The only way I know how to do that, is to put myself in laughable situations. What about bowling? You can't possibly fall doing that."

"I have never done that either. Can't you break a nail? I just got my nails done." I looked down at my perfectly painted fingers.

"You should kill yourself with that one. You have got all these excuses as to why you can't do something. Why don't you come up with something that you want to do?"

"I can't think of anything either."

Lacy said, "Girl, we have got this banging ass apartment yet we never entertain. We have the pool ten steps away and we haven't even taken a close look at it, let alone get in it."

I was getting frustrated. "If there's something you want to do, do it. Don't wait around for me."

"Will you wait a minute? I was only suggesting places to go because it will give us a chance to get out and meet new people."

"I'm not interested in meeting new people. I have all the friends I need right here. Don't you remember how difficult it was for me to get use to you?" I walked into the kitchen and poured myself some soda out of the bottle in the refrigerator. I avoided looking at Lacy because I didn't want to see the look of disappointment on her face. I knew she meant well but it was difficult for me to change who I was.

"God, yes. I remember. You were simply hateful. And don't think I don't know it was you that tried to poison me with those damn cookies. I might not have said anything about it, but I know."

I spit my drink out over the kitchen counter. I coughed so hard, I thought I was hacking up a lung. "I don't have any idea what you are talking about," I said once I finally caught my breath.

"Don't lie about it now. I knew you got me as soon as my face started swelling up. Served my ass right for touching your cookies in the first place."

I was flabbergasted. The whole time, I thought I had pulled a fast one but Lacy knew about it the whole time. I looked at her with narrowed eyes. "If you thought you knew, why didn't you report me to the police or Mrs. Gates?"

"For what? They were your cookies. What you did with your cookies was no crime. I had no business taking them. Of course, I was a little salty at first. I wanted to fuck you up real bad because I could have died behind that shit. But, at the end of the day, I couldn't blame anybody but myself. I just know not to touch your motherfucking cookies anymore."

I tried my best to keep a straight face and continue to deny any wrongdoing, but I couldn't. The whole situation was suddenly hysterical to me. I laughed, long and hard, until tears were running down my face. It was the kind of laughter that made your belly hurt when you finished. It felt good.

"Oh, so now the shit is funny? I almost died." Lacy looked angry.

I sucked in my smile. "I don't know what you are talking about." I was neither going to confirm or deny any knowledge of the incident. Some secrets were best kept close to the chest. I thought this was one of them.

"You can play dumb all you want. I know, you know, I know. It's cool. Really, I'm not mad. I'm just thankful your friend Brody was around to save me. Without his help, I would be fertilizer by now."

I put my glass in the sink and ran some water into it. "You probably ate something else that didn't agree with you and didn't know it." I walked into the living room and picked up the remote to turn on the television.

"Why are you turning on the television? I thought we were going out somewhere," Lacy whined.

"We were but you couldn't make up your mind where you wanted to go."

"I couldn't make up my mind? I gave you three choices. If you have got any other ideas, please share."

"I'll think about it while you go get showered up."

"Okay, cool." Lacy trotted off to her room.

I released a pent up sigh of relief when Lacy allowed our conversation to drop. I didn't like to be reminded of those times when I first met Lacy at the group home. I was so bitter from having had four years of my life stolen from me due to a stupid prank. It was a terrible time for me.

I went up to my bedroom to find something to wear. Since I had already taken my shower, I only had to change. For what, I didn't know. I walked over to the bannister and called down the stairs. "What are you putting on?"

"You haven't said where we were going."

I was getting so irritated, I wanted to scream. I didn't understand how this whole conversation started. I was perfectly content sitting at home. I was brushing my hair when the perfect idea came to me. "I got it. Jeans and sandals will be perfect, and hurry up," I called down the stairs.

"You came up with something? Great, I will be ready in fifteen minutes."

***

"Where are we going?" Lacy asked as she wrapped a scarf around her head.

"North Carolina." I yelled back over the rushing wind. We had the top down but the windows rolled up. Even so, it was difficult to hear when Lacy used her normal talking voice.

"Are you freakin' kidding me? What in the hell is in North Carolina?"

"It's really not that far. I went up there with Brody one time. You are going to love it." I patiently explained like I was talking to a petulant child instead of an adult.

"What are we going to do? Just drive there and come back?"

I could hear the annoyance in her voice. "Part of me wants to keep it a secret, but I can tell you are going to bug the shit out of me until I tell you."

"That's not fair. I just want to know. What's the harm in that?"

"Okay, but you have to promise me you are not going to laugh at my idea."

"No way buddy. If you tell me something jacked up, I can most assuredly promise you, I'm going to laugh."

"Then, I guess I won't tell you." We drove for several seconds before Lacy gave in.

"Fine, I won't laugh." She sounded salty when she said it so I snuck a peek to make sure she wasn't tripping.

"I've always wanted to go gem mining or even gold mining. I saw this place the last time I was up here, so I thought we would go there."

"Gold mining? You mean like we saw on that television show, "Gold Rush?""

"Sort of, but not that complicated."

"Will we have to climb and look under rocks and shit?"

"I sure hope not. If that's the case, we will swiftly turn around and call it a day."

"Why didn't you look the place up on line and check it out first before we took the trip?"

"Did you have something else in mind to do? I thought this would be different. Can you at least try to keep an open mind and see what happens? If we don't like it, we haven't lost anything but gas and time."

"Girl, chill. I'm down for whatever. I was only busting your chops because I got it like that."

I snuck another look at Lacy and she was smiling from ear to ear. I wanted to be mad at her for busting my chops, but her smile was infectious. "Why you do that? You know I was nervous about telling you. You just got me all worked up for nothing."

"'Cause it's fun getting you going. At least it got you from dwelling in the past. I'm actually pretty excited about this adventure especially since I've never done it either. I'm not sure about how I'll feel if I mess up this shirt, but it's all good. How long before we get there."

"It's about an hour and a half from our building. Turn on the radio and chill. Enjoy the breeze. We are going up in the mountains too which is pretty cool. Damn it, I should have bought a camera."

"What do you need a camera for? Your phone has a great camera. It doesn't make sense to carry both."

"I don't know why I forget about my phone. I keep wanting a phone to be just a phone. See, I knew you were good for something."

"Fuck you Jordan. I'm good for a lot of things. If you don't know, then you better ask someone." She chuckled.

Just like that, my mood changed again. My moods were swinging like a pendulum, back and forth. One minute I was happy and relaxed and the next, depressed and stressed. This was one of the symptoms of my disease. Normally, my medications were pretty good at keeping me regular, but I was beginning to think I was in need of a tune up. "How come you don't have up and down mood swings? How is it that you are consistently happy all the damn time? Shit is annoying."

"I get my bad days just like everybody else. I just try not to let it show. Besides, I think my expectations are lower. I don't require much to make me happy so each day I'm constantly finding something to smile about."

"What the fuck does that mean? Your expectations are lower? Are you trying to say mine are high or unrealistic?"

"This don't have nothing to do with you boo. You asked me how I was able to be the way I am and I'm trying to explain it the best way I can. You have to find what works for you."

For some reason, her words troubled me. She was actually younger than I am. Yet, in so many ways, she appeared wiser. I actually felt a little bit jealous. "I wanna be just like you, when I grow up." We both started laughing.

"Wow, look at those trees? We are really getting up there. Is that smoke?" Lacy asked while pointing out the window.

"Haven't you ever heard of the Smokey Mountains?"

"Stop lying, they actually smoke? Are they really on fire?"

I was happy that I wasn't the only one who thought that about the smoke. "No. It's actually a foggy haze caused by the humidity in the air. Kind of cool, ain't it?"

"Yeah. I wonder what it would look like up close. I mean if we were right in the middle of it. Would it be like an optical illusion or something?"

"If you are hinting to me that you want to do some hiking, I'm not biting that dog."

"No, you don't have to worry about my going down in the woods. Niggers in the woods are not a happy mix. These mountains are also known for black bears. I'm good."

"Thank God. I was hoping I didn't have to leave you here," I said laughing.

"Oh hell no! You mean you would leave me? What kind of shit is that? You know I would never leave you."

"You should kill yourself for saying that. I didn't even leave you in the group home for long. So you know I wouldn't be leaving your ass in some damn woods."

"I was about to say, I might love you like a fat kid loves cake, but don't get it twisted."

Lacy was dead serious. I knew firsthand how Lacy settled her problems so I wouldn't be challenging her on that. She wasn't going to have any problems out of me.

CHAPTER TWO
LACY BATES

I was excited about our impromptu trip. We stopped at one of the most colorful places I had ever seen. The mine was in the middle of a small Indian village. The streets were alive with tourist walking and shopping. Tiny shops lined the narrow streets bustling with people. We were in the Cherokee Village, one of the few reservations in North Carolina. Every shop hyped their authentic artifacts and fudge. I was sure the fudge was more of a lure than the actual mining we had planned to do.

"I already know which shops you are going to," I said laughing.

"You know it. When I came up here with Brody, all of these shops were closed. I just want to go in and sample some of the fudge before we go."

"Sample? That's all you're going to do?"

"What? Can I at least get a little to take home? It would be a sin to come all the way here and leave some of this chocolate heaven behind. Before you turn your nose up, you should try some too."

"I'm not turning my nose up at it. I'm just watching what I put in between these lips before it settles on my hips."

"Do you boo. I'm getting some."

We were driving slowly through the village. The ratio of motorcycles to cars was two to one. "Have you seen any other black people? 'Cause I'm looking and I ain't seen one."

"I know right. I was just thinking the same thing myself."

"You sure it's safe for us to get out of the car? Those motorcycle riders are looking kind of rough."

"They are not going to kill us in broad daylight."

"Well let's just make sure our black asses are back in the car and headed down the mountain before the sun goes down. I'm not trying to have them making an example out of us."

Jordan laughed out loud. She pulled off the main strip and stopped in front of Gem Stone Mines. She popped the trunk as she turned off the car. "Let's put our purses in the back. I don't know how physical this is going to get and I'm not trying to mess up my purse."

I asked, "Ok, but what about money? I doubt they are going to let us do this shit for free."

"Don't worry about money. I got this one. You can comp our next little adventure." Jordan pulled several twenty dollar bills from her wallet and zipped up her tiny purse. I admired the fact that she could get away with carrying such a small bag. I, on the other hand, couldn't function with anything less than a mini duffle bag. I had a little bit of everything in my bag. I was always prepared for anything. I decided against putting my bag away, instead I used the shoulder like straps to secure it on my back. It might not make any fashion statement, but I wasn't about to be caught off guard if something went down. As a rule, I never left home without it. I even tried to talk Jordan into carrying one herself. She claimed she didn't need to as long as she had me. I had mixed emotions about this because there might come a time when I needed her ass to save me. Like the time we ran up on someone from Jordan's past. If I wasn't carrying my knife, we would have had to let the chick get away. I cut that bitch deep, to the white meat, and today she's a non-motherfucking factor. I didn't believe in wasting opportunities. The God I served, set it up and I gift wrapped it.

"Lacy, you are not going to need that big ass bag. You can't even call that thing a purse." Jordan chuckled.

"Don't start with me about my bag. You already got me in the fucking mountains where the only thing I see resembling a black man, is a fucking bear. If these motherfuckers forget what year it is and try to come at me all sideways, I will be ready for it."

"Alright but don't be asking me to hold your bag, cause I'm not about to do it." Jordan closed the trunk with a soft thud.

"Duly noted. Now can we go ahead and do this?"

Two enthusiastic white men approached us as soon as we approached the shop. I slowly removed my bag from my back and slung it over my shoulder for easier access.

"Welcome to Gem Stone. Is this your first time here?" One of the men extended his hand to Jordan. I kept my eye on the other one who had his hands in his back pocket.

He nodded his head as our eyes locked. It was almost like we were silently communicating. My look said, 'don't start none, won't be none'. I nodded my head back. It wasn't so much that I looked the part of a gangster thug, because I really didn't. I was short, almost petite. I tipped the scale at a measly one hundred and twenty pounds but most of it was taunt muscle. Not an inch of flab on me. People usually look at me and laugh when I get angry, until I have to shut it down. "Yeah, first time," I answered.

The first guy went on. I suspected the other guy didn't do much talking. He was probably there for muscle with no brains. "Let me tell you what we do here. While this site is an actual mine, we don't do mining here. These mines have been worked more than a Las Vegas prostitute." He paused to laugh but when he noticed he was the only one laughing he continued. "We get our dirt from other active mines across the country. We sell the dirt by the pail or bucket. Either one you get, will be rich in gems. It's our guarantee to you."

"I don't get it. How are you making any money this way? What's the catch?" I knew everybody had an angle and I wanted to know what theirs was.

The other guy finally spoke. "There ain't no catch." He spat out a wad of tobacco juice, near my feet. I watched as a small amount dribbled down his chin.

"Ewe. You need to wipe that crap off your face. It's nasty." I turned my head away in disgust. I had heard about people chewing tobacco before. This was the first time I had seen it up close and personal. The guy smiled, showing badly discolored teeth. It was no wonder he didn't talk much. He wiped his mouth with the back of his hand and I looked the other way thanking God that I didn't shake his hand. This fool was about to get me in trouble and he wasn't even aware of it.

"Where you ladies from?" the first guy asked. He seemed like he was trying to divert my attention from his partner. I was glad because I didn't plan on looking at him again. I felt like the sadistic son-of-a-bitch took pleasure in grossing me out.

"Atlanta," Jordan answered. I nudged her in her side. I didn't want her to volunteer any more information about us.

"So, where do we do this mining?" If they mentioned anything about going in a dark cave, I was out. Even though it was broad daylight, I felt like this was the type of place folks could disappear from. Since no one knew where we were, we would never be heard from again.

"Right here, little lady." The man said pointing to some long wooden boxes. I took a step closer to see. I knew that I had an overactive imagination but they reminded me of long narrow coffins. The boxes had water running through them. "First you pick your bag or bucket of soil. You pour a little of it in this here box and swish it around in the water. When you find a stone, put it in this bag."

"I am so confused. How will we know a stone from a rock?" Jordan asked with this perplexed look on her face.

I was glad she asked the question because I didn't have a clue either. The man handed us both another smaller wooden box with a screen at the bottom of it.

"If you come across something and you are unsure about it, put it in the bag. We have gemologist inside who can tell you what each stone is and more importantly, how much it's worth. We also have this chart here that shows you what most of the stones look like." He pointed to a poster on the wall which I couldn't see unless I stood up on the box to look.

"Jordan, it sounds like fun. However, I don't think I want to do an entire bucket. Let me try a bag and see how I do before we commit to anything else."

"Sounds good to me."

Jordan was all amped up and ready to go. The guy handed us two bags. I poured a little into my box and set the bag on the floor.

"Be careful you don't drop your box in the water. Once its contents are flushed away, it's gone," the guy with the nasty teeth said.

There was nothing like a little pressure. Jordan and I didn't speak as we worked. The more gems I found, the more excited I became. I might have done such a great job at cleaning my rocks but I was eager to find out what I had in my bag. Unlike Jordan who took her time examining each and every clod of dirt, I rushed through the process much like a child trying to get to the center of a tootsie roll pop.

"I'm done," I exclaimed as I patted my hands together to clear the dust from my fingers.

"You cannot be finished that entire bag. Stop lying." Jordan looked around on the ground searching for my bag.

I had balled up the empty bag and stuck it in my back pocket. "I promise you, I'm finished. I'm ready to go see what this stuff is worth." I rushed off before Jordan could object, knowing full well she would want us to do this thing together.

"Wait. Let me see how many you have collected."

I reluctantly showed her my bag which had about seven mid-sized stones in it. "See."

"Dag, is that all you have? I've got twice that much and I'm only half way finished with my satchel."

I felt guilty that I had wasted Jordan's money by rushing through my mining. Unfortunately, there was nothing I could do about it because I had dumped the rest of the dirt into the trough. Something about this experience brought out the little kid in me, who rushed through opening all of their gifts to see what Santa had brought without appreciating what I received. I felt like each stone was a present and I couldn't wait to unwrap it. "I guess I got a little over zealous."

"You ain't even lying about that. Don't worry about it. I don't have to finish up my bag here. I can do the rest of it at home."

"No, that's not fair to you. I was acting like a big kid. I'll wait for you to finish. This way we can have them examine all of the stones at once."

"You sure?" Jordan never stopped working on her bag of dirt.

"Yeah, it's cool. I'm going to walk over to the other side to see what they are doing with the gold mining." I stuffed my bag of rock into my shoulder bag to keep from lugging it around.

Jordan waved me away. "I won't be long."

We were the only black people at the mine so I was careful about walking up on folks without them knowing I was coming. It still amazed me that in this day and age black people were still the most hated race of people in the world. Every time I walked pass a white person, they clutched their purses like I was born to steal. It hurt my feelings. I looked back over my shoulder and noticed the spitter following me with his eyes. He made me feel creepy. I crossed over to the other side of the enclosure. It also had a long trough with water flowing through the bottom of it.

"Are you going to try your hand at panning for gold, little lady?" the original salesman asked.

"No, I was just looking."

"You should give it a try to get the whole experience you came for."

Part of me really wanted to try it but the other part of me didn't feel like going through another bag of dirt. "I'm really just trying to wait for my friend to finish with her bag of dirt." I would have walked away at this point but there really wasn't any place left to go but inside the office.

"If you are not going to try it, then at least let me show you how it's done." The man picked up a shallow pan and used it to scoop up some sand from the bottom of the trough. "See these ridges on the pan? You want to keep the water below this level. Shake the pan, creating a wave motion that shifts the sand off the gold. The gold, if there was any in here, would sink to the bottom of the pan while the sand rinsed off into the water."

"Looks complicated to me." I was completely bored and uninterested with the process.

"It's all in the wrist. Takes practice, but the rewards can be great. I'll be honest with ya though, the chances of finding any real gold in this stuff here, is slim to none. With the prices of gold today, you can bet your sweet fine ass, they went over this here dirt with a microscope, before they sent it to us." The older man winked.

I was rather appalled that he would say this to me. "If you feel that way, why are you scamming people out of their money?" He didn't know how close to pissed off I was.

"People don't come here to actually get gold. They only want the experience, to say they have done it."

Now that he broke it down to me like that, I couldn't be mad. Basically, it was a tourist gimmick and he found a way to make money off of it. "Thanks for the lesson. I'm going to check on my friend. She should be finished by now."

"No problem, little lady." He rinsed off the pan and put it back on the stack. He dried his hands on his filthy pants. I didn't notice the dirt, until I followed his hands. I looked down at my own legs and noticed a fine line of dirt on my copper toned skin.

"Fuck," I exclaimed as I fervently tried to dust myself off. I had not counted on getting dirty.

"I guess we should have warned you about the flying dust. It goes with the territory," the spitter whispered close to my ear. I jumped away from his close proximity as my hand reached for my knife.

I pointed to the nicer of the two men. "You better get your boy. I have had about enough of his nasty ass."

"Cecil, leave this pretty little thing alone. She don't want your old ass! Don't pay him any mind. He's harmless. We don't get many pretty girls coming through these parts. Can't blame a man for trying," the man said winking.

I thought I was going to gag right then and there. The very thought of this lecherous old man breathing on me, gave me the creepy crawlies. I was ready to go. I warily backed away from both of them. If this was customer service, they sucked. I rushed back over to Jordan as she was finishing up.

"Girl, these motherfuckers is crazy. Those old men were hitting on me."

"Now that is funny. Did you tell them to dream on?"

"I almost threw up in my mouth. Let's get out of here before I have to cut one or both of them."

"I'm done. Let's go see what we got." Jordan squealed with delight.

I'd almost forgotten about sitting with the gemologist. "Fine, but I'm picking our next excursion. Preferably with some other black folks."

Jordan placed her hand on my arm. "I know this isn't your cup of tea. Thank you for indulging me in this."

"I didn't say I didn't like it. I'm just not thrilled about these crusty ass men. The rest of it was cool."

"Good. I'm glad."

***

We were back home, sitting on the couch watching our favorite black soap opera, The Have And The Have Nots, when Jordan paused the recording. "I've been thinking about what you said about going somewhere on a trip with a lot of black people. It got me to thinking, and I was wondering what you thought about maybe going to Jamaica or the Bahamas?"

"Those places sound nice, but what about Miami?"

"Are you kidding me? Florida won't get any of my money after they let George Zimmerman get away with killing Trayvon Martin. I would rather set my money on fire than spend a dime of it there. Believe that."

"Oh yeah, I forgot about that boycott. You're right. There have to be other places, inside the United States, that we could visit." I got up to go into the kitchen to fix myself something to drink.

"Why do you want to stay in the United States? What's wrong with travelling outside of the states? Seeing the world?" Jordan followed me into the kitchen, seemingly forgetting about our television show.

I knew we were going to have this conversation eventually, but I really didn't want to have it now. "I don't have anything against travelling. I just thought there might be other places that we could visit first." I got my drink and left the kitchen with Jordan hot on my heels.

"You know I can tell when you're not telling me the truth right?"

She could see through me as if I were made of glass. It was both a blessing and a curse. Especially, right now. "Fine. I was going to tell you this later anyway. It just never came up. Remember when I told you about this guy who took my bag with my identification in it?"

"You mean the day you were in the park and passed out?"

"Yeah, the day you poisoned my ass. Anyway, I never did get around to replacing my identification."

"For heaven's sake, why not? It doesn't take all that long. All you have to do is go down there with your birth certificate, something with your address on it and your social security card. At most, it will probably take two hours."

"I know what it takes. I just don't have all that stuff." I was feeling guilty for not having admitted this to her before. Jordan had been so good to me. I didn't want to give her any reason to regret letting me move in with her.

"Is that why you haven't gotten a car yet?"

"Yeah. I mean, I know how to drive and shit but getting that license is going to be a bit of a problem."

"Why is that? Make me understand. Did you fail the test or something? I could teach you how to do it, or help you study for it. It really wasn't that bad."

"It's not the test. It's more like proving who I am. I don't want to necessarily let people know about me."

Jordan had this perplexed expression on her face. I knew I was talking in circles but she had to see this was difficult for me. We always said we would have a conversation in which I told her my story. Thus far, the topic had never presented itself.

"Girl, I don't know what you are saying to me right now. If you can't prove who you say you are, how did you cash that check I wrote to you?"

"I didn't cash it."

"Don't tell me you are walking around with a check for a million dollars in your purse. What have you been doing for money?"

"I haven't needed any money. Every time we go somewhere, you are always reaching for the check. Besides, I get a little something from the state. It's enough to pay the rent with some extra."

"Are you telling me you don't want my money? Is that it?" Jordan was getting a little upset. I could tell by the way her brow creased in the middle.

"I ain't no damn fool, of course I want it. I just have to figure out a way to get to it without alerting the authorities that I'm in the area." I stole a look at Jordan expecting to see a worried expression on her face. She surprised me when it was not there.

"Authorities? Why would the authorities be looking for you?"

Nervously, I twisted my hands together. My mind was racing trying to think of an acceptable response to her question but the only thing I could come up with was the truth. "I'm not exactly sure they are looking for me per sè. But in case they are, I'm not about to gift wrap and deliver myself to them."

Jordan got up from the sofa and went to the bar. "I have this feeling that I'm going to need a drink behind this story. Shall I pour you one too?"

Even though we were both legally under the drinking age, we had a completely stocked bar. It was one of the many amenities of our luxurious Buckhead condo. Minutes from downtown Atlanta, our penthouse suite was to die for. We were the youngest tenants in the building. Jordan actually rented the space and only charged me a measly five hundred bucks to stay there.

"Yes, I think I'm gonna need one too. Pour me whatever you are having, but put more soda than booze in it. I just took my medicine and I ain't trying to flip out up in here." I waited until Jordan settled back on the couch before I began.

"Okay, lay it on me." Jordan's smile was patient and reassuring.

"I haven't told this to anyone." I took a huge sip of my Patron and coke.

"Will you relax, it's just me your talking to. We don't have any secrets. Right?"

I knew she was trying to put me at ease but it did not stop me from feeling nervous.

"Mrs. Gates' actually took me into the group home because she found me living on the streets."

"So, the part about you aging out of the system was a lie?" Jordan asked.

"Yes. Mrs. Gates came up with that one. Had I known she was going to turn out to be such a controlling witch, I might have taken my chances on the street."

"I know that's right. The way she treated those girls in the home was uncalled for. She didn't have to impose such restrictions on them. Most of us were smart enough to do the right thing. For the ones that didn't, she should have used the time to teach them to do better."

Part of me wanted Jordan to keep on talking, but the other part of me was ready to lay my cards on the table while I still could. I jumped in before Jordan could say anything else. "She wasn't all bad, she did have a heart. She just didn't show it all that much. She was better, in the beginning. I was one of the first girls in the house."

Jordan's brow creased in the middle. "Seriously? I don't know why I thought you were relatively new."

"Probably because you came in and trumped me in everything. You got the best room with little or no restrictions. Although I wasn't trying to get out in the world, I wanted to be able to go out when I felt like it. You know what I mean? If you noticed, once the novelty of leaving the home wore off, I pretty much stayed in the house."

"I honestly wasn't focused on anybody else but me. I was just starting to remember things from my past. Besides, I kind of hated you, so you weren't even on my radar."

We both shared a laugh. I appreciated the way Jordan was allowing me to tell my story, my own way, without a lot of questions. "I was living on the streets because of an altercation I had with my mother's boyfriend. He liked to put his hands on me, if you know what I mean." I shuttered as a particularly vivid memory popped in my head.

Jordan clutched my hands which were in my lap. "Oh, Lawd."

"He used to touch my sister first. Then he decided there was enough of him to go around for both of us."

"My God, he didn't..."

I couldn't say yes. I could only nod my head in the affirmative. Every time I thought about it, I felt dirty. Even though I was an innocent and unwilling participant, it still hurt. I shook off the tears I felt were coming, while stifling the urge to wipe my face clean of the dirt I feared was clearly marking me.

"What a low-down motherfucker! What did your mother say? Did she know?"

"She knew. She had to. She might try to say she didn't know. However, I know she's not that stupid. When she would come home from work, she saw the busted lips and black eyes. She never once questioned what happened to us. One day he broke my sister's arm. He told my mom I did it. She whooped my ass behind that shit. My sister gave up, then she ran away."

"Why didn't she take you with her? You were both going through the same shit? I don't understand that."

I shook my head. "I don't know. I never got the chance to ask her. She just left one day and never came back. Momma said I ran her off." I was trying very hard not to breakdown, but I could not hold back my tears. It was still too painful for me to talk about. Jordan scooted close to me and took me in her arms. I was immediately transported back to the times my sister used to comfort me after each brutal encounter with my mother's boyfriend. Believing that she would abandon me was the worst. Not knowing what happened to her was slowly killing me. This was one of the reasons why I worried the fuck out of Jordan until she finally decided to be my friend. I missed that companionship. It was a tough sell that almost got me killed. In the end I believed it was worth it.

"This is terrible. Honey, I'm so sorry."

I clung to Jordan as I truly cried for the first time since I had left my mother's house. Even though it had been over two years since I had seen my sister, in my heart it felt like it was only yesterday. Jordan continued to stroke my back while making cooing sounds. I cried until I felt like I had no more tears left. When I finished, I pulled away feeling ashamed for my weakness. This crying shit was so out of character for me.

"So what happened to the pedophile after she left? Did he straighten up and fly right?"

"For a while, he kept his distance. I was so hurt that my sister left me, I started failing in school. I went from a straight A student to a D student in one semester. The school sent home a note, which my dumb-ass gave to my mother. She pitched a bitch and sent her stupid-ass boyfriend to the school on my behalf. He fed them this bullshit story about my mother being deathly ill as the reason for the slip in my grades."

"Why didn't you tell them it was a lie? Especially since you had their attention."

"What was I supposed to say? That this miserable shit climbed into my bed at night and fucked the brakes off me? Do you understand how hard that is to tell someone?" I was no longer sad. I was pissed at the abuse and injustice I suffered.

"Well, yeah. That's exactly what you should have said. It was the truth. It might have been hard, but it might have saved you some pain."

"I tried to tell, but I couldn't. The first time it happened, I was twelve. He said it was the way grown-ups showed each other they loved them. I kept telling him I wasn't a grown-up but he wouldn't listen. Then he used to tell me my sister did it and she liked it. 'Don't you want to be more like London?' That was the worst part. He kept throwing her in my face, making me think something was wrong with me because I didn't like it."

"What a sick bastard. Did your sister know he was touching you?"

I finished my drink in two quick gulps and went back to the bar and fixed myself another. "Yeah, she knew but there wasn't anything she could do, she was only fourteen. It wasn't like we could kick his ass or something like that."

"Did he make you watch while he was doing her?"

I shuddered violently again. Jordan had pricked a sore spot. I felt cold and hot at the same time. "Sometimes. Mainly when he wanted to punish me. I didn't like to see him do it to her. She would cry so hard."

"Disgraceful. I wish I could get my hands on that slimy pervert. I would cut his dick off to the nub."

"I got the bastard. That's why I was running. I don't know if I killed him. I gave it my best shot though."

Jordan gasped. I'm not sure why she was surprised. It wasn't like she hadn't seen me kill before. I wasn't proud about what I had done. To me, it was my only way to survive. I couldn't keep allowing him to do that to me. Each time he touched me, I felt like I was dying inside.

"What did you do?" Jordan's voice was barely above a whisper. She acted as if someone else was in the room and could potentially hear us. She made me want to whisper too.

It took me a few seconds to answer her. Those horrible images of him floundering in the tub kept flashing before my eyes. "I tried to slice off the fucker's balls with a straight razor. Then I took all the money he had in his wallet and hopped the bus to Atlanta." I watched and waited for Jordan to recoil from me.

"Good for you! What about your mother? Did you ever try to reach out to her?"

"For what? She never helped me, or my sister, while we were being abused. Far as I'm concerned, she can go fuck herself." My heart was thumping wildly.

"I can't say I blame you there. I don't get it."

I was confused. "What don't you get?" I had explained everything to her, step by step.

"I don't get why some people bother having children. I don't understand why it's so easy for them to have us and then abandon us. It ought to be more difficult. I can't imagine going through the process of getting pregnant, carrying the baby for nine months and then nothing."

"Hey, I agree with you. I think it's way too easy for people to have kids. They should have to pass some type of test before they can have a child."

Jordan shook her head no. "I used to think that as well. But then people would complain that the government has too much control over their lives. I can see it now, people having babies in their homes, without the benefit of medical attention. It would be a giant step backwards."

"That may be, but there should be a happy medium. As educated as we have become, how could something so simple and natural be so fucked up? Innocent children are being born without a chance to survive because the very people who are bringing them into the world are trying to take them out." I started crying again.

It was Jordan's turn to get another drink. If we weren't careful, both of us would end up drunk as hell. I was already feeling the effects of my two drinks back-to-back, in a relatively short amount of time.

I said, "You know we can debate this for one hundred hours and still not come up with a solution. At the end of the day, the only things we have control of is ourselves. When we have children, then we can change it for them."

Jordan shook her head. "Yeah, that's if I decide to have children. The way I feel right now, I'm not interested in bringing anyone else into this world. It's way too hard."

"I feel you. Hopefully, you will change your mind when you find that special someone. A child is the ultimate gift you can give your mate. I believe that, despite what was done to me as a child."

"I hope my feelings do change."

"They will. You have too much love to give to keep it all to yourself. So let's backtrack for a minute. You need to find out what happened to this prick. You just might be in hiding for nothing. If you didn't kill him, you would have been justified in injuring him."

"I thought about it, believe me. It's scary. I wouldn't even know how to start looking though. I'm not about to just walk in there and say, Momma I'm home and see if he falls from the ceiling like a damn bat or vulture."

"Hell, you said yourself we could find anything we wanted on Google. Let's do a search on that motherfucker."

"Yeah, but that is kind of risky. Haven't you ever noticed that every time you do a search on something, especially if you are trying to buy something, Google ads for the same item or company show up all over your newsfeed? That lets me know there is no such thing as privacy in cyberspace. If I do any research, the internet is not the way I want to do it. Not for this."

"We could hire someone to help us. Someone we can trust, like Brody maybe. We also have to find out what happened to your sister. She has to be out there someone. Who knows, she might even be in Atlanta too."

I hung my head as the weight of her words bore down on me. "She's not in Atlanta. That prick told me he killed her. That's why I stabbed his ass."

Jordan's mouth dropped open. Obviously, she didn't see that one coming. "Don't you see he might have been lying to you to control you? We have to find out for sure. We should call Brody. You trust him, don't you?"

"I trust him to a certain degree but I don't know if I want to share with him why I need to know these things. He might feel compelled to turn my ass in."

"We could just ask him to help us find out what happened to your sister. Anything else, we could play that by ear."

"I guess that is alright if we could just limit it to that. I don't want him to contact my mother under any circumstances. She doesn't need to know where I am. I don't want to have anything to do with that bitch. She had her chance to protect us and she didn't. She can catch fire as far as I'm concerned."

"I feel you. I almost want to check on my own mother to see if she's alive. Not because I fucking care if she is or not. I just want to know."

Everything we talked about culminated to this moment. My heart started racing, knowing that this could be a defining moment in our relationship. I cleared my throat. "Do you really want to know, or are you just saying it?" My foot tapped repeatedly on the floor as if it had a mind of its own. I placed my hand on my knee to keep it still.

Jordan gave me a side-eye which I could have been interpreted two ways. Either she wanted to know, or she didn't. I wasn't going to assume. She was going to have to tell me.

"Of course I would want to know. If the bitch is still alive, then I fucking underestimated her."

"She's not." I waited for an explosion of some sort from Jordan.

"Good." Jordan finished her drink and poured another.

"Aren't you even going to ask me how I know this?"

"Not really. I don't care. If she's dead I don't have to waste any more time thinking about her. Case closed."

It was my turn to be amazed. I wondered if that would be enough for me. I didn't think so. I would probably want to go and spit on my mother's grave or pee in her ashes.

"What about my sister? Is she gone too?"

This time, there was a noticeable hitch in her voice. I didn't want to answer, but I didn't want to lie either. I nodded my head yes.

"Good. You are the only family I have left. I'm going to call Brody tomorrow and ask him to come over. He's a reporter. He knows how to snoop around without calling attention to it. I'm going to bed now." She put her glass in the sink and went up the stairs to her room.

"Goodnight." I called up the stairs as if she could hear me through her closed door. I prayed for a peaceful night sleep for both of us as I turned off the lights and retired to my own bedroom.

CHAPTER THREE
JORDAN BREE

If I used a syringe, I couldn't get the coffee in me fast enough. I was sitting at the table in the kitchen, filling cup after cup, drinking it so fast, it was burning my tongue. I had a slight headache which I wasn't sure was from the alcohol I had the night before or my lack of sleep. I tossed and turned so much after my conversation with Lacy it was pathetic. I almost got up, but I didn't want to continue our conversation, just in case Lacy was still in the living room. Last night, was probably the first night that I regretted not living alone. I wanted to grieve on my own, in my private way. I felt like such a hypocrite. I professed to hate my family but deep down inside, I really did care what happened to them.

I assumed drugs killed them. Regardless of whether or not I had a hand in their deaths, knowing they were dead still caught me off guard. I kept wanting to get out of the bed and ask Lacy how she could be so confident about their deaths. If, in fact, drugs killed them, neither of us were there when they took the drugs I had given them. This is what made me feel like a phony. When I bought the drugs, I knew there was an eighty percent chance my mother would steal them and overdose.

Saying no wasn't in her vocabulary. Once she stole the drugs, I didn't want to know what she did with them. Now, I had to know if what I did caused her death. I cleaned up our glasses from the night before and left them to dry on the counter. I straightened all the pillows and wiped imaginary dust from the table tops. When I couldn't take it anymore, I knocked on Lacy's door.

"Come in."

"Hey, did I wake you?" It was a stupid question and I knew it. Of course she was sleeping, what else would she be doing?

"No, I was just laying here. My head hurts a little and my eyes feel so puffy from crying."

"I feel you. I feel like shit too. I tossed and turned all night."

"We both should pop some Tylenol and have a good breakfast."

"I'm not even hungry. I chugged about ten cups of coffee. If I put anything else in my belly, I'll pop."

"Maybe I should try some coffee too. Let me throw on some shorts and I'll come out there."

"Okay," I backed out of Lacy's room suddenly feeling like an intruder. It wasn't the first time that I had been in her room, so I wasn't sure where these feelings were coming from. Perhaps it had something to do with my waking her up. I put some water in the coffee pot while I waited and turned it on. She was out in five minutes. Her hair, which was previously all over her head, was pulled back nicely in a ponytail.

"The water should be hot in a minute."

Lacy pulled out a chair and sat down. She rested her chin on her hands. "What time is it?"

"It's early, a little after nine. I'm sorry. I was driving myself fucking insane."

She lifted her face from her hands. "What's wrong, boo?"

"I've been up all night trying to figure out how you could be so certain about what happened to my family."

"Oh," she looked down at the table. After several seconds she got up and went to her bedroom. The teapot started whistling. Confused, I went to turn it off. The shrill noise wasn't helping my headache. Lacy came back in the room and placed a newspaper on the table. I picked up the paper as she went to fix herself a cup of coffee.

"What's this?"

"Their obituaries. Ever since I've been on the run, I've been obsessed with reading them. Both your mom and your sister are listed. I'm sorry."

I couldn't bring myself to look. Knowing they were dead was enough. I didn't need to see their names in ink to believe it. "How come you didn't show me this before?"

"I wasn't sure you wanted to know. I kept it in case you ever expressed any interest."

"Wait, this isn't making sense. I thought obituaries were put in the papers by family members. I sure as hell didn't do. So where did it come from?" I thumbed through the pages trying to work up the courage to look for myself.

"Maybe they listed it because of the bizarre circumstances." Lacy shrugged her shoulders.

"What bizarre circumstances? Niggers die in the projects from drugs every day. If the newspaper wrote about everyone, the paper would be as big as the yellow pages."

"Your mother died one day and your sister died two days later."

I started laughing uncontrollably. This shit was too much.

"What the hell is so funny?"

"If they didn't die on the same day, then that means my mom didn't share. She used until she couldn't do any more and my sister found her stash later. Her dumb ass probably thought she would beat the odds. She used to think she was exempt from shit. Wouldn't even admit she had a problem. Serves her ass right. "

"Wow, you sure know your family. I couldn't understand how it happened. Especially since they were both found at home."

"Thank you. It is better to know. Now, I won't be looking for them on every corner. Maybe now they will have some peace."

"I know what you mean. I wish I had the same type of closure."

"I'm going to call Brody now. I am so sure he can help us without getting all into our business."

"All you got to do is throw that pussy power on him and he won't stand a chance."

"Ewe. You can be so disgusting sometimes," I said laughing.

"What did I say? It ain't nothing wrong with using what you got to get what you want." Lacy twerked devilishly low to the ground. Her ass was popping and going in circles like she needed money for the rent.

"Girl, you are a mess. I can get what I want without all of that." I pretended to be annoyed when in actuality, I was secretly thrilled. I had been trying to think of a reason to invite Brody over to our home and this would be the perfect opportunity.

"When are you going to call him?"

"We have to get our stories straight first. What exactly are you willing to tell him about your situation? I don't want you getting mad at me if I spilled something I wasn't supposed to."

"That's a good idea. I don't think we should tell him about my cutting the boyfriend. I think we should stick to finding my sister. If he does find anything, he will probably get information about my mother too. He will know pretty quickly if that prick is still in her life."

"Lacy, until we find proof otherwise, I think we should assume that your sister is still alive. That asshole probably told you she wasn't just to keep you in line."

"True. I hope it was a lie. But then again, if it is, then it will mean that she actually left me there alone."

My heart went out to her. I didn't know which one of those two scenarios would be better for her. Since I knew what it was like to feel abandoned, I truly sympathized with her. "What do you think about inviting him over for a pool party? You were saying that we had not used it since we moved in."

"If you are not planning on seducing him, why would you want him over here when you're near-naked? I think it's going to be hard for him to concentrate. Pun definitely intended."

"That's because you have a gutter mind. Brody is a grown man and knows how to control his animal urges."

"Being grown has nothing to do with it. I just think inviting him over here to test his strength is wrong. It won't just be you in a bathing suit. I'll be wearing one too. He won't know where to look."

"When you put it that way, you might be right. Maybe we should invite him over for dinner. This way, we could talk without fear of being overheard."

"That's better. If you want, I'll make myself ghost so you can give him a little bit to go."

"Thanks, but that won't be necessary. If I feel the need, I'll just go back to his place."

"Handle your business then."

I went into my sitting for a little privacy to call Brody. Even though I didn't have anything to hide from Lacy, she didn't need to see how nervous I was to talk to him again. I had been keeping my distance from Brody ever since I got this apartment. He was so easy to be around. I didn't want to develop a dependency on him. I wanted to find my own way in the world and I couldn't do it if he was always there.

"Hey Brody, what's up?"

"Hey yourself, stranger. I was beginning to think you had forgotten all about me."

"You know I could never forget about you. You pretty much saved my life." This wasn't an exaggeration either. If it wasn't for Brody's investigative talents, I might still be locked up in a hospital for the mentally insane. Brody's exposé caused a major reform in the way mental patients were treated and it shut down a number of the hospitals in the state. As a result, I was filthy rich too!

"If that's the case, why haven't I heard from you?" Brody teased.

"Oh you know how it is. I had a lot of things to get straight after I left the home. Then Lacy moved in, and we needed to get in stride. Things are looking good now."

"I've really missed you. I'm glad to know that everything is okay."

My heart skipped a beat as I listened to his silky voice over the phone. His voice was so damn sexy to me. It should have come with a cautionary warning while listening to him. It was the type of voice that made you want to check your panties at the door. That was another reason why I was reluctant to see him again.

"Things are better than okay. In fact, Lacy and I are celebrating our first month in the apartment and we would like to invite you over for dinner tonight. If you're free."

"Are you kidding me? Ain't no way I'm turning down a home cooked meal."

"Who said anything about cooking," I joked. My mind was already churning with the possibilities.

"Damn, you sure know how to bust a man's bubble."

"I was just kidding. What do you like to eat?"

"I'm a man of simple taste. Meat, potatoes maybe some bread. You can't go wrong with that."

"Boring. Why don't you challenge me with something a little more complicated," I teased.

"I didn't know you wanted to get all fancy. If that's the case, I'm a real seafood lover. You name it, I'll eat it."

"What about some pan seared Swai with some roasted tomatoes and dirty rice?"

"Girl, you are going to make me marry you. What time do I need to be there?"

"Say six o'clock. I have to go to the grocery store and I'll need some preparation time."

"I promise you I will be on time. Just give me the address."

I could barely hear him. My heart was beating so fast. I couldn't believe the effect he had on me. It was just a phone call for crying out loud. "Okay, we'll see you tonight."

"I can't wait."

I hung onto the phone for several seconds before I hung up. I turned around and Lacy was staring at me from the door with a big old smile on her face. *Damn, I thought I had closed the door.*

"What?"

"Look at you. Your face, it's all flush!" She walked over to me and grabbed me by the shoulders, forcing me to turn and look in the mirror. She was right my face was visibly colored.

"So." That was the best I could come up with. There was no use trying to deny it when the evidence was there in plain sight.

"Something tells me I'm going to be wearing my headphones tonight."

"I don't know why sex is the first thing you think about. Can't a girl have some class about her?"

"What has class got to do with this? Hell, it ain't like y'all haven't slept together before. He popped your cherry for Christ sake, get a grip."

I opened my mouth to respond and shut it immediately. What the fuck was I to say behind that? She was absolutely right. It wasn't like this was our first time or anything like that. It was just different for some reason. Maybe because he was coming to my own home. Maybe it was because I remembered how it felt. But whatever the reason, I had to pull it together and do it quick.

"Grab your bag. We have got some shopping to do."

"What are you making?"

"Swai."

"What pray tell is that?"

"Shark."

Lacy had been right behind me on the way out the door but she stopped in her tracks.

"Get the hell out of here. What do you know about cooking or eating shark?"

"The cooking channel boo." We both laughed as we climbed into my car.

"That is ambitious for your first time cooking for him. Why didn't you stick with hotdogs and hamburgers on the grill? At least if you fucked it up, you could blame it on the wind or something."

"Here's the thing I learned off Real Housewives of Atlanta: you start off cooking this fabulous meal giving yourself enough time to experiment. You always have a backup plan in case you fuck it up."

"What's your plan B since you have already told him what you're making?"

"That's easy. There are at least two restaurants within five miles of here that make that shit every day. One of them delivers."

"Damn, you are a motherfucking genius," she said.

"No I'm not. People can say what they want to say about these reality shows. You can learn something from them if you look past the drama."

"Oh, I agree with you even though I kind of like the drama."

"Don't get me wrong, I like it too. Sometimes it's so real. The only time I get pissed off with it is when the women fight with each other. It breaks my heart that black women in particular, can't seem to go nowhere in public without acting a fool."

"Girl you should kill yourself with that one. That is what they want you believe but it ain't true. If that was the case, there would be signs up in all the restaurants, bars and movies, banning bitches from entering in groups."

"If you think large groups of women don't get the side-eye, you haven't been paying attention. Restaurants hate to see them coming because women typically tip less than men. It's a wonder they don't spit in our food."

Lacy gently punched me in the shoulder. "Why would you say some shit like that? Now I'm going to be inspecting my food every time I go out to eat. Ain't nobody got no time for that."

"You're safe. You don't hang out with a bunch of women. But it does make me wonder how we would fare with a larger group? I mean we get along great. I wonder what would happen if we decided to expand our circle?"

"I'm going to tell you right now. I would be jealous as hell. Especially if I saw you were having more fun than I was."

I took my eyes off the road for a minute. "Are you serious?"

"Hell yeah. Don't you remember how hard I had to fight for this friendship? I wish another bitch would try to come in and take my place."

I could not contain my laughter. Lacy was so funny sometimes. She loved hard. She hated harder. She didn't have to worry about me jumping ship. What she did for me when she took out one of my arch enemies sealed our relationship for life.

"The only thing that pisses me off, is that all of the drama mamma shows are being filmed right her in Atlanta. Makes the world believe ain't nothing here but a bunch of nuts."

"Your right. Real Housewives, Love-N-Hip Hop, Married to Medicine, The Braxton's and Honey Boo-boo."

"You did not just add Honey Boo-boo to the list!" I started laughing so hard I was crying. "You are going to make me wreck my car." It was a good thing that we had reached our destination because I couldn't stop laughing.

"You have seen that show."

"Ain't no drama on there. They are just ignorant."

"It still affects how the world sees us. About the only show that I know of that is filmed here where there isn't a bunch of foolishness, is T.I. & Tiny. I actually love his family values."

"That is so true. I love seeing them together. Kind of gives you hope for finding a good man."

Lacy said, "Humph, I'm sure he did his share of dirt too." She opened the car door and got out.

"That may be but I'm not looking for shit on him either. A woman's got to have something to believe in. Even if it is someone else's man." I got out of the car as well.

"So let's talk about this because I really do want to know. How do you feel about snooping? Would you go through your man's things if you thought you could get away with it?"

We were walking through the open styled farmer's market. "I honestly don't know. I believe there are consequences to being nosey."

"What about the ones for being ignorant?"

"True. I guess it would depend on the situation. You have to make a decision before you look. If I feel like I have nothing to lose, I'll do it. But, if I'm not ready to say fuck it, and walk away, I won't."

"Damn. Why wouldn't you make that decision after you find something?"

"Because either way there is going to be repercussions. If you find something that you didn't want to see, you are going to have to do something or be miserable. Like, for example, say you go over to your man's house and see a box of condoms on the dresser. He takes a shower and you count how many are in the box. The next time you come over there, you count them again and some are missing. He didn't use them with you so then it becomes a moral dilemma. Do you cut this motherfucker's dick off or do you walk away?"

"I can see you walking away, but I think I'd go for the dick. I might even keep it for sentimental reasons."

"Lacy, sometimes you scare me. You have the biggest heart of anyone I know, but you can be so ruthless." I knew I had touched a nerve almost immediately. I wasn't trying to hurt her feelings but I obviously had.

Lacy stopped walking. "Tell me what you need and I'll go get it. This shouldn't take forever."

"So are you mad at me now?"

"I'm not mad. I just don't want to be in the store all day." Lacy was resting her arms on the shopping cart and for a split second, I thought she was going to ram me with it.

It was my turn to get annoyed. "If you had something better to do, you should have said so." I walked off looking for the fresh fish. This wasn't a market that I frequented so I didn't know where anything was. Since I was cooking something I believed to be both exotic and different, I didn't think I could have found it at my local Krogers store. With each angry step I took, I started to realize how stupid it was for me to be upset with Lacy. I turned around to go apologize and walked right into her. "I'm sorry. You know I don't have any filter and if I think it, I'll probably say it. I didn't mean any harm."

"I know. It was the only thing that stopped me from running this cart into your ankles." Lacy smiled a sly grin. I was glad she didn't do it too because that would have hurt like the dickens and we would have been fighting in this market thus proving that black women couldn't get along.

"Let's get what we came for and get out of here. I have got a lot of work to do. Do you want to pick out something for dessert while I get the fish?"

"Sure, what were you thinking about having?"

"I don't really care. To be honest, I don't even know if Brody likes desserts. Seems like all he talked about was working out and shit. You two are just like peas in a pod in that area."

"Girl please ain't nothing wrong with a fit, fine ass. I'm not mad at the brother. As far as dessert goes, when all else fails, get chocolate. If he doesn't like it, there will be more for us."

"I know that's right. I have never met a chocolate cake that I didn't like." Lacy didn't appear to be angry at all when she walked off but with her, I never knew what she was thinking. We were so much alike in a lot of ways which was the makings of a good friendship. Where we differed is how we handled certain situations. Her approach was more hands on than mine. These were the thoughts that woke me up at night.

I took my list from my purse and picked up the remaining items for our meal. As I shopped, I could not hide the big old grin that kept trying to pop out on my lips. I was a little bit scared about seeing Brody again. He was the first man to show an actual interest in me and it gave me goose bumps just thinking about him.

"Feast your eyes on this." Lacy held a clear plastic container with this monstrously big cake inside.

"Oh my, that cake is humongous. Where did you get that from?"

"I got it from the bakery in the corner. It's called seven deadly sins. It's supposed to be seven different cakes all in one."

"That's what I'm talking about. I say fuck the fish and we can eat the cake Annie Mae."

"I knew you would say that, but you better be thinking of your man first. He ain't gonna want to just eat cake. You said it yourself he's a health nut. We can OD on cake after he goes home."

"Well, I hope that cake tastes as good as it looks. I'm ready to go."

"Are you sure you have everything? I'm not trying to go back to the store after we get home."

"If we don't have it in this buggy, we aren't going to get it. I decided to put some crab meat in the fish so it should be good."

Lacy frowned. "You are going all out for that man aren't you?"

"What do you mean? You like Brody don't you?"

"Of course I like him. Remember, he did save my life."

"Then what's the problem?" I was getting a slight attitude.

"I didn't say it was a problem, I was only making an observation. Don't get your panties all twisted about it." Lacy sulked.

I could tell where this was going and I wasn't feeling it. For whatever reason, Lacy was priming herself up for a fight with me. She did it sometime when she wanted to be left alone. "Lacy, I'm not going to fight with you. If you have something you want to say, please say it so we can get on with our day."

"Ain't nobody trying to fight. You are just being overly sensitive."

I paused as I considered her response. "Am I?"

"Yes, now let's go before we really do get to fighting."

We didn't talk until we had all the groceries in the car and we were headed home. The air inside the car was tense and I didn't know what to do to make it better. It was possible that I was projecting my own insecurities on Lacy, but if I was, I was unaware of it.

"Are you having second thoughts about my inviting Brody over? If so, I could always take the meal over to his house."

"I can't tell you who to invite into your home."

I drew back offended. "Lacy, it's our home. I mean what I say. Even when I'm crippled crab crazy, I don't want you to ever feel like you are out of place in your home. I would rather you nut the fuck up and send everybody out, including me, before I let that happen."

"Yeah right. Where they do that at? I can see it on the news if I ever twisted my lips to tell you to get out your own apartment."

"You have the right to tell me anything you like. Whether I listen or not is another matter." We both were laughing as we got out of the car. "But on the real tip, we both need to make more friends before folks start treating us like a married couple. I don't want to have to bust somebody in the mouth for saying something stupid based on their perception."

"I think you're right. I'm going to have to work on my social skills. Sometimes, I'm not the friendliest witch to be around."

"I'm glad you said it before I did, but you're right. We both need to work on our people skills." I grabbed the last bag as Lacy unlocked our front door. This was our first major discussion since we moved in together. I thought it went well and I was hopeful about other future discussions going as well.

As long as we were honest with each other about our feelings and didn't let problems fester, we should be good. At least, I hoped so.

"Wouldn't it be great if you could invite someone over and we could double date?"

"Well damn, I didn't realize this was actually a date. I thought you were inviting him over to help me with my little problem. If you want me to go hang out somewhere else, all you had to do was say it." Lacy folded her arms across her chest and stared out the window.

This wasn't what I meant at all. Was it so wrong that I wanted her to feel as happy as I felt about the prospect of seeing Brody again? "Girl, stop trippin'. Ain't nobody asking you to leave."

"You are the one babbling about date night like you want to be alone and get all sucky face with Brody."

"If I wanted to suck his face, I would go over to his house. I told you that. This ain't about him and you know it. What's really going on with you?"

"I don't know," Lacy said in a small child like voice. This voice scared me. It wasn't so much that I had to lean over to hear it but for the first time since I have known her, I actually detected what could only be a quiver of fear in her tone. Fear wasn't an attribute that I thought Lacy capable of.

"What do you mean you don't know? You are feeling something."

"Can you just lay off for a fucking minute?"

"Will you tell me what's wrong then?"

"I don't even know how to describe it. I just feel really funny."

My mind was whirling through different scenarios of what could have happened to upset her and I was coming up with blanks. "I'm going to let it go for now, but I have got my eyes on you."

CHAPTER FOUR
LACY BATES

I was feeling a little bit guilty because Jordan gave me an opportunity to lay my cards out on the table and I didn't take it. I had been keeping several secrets from her and the guilt was tearing me up inside. Meeting Jordan changed my life in so many ways. In a short amount of time, she had become closer to me than my own sister. However, I was still holding on to some things I really needed to let go.

"Do you need any help?" Jordan must not have heard my slipper feet on our hardwood floors because she damn near jumped a foot in the air. She was leaning over the counter with a knife in her hands apparently reading her recipe.

"Girl, you know you should not be sneaking up on a black woman with a knife in her hands. I might mess around and cut you by mistake. You know how scary we can be."

"I wasn't trying to sneak up on you. You had your head in that paper so you didn't hear me coming. Besides, I have good reflexes. I wouldn't stick around long enough for you to get me," I said laughing.

"Still, you should be more careful. You know I watched that show last night, Paranormal Witness. My nerves are still bad."

"That's what you get for watching that crazy mess on television. I heard you in there last night jumping around and shit."

"Girl that shit be good. I like to be scared a little bit as long as it doesn't happen in real life."

"Do you really believe in that stuff?"

"Hell yeah! I believe it. Don't you? I mean, have you ever had something strange happen that you just can't explain?"

"I had some shit happen that I didn't understand before but I don't think it has anything to do with ghosts and spirits. I believe there is a logical explanation for everything."

Jordan put down her knife. Her face was somber. "Then how do you explain your belief in God. Logically, he can't exist, but I know for a fact you believe in him. He parted the red sea, turned water into wine, made a burning bush talk, yet you don't question that. That's the way I feel about ghosts and spirits. I also know you believe in heaven and hell and the existence of the devil. Now that's one hell of a spirit for you."

"When you put it that way, I guess I do believe. I guess my doubts come in when you have people who say they can talk to the dead. Those are the people I don't believe. They cheat folks out of their money thinking they are talking to their long lost cousin or something."

"I agree. There are some people out there doing that too. But for every twelve that are fake, I think there is one that is totally legit. I just don't believe that once we die it's over."

"You are really starting to creep me out."

"Why? I'm more afraid of the living than the dead."

"I think we are going to have to agree to disagree on this one. You can have all the beliefs you want. Let's get this straight right now. I'm drawing the line about doing any freaky shit like séances and stuff in this house."

"Girl bye. Ain't nobody talking about doing any of that stuff. I just said that I believe in it to a certain degree. That doesn't mean I'm about to try any of it out. Besides, I have cooking to do."

"I asked if you needed any help."

"Oh, right. You sure did. Can you go through that crab meat and make sure there are no shells in it? It would really be a big help."

"Ewe, I'm not trying to have my hands smell all fishy."

"Jesus H. Christ. That's what soap is for."

"Jeez, I'm just joking. Lighten up."

I took the crab meat and a large bowl over to one of the bar stools and had a seat. I really didn't mind helping Jordan. It gave me something to do. Besides, I wanted to clear the air before Brody got there.

"Can I be honest with you?" Jordan asked.

I stopped picking through the crab as my heart rate accelerated. Every time someone asked me that question, it seemed like something bad would happen to me. "Of course," I answered between lips that suddenly became parched. I felt like all the fluid in my body had evaporated.

"I'm nervous about seeing Brody. I don't know why, but I'm almost giddy with it."

"Oh, that's all? I mean, it's only natural you should feel that way. I think. You have to remember you are talking to a girl who has zero experience with men. I have never had sex with anyone unless it was forced on me. So, I don't know how you are supposed to feel in a situation like this."

Jordan grabbed a dish towel and wiped her hands. "I keep forgetting about that. I'm sorry."

"No worries. I don't think about it much anymore."

"I still think we should try to find you someone. I mean, it's not like Brody is my man or anything like that, but at least he's a man and he appears to be interested in me. I want that for you too."

"I want that for me too. Speaking of which, were you serious about my inviting someone over for dinner tonight?" I asked sheepishly.

Jordan stopped washing the fish and smiled at me. "Of course I'm serious. I think it would be fun."

"Well, there is someone that I could invite."

"Say what? Have you have been holding out on me Missy? I'm not sure I like that."

"No, not really. I haven't actually told this guy who I am."

"Huh? What are you talking about? You are not making any sense."

"Remember that show we watched the other night on television?"

"That stupid show about internet dating?"

"Yeah, that's the one."

Jordan picked her knife up and resumed cleaning and dressing her fish. The skin around my neck started to feel tight and I gently pulled at it.

"Oh, Lord, please don't tell me you have fallen for some guy you have been talking to on line. Didn't you see the same show I did? Those things never turn out right." Jordan was wielding the knife as she talked.

"Sometimes they do. You have only watched one show. I have been watching it for two seasons."

"Even still. You are so pretty, why would you have to find some guy off the internet?"

"I'm not exactly putting myself out there to meet anyone now am I?"

"Well that's true. You don't go anywhere except when you are out running and shit. But surely there is a better way than this blind date type of shit."

"It's not exactly blind. I know who this guy is. He just doesn't know who I am."

Jordan put down her knife again seemingly finished with her preparations. She washed and dried her hands. "Okay, I'm totally confused now. What did you do? Surf through some nigga's pictures on Facebook and picked one out?"

"If you are going to make jokes about it, then I'm not going to tell you."

"Sweetie, I'm not making fun of you, but you know how this sounds. It's so...desperate."

"I am not desperate." I pushed the crab meat away from me angrily. I knew telling her wasn't going to be easy but I never imagined it to be like this.

"I didn't say you were desperate. I just said it sounded desperate. There's a difference."

"Well it sounds like the same thing to me. Forget it. I'm out of here."

"Lacy don't run away like that. You know I'm crazy. Finish telling me what you were trying to say."

I was a little pissed off. I didn't like for people to poke fun at me. "It ain't no big deal. It was just something I was thinking about." I was sulking because this wasn't going the way I wanted it to go.

"Really, come on. I'm not judging you."

I thought about it for several seconds. I really needed to tell someone my plan just in case shit got a little ugly. Jordan was my best friend in the whole world, so I had to take a chance and hope that she wouldn't get mad at me. I went to the refrigerator and grabbed a beer. I didn't even like beer, but I needed the fake courage it gave me. "Like I was saying before I was so rudely interrupted. I'm talking to this guy but he thinks he's talking to you." I guzzled the beer while I waited for her to comprehend what I had just said.

For several heart beats Jordan didn't move. It was almost as if she was encased in ice. Slowly, she thawed. "Are you fucking kidding me? You used pictures of me to meet this creep? Why in the hell would you do that and drag me into this mess?" Jordan shouted.

"I um—" I knew she was going to freak a little bit, but she seemed angrier than I anticipated. I didn't know why she was trippin'. I was going to tell the guy the truth eventually.

"What kind of bullshit is that Lacy? I'm not playing that little game with you. You need to fix this shit and quick. People could get fucked up if you know what I mean. And why the hell wouldn't you use your own picture? That's what I can't understand and you better not have a television crew lined up to call me on my fucking phone either. I'm not playing with you Lacy. I will hang the fuck up."

"Will you pipe the hell down? I didn't do it this way because of the television show. I did it because I didn't know if the guy would agree to meet me if I told him who I was."

"Grab me one of those beers too. You are making my head hurt."

I opened the frig and grabbed two more beers. I slide the bottle over the counter hoping that she didn't use it to bash me in the head with it. Jordan had a little temper on her and I didn't want it flaring up on me again. "This all goes back to that night at the festival in Atlanta and I almost died?" I didn't mention the fact that she was the one trying to kill me as I was sure she got my drift.

"Yeah," she replied hesitantly.

"And the dude who pretty much left me for dead."

"Go ahead."

"I want to see that fucker again. I knew he wouldn't agree if I came right out and told him who I was."

"And you want to bring him here? To our house? Girl, are you crazy?"

"Damn, hear me out before you start saying no and shit."

"Okay, but it better be good. This is sounding like some bullshit to me."

We both sucked down some more beer. "We were both a little high so there is a very good chance he won't remember who I am. I was thinking if I invited him here and things went to the left, you and Brody could stop him from going off on me. And, since Brody was actually there when the shit went down, he won't be all surprised about what happens."

"What do you expect to get from confronting the dude? Surely you don't want a relationship with him."

"Hell no! I don't want a relationship with him. I just want him to look me in my face and tell me why he bailed on me." I tossed my empty beer bottles in the trash. I was feeling a slight buzz.

"I don't know, girl. This sounds risky to me. If we do this, we are going to have to let Brody know about it before the guy gets here. Have you already invited him?"

"No, I wanted to ask you first. He might even say no."

"Damn. This shit is wild. What did you do? Did you set up a Facebook page for me? I think I need to see this page before I agree to anything. I don't know if I like my face out there on the internet."

"I made the page private. Besides, I couldn't very well put my own face out there because I still don't know if folks are chasing me or not." I went in my bedroom and grabbed my laptop. I signed on and put it on the kitchen counter for Jordan to see.

"So, this is Facebook? What's the big deal?"

"It allows you to connect with people all over the world."

"A telephone will do that sweetie."

I sighed. "This is another way. It started out being popular with folks our age in college. Now everybody and their momma uses it."

"Sounds like a lot of work. Where is this page you told me about?"

I clicked on the tiny image I made for her profile page. "See this little picture of a wheel, if you click it, it shows your page as private. Only people who you invite as friends can see your page."

"How many friends do I have?"

"One. I didn't really use your real name, just your picture."

"Where the fuck did you get that picture. I look like a hooker?"

"Girl, shut up. You do not. I took it the day we went shopping and were trying on all those clothes."

"Well, I left that outfit at the store on purpose. I think you should change it to something more conservative."

"Honey, hush. You looked good but I can change the picture with no problem. I didn't set the page up for any other reason than to trap Seven and it worked."

"Who the fuck is Seven?"

"That's the guy's name I was telling you about. Damn. Keep up."

"What kind of name is that? Is it his government name?"

I laughed out loud for the first time since we started talking about this. "Yeah, I checked. His mother must have had a sense of humor."

"You ain't even lying. When will our people learn that names mean everything? Folks are getting turned down for jobs because they have these wild ass names."

"I know right. I teased him about it too. So what do you say? Should I send him a message and ask him to come over?"

"I guess so, but you better call Brody and tell him what's about to go down. If he's not on board with this shit, I don't think we should do it."

"Let me just see if he's gonna come or not. We might be getting all worked up over nothing." I switched over to Seven's page and sent him a private message. I was nervous as I did it too, because if he said no, or didn't show up, it would be like he was rejecting me twice. As it turned out, I didn't have long to wait for an answer. He responded immediately.

"That negro must live on Facebook. He's already responding to my message," I said laughing.

"Oh, Lord, I hope I don't live to regret this. What time is he coming?"

"I told him seven."

"Fine, I will be good and liquored up by then. I'm leaving it up to you to talk to Brody."

Jordan finished seasoning and stuffing the fish and put it in the oven to bake while I cleaned up the kitchen. She hung her apron behind the door and went up to her bedroom and shut the door. My hands were shaking a little as I picked up the phone to call Brody.

CHAPTER FIVE
BRODY MASON

I was nervous as a cat in a room full of rocking chairs. One false move and my tail could get squashed. Being with Jordan was unlike being with any other girl I had ever met. Most of the time it left me feeling like a puppy begging for table scraps. The funny thing is, those scraps tasted better than any steak I had ever eaten. The fact that she could cut me off without notice, unnerved me. I was used to calling the shots and this time it was different.

My common sense was telling me to run as fast as I could, but my stupid heart wouldn't listen. It wasn't the physical aspect of our relationship that kept me going. That is, if you could even call what we have a relationship. We had hot steamy sex once. That was it. Although it was good to me, it was also a little scary too. Jordan practically forced me to do it. For the first time in years, I even had doubts about my prowess. Jordan had me feeling emotions I didn't even think I possessed.

I was about to walk out the door when the phone rang. Any other time, I would have let the answering machine get it, but once again, Jordan had me walking the walk of a sprung nigga.

"Talk to me." I was so confident it was Jordan. I didn't even bother to look at the caller ID.

"Uh, is this Brody?"

"Yeah, who's this?"

"I'm sorry. It's Lacy."

"Oh hey, Lacy. Is everything okay?" My heart started to race with just the thought that something could have happened to Jordan.

"Yes, everything is fine. I told Jordan I wanted to ask your help with something. I was wondering if you could possibly come over earlier than six."

I looked at my watch as a habit even though I knew I didn't have any place else I needed to be. "I was about to run out to the store and pick up a bottle of champagne to christen your new apartment. I could come on over right after that if you want."

"That's sweet of you, but I'm pretty sure I speak for Jordan too when I say, we don't need the champagne. I hate the stuff and I don't think she likes it either."

"Oh, okay. You want me to get some wine then?"

"Trust me. We are good. We have more liquor then the neighborhood bar. Just come on over when you get ready."

"Cool, see you in a little bit." I wasn't sure how I felt about knowing that Jordan and Lacy had a large supply of alcohol in their home. Both of them were still young, with varying degrees of psychological issues. I had to keep reminding myself how I behaved when I was their ages. Compared to me, they were angels.

***

I rubbed my hands down the legs of my jeans before I announced myself to the doorman of Jordan's apartment building. The downtown building was so swanky and posh, I almost felt intimidated. As daunting as it may be, I liked the fact that she chose such a secure building.

"Miss Bree is in the penthouse, Sir. Kindly press P in the elevator. She is expecting you," the doorman said with a polite nod of his head.

"Thanks," I mumbled. I could already tell that I wasn't going to be making too many late night trips to her house if it meant I had to announce my intentions every time I visited. I started laughing almost as soon as this thought cleared my head. At the rate I was going, I was lucky to even be here right now, let alone in the future.

During the express ride to the penthouse, I had the opportunity to compose myself a little. I stepped off the elevator and tried not to over think why I was actually here. There were two apartments on this floor but I didn't have to guess which one of them Jordan occupied because Lacy had opened the door waving excitedly.

"Brody, you are looking good! Come on over here and give me a hug. If you weren't my girl's man, I would be hitting on you my damn self," Lacy said laughing.

For a moment, I thought my ears were deceiving me. When did I become Jordan's man? Instead of playing into Lacy's choice of words, I went with it. "Girl, look at you! Life in the penthouse certainly agrees with you." I gave Lacy a big hug, lifting her tiny frame off the floor and twirling her around. This was my first time seeing her all dolled up and I liked what I was seeing.

"Get in here before our neighbor comes out to see what all the noise is about."

"You got a nosey neighbor?" I asked chuckling.

"I'll say. He's an older white guy. I don't think he likes us being here very much."

"He probably doesn't. I doubt it if too many of us are able to afford an apartment in a building like this. However did you find it?"

"Jordan's lawyer hipped us to it. It came furnished so it suited our needs. In any event, we like it and you are our first official guest."

"I feel so honored." I tried not to appear obvious as I looked around the apartment for Jordan. I thought I was being discreet, but I was stone cold busted.

"Hold on buddy, Jordan is still getting dressed. I told her I wanted to speak with you alone so she's taking her time."

"Uh, that's not a problem. I was just checking this place out. It's nice."

"We even got our own pool and hot tub," Lacy said as she walked over to the terrace doors and slid them open. I followed her out onto the balcony in awe. Compared to this place, my apartment was a dump.

"Damn! Talk about living large. I don't even want to know how much something like this cost."

"I know right. It's a big difference from where we came from!"

I followed Lacy back into the apartment and took a seat in the sunken living room. The modern furniture gave the room an elegant feel to it without being overly pretentious.

"Something smells good too," I said as I rubbed my belly. Truth be told, I wasn't hungry at all. The problem with my stomach was mainly nerves.

"Do you want something to drink?"

"I'll take a beer if you have one."

"Yeah, we got some." Lacy came back and handed me a beer and took the seat next to me on the couch.

"Thanks." I was trying hard to think of something to say to Lacy. I didn't really know her well and this was the first time we were alone together outside of the time I visited her in the hospital.

"I never got the chance to really tell you how much I appreciated all that you did for me and Jordan too for that matter."

"Ain't no need to thank me, I just did what needed to be done."

"That's kind of why I wanted to talk to you and my request is two-fold."

"I'll help you all I can, Lacy."

"Thanks, but don't be so fast to agree until you have heard what it is I want."

"Okay, point taken. What's up?"

"I know who the guy is that left me that night in the park. I want to confront him. I don't want it to be this big fight, I just want to ask him why he left me."

"That sounds reasonable enough. I would want to know too. But I thought you didn't really know the dude."

"I don't really, but I made him show me his license before I got into his truck."

"That was smart. Did you call him?"

"Not exactly. See I wasn't sure how I wanted to handle it or if he would even remember who I was. I mean, we were kind of high, if you know what I mean."

"Oh, I get it. You don't have to explain it to me. I know how those outdoor festivals can be."

"Exactly."

"So what do you need me to do? Track him down for you?"

"No, I actually found him on my own. I need you here as a buffer if things go left when I confront him."

"Wait, you mean he is coming here, tonight?"

Lacy nodded her head yes. I felt a small prickle of dread form in the pit of my stomach. I wasn't trying to get into any beef with some cat I didn't even know, but it was too late to back out now.

"He's coming, but he doesn't know he's supposed to meet me." Lacy dropped her eyes to the floor.

"What's that supposed to mean?" I asked as my misgivings grew.

"Well …"

As much as I wanted to see Jordan, I wasn't there for any bullshit. "Come on Lacy, spill it."

"Long story short, he thinks he's coming here to meet Jordan. I made a fake profile on Facebook and used her picture. Before you get all mad, Jordan didn't know anything about it until after I did it. She said she would play along, as long as you agreed to it."

"Wow. You do know this could go very badly don't you. People don't like to feel set up."

"I know. Do you really think he would have come if I told him I was the girl he left to die in the park?"

"Well, you got a point there. But still …"

"It was the only thing that I could think of other than showing up at his house. At least this way with witnesses, I know he won't try anything if he gets all mad and shit."

"Damn, Lacy, I wish you would have talked to me about this before you did it. I think we could have figured out another way for you to get the answers I feel you deserve. But you have done it now, so we will deal with it. As long as he doesn't put his hands on either of you girls, I'm cool."

Lacy reached over and gave me another hug. I heard a door close and I stole a look. Jordan was walking down the stairs in this amazingly long white dress. She looked like an angel to me. Her hair was hanging long and flowing as she practically glided down the stairs. Her entrance reminded me of an old fashioned Hollywood flick that was shot in black and white.

"Hey, Brody."

If she knew the effect she had on me, she didn't let it show on her face. I disengaged Lacy's arms and stood up to greet this woman of my dreams.

"Jordan, you are looking lovely as usual." I stood with my arms at my side unsure how to properly greet her.

"What? I don't get a hug?" Jordan asked smiling.

"Of course." I stepped forward as a slow smile spread across my face, almost like a flower in full bloom. I was immediately in sync with everything about her. From the way she curled her hair, to the perfume she wore that was tantalizing my nostrils. I wanted, no needed, to touch her. I pulled her to me and I inhaled her scent deeply. For a moment, it was like we were alone in the room as Jordan seemed to melt in my arms.

"Oh, for God's sake, get a room," Lacy said laughing breaking our spell.

Jordan pulled away first, but she continued to hold my hand as she gently pulled me over to the couch.

"Ignore Lacy. She's wanted to tease me all day."

I was confused by this but I tried not to let it show on my face. What was there to tease Jordan about? Could she have been as nervous or excited as I was at the prospect of seeing each other again? Did I dare suggest we get that room? Despite how good that sounded to me, I knew that wasn't the right answer. "Uh oh, have you two been cutting up?" I took a healthy swig from my beer.

"Whenever I get in one of my moods, Lacy tells me to go get some dick. She thinks that's the cure for everything," Jordan laughed out loud.

To my utter dismay, every drop of the beer that remained in my mouth was now on the coffee table. Lacy ran over and started hitting me on the back.

"Damn, Brody. You alright?"

I was mortified. I had beer dripping down my chin into my lap. What was I to say? "I am so sorry. That went down the wrong way. Where's the bathroom?" I didn't even want to look at Jordan.

Lacy was still laughing. "Second door on the right. Holla, if you need some help. I'm sure Jordan can clean you right up."

"Leave the man alone," Jordan hissed.

I felt like such an idiot. If I could have discretely gone out the door, I would have. I hadn't pulled such a punk move since I was in grade school. I couldn't even laugh it off, I was so embarrassed. I used a few paper towels to wipe away most of the mess. Luckily I was wearing dark pants so the stains didn't show up as well. I wiped my face as I looked in the mirror.

"Get a grip man. It's not that serious," I mumbled to my reflection. I wasn't really in the habit of talking to myself, but I actually felt better with the reassurance.

Lacy was waiting for me when I came out the bathroom.

"Brody, I'm sorry. Do you forgive me? You guys look so cute together. I can't help it when I tease you. Y'all just need to fuck and get it out the way."

"I heard that!" Jordan yelled from down the hall.

This was a big joke to both of them and it was starting to get on my nerves. "I don't know what's up with you two tonight, but I think I should leave before I make an even bigger fool of myself." I was not about to be toyed with. I cared too much about Jordan to be the butt of their jokes.

"No Brody. I promise I'll behave. It's just seeing you together. I promise I'll be good." Lacy pleaded.

"Yeah, and if she doesn't behave, we can get her back when that guy gets here." Jordan added.

Jordan was right. I had forgotten about the little dilemma that Lacy wanted my help with.

"Yeah, that's right. Payback can be a bitch." I boldly teased. For a split second, Lacy had this worried expression on her face but she quickly adjusted it. She was good. I was going to have to teach her how to play poker. She would be killer in a game. I would bet all my money on her.

CHAPTER SIX
LACY BATES

I was anxious to get this meeting over with. I glanced at the clock for about the hundredth time in five minutes. Yet Seven was still not here. I tried not to let my apprehension show as I prepared cocktails for Jordan and Brody, but all this pretending was getting on my nerves. I hated to be kept waiting, especially by a low down dirty dog like Seven, or Hector, as his momma named him.

"Girl, sit down somewhere. You are getting on my nerves with all this pacing back and forth. The nigga is going to be here. Stop sweating it."

"I am not pacing. I'm working out a kink in my knee that I got while running."

"In six inch heels? How's that working out?" Jordan snickered.

Jordan had jokes now but she wasn't all ha ha and shit before Brody got there. She changed outfits six times until she settled on the white dress she was wearing. I almost reminded her of it but decided against it. "Can I get you guys something to drink?"

Brody laughed "If you give me one more drink, I'm going to have to crash on the sofa."

"Fine, I'm nervous. Shoot me." I admitted.

"I'm trying to understand why though. What exactly do you hope to accomplish by inviting him here? I mean if he says he's sorry and all that, would you consider dating him or something like that?" Jordan's hair hid her eyes so I didn't know if she was messing with me or not. She knew I didn't give do-overs, so I didn't know why she was playing me in front of Brody.

"You already know the answer to that one so don't trip." The house phone rang and I momentarily froze.

Jordan smiled slyly. "Hello. Lover boy is here. Aren't you gonna answer it?"

"Jordan can you answer the door? He might leave if he sees it's me." I stood there wringing my hands with my feet locked in place.

"Sweetie, I'll answer the door, but first you have got to answer the phone."

"Huh? Oh, my bad." I snatched the phone from the wall feeling like the village idiot. "Yes, send him up." All of a sudden all my emotions started to collide. "He's here." I whispered.

"Damn, girl! Are you sure you want to do this?" Brody asked. I could tell he was ready to bust out laughing.

"Be quiet Brody. You sit here with me like we're together while Jordan answers the door." I felt better issuing orders.

As Jordan walked to the door, she said, "Just so you know, if this nigga tries to kiss me, I'm kicking him in the balls."

Brody chimed in, "And I'm punching him in the face."

It was a good thing I didn't have any serious designs on Seven or his ass would be toast. I practically fell over the sofa as I tried to jump unsuccessfully over the arm in my short skirt and heels. If Brody hadn't caught me, I would have rolled to the floor.

"Whoa, Nelly."" he said between chuckles. It was a good thing I owed him my life or he might have been in trouble too.

"Just act natural," I said as I smoothed my hair back in place. I leaned in closer to Brody pretending to be in deep conversation.

Jordan let him ring the bell twice before she opened the door.

"Jordan? Wow, I can't believe it. You look just like your picture!"

"You are a bit of a surprise yourself."

I could smell Seven even before I could see him. The strong aroma of weed was overwhelming. There was an awkward moment of silence and I almost stood up to see what was going on by the door. Brody, hand on my wrist, stopped me from getting up. "It's okay, I'm watching. That dude is high as hell but he doesn't look crazy," he whispered.

"Figures," I snorted. I wasn't the least bit surprised. We were high together less than five minutes after meeting each other.

"Come on in. I hope you don't mind, I invited my girlfriend and her boyfriend to join us."

"Why should I care? It's your place. And it's mighty fine too, just like you. Man, when you first poked me on Facebook, I thought one of my boys was fucking with me."

"Really? Why's that?' Jordan's voice was unusually low, indicating her discomfort.

"Are you kidding me? Look at you. You are gorgeous."

I felt Brody tense up next to me and I grabbed his wrist to keep him from getting up. I was pissed off because Seven had used the same lame duck line on me when we first met. He couldn't even be fucking original.

"Seven, uh, these are my friends, Brody and, uh, Lacy." If Seven noticed her hesitation, he didn't let on.

"Hey, how y'all doing?" Seven asked as if he couldn't care less. It was obvious to me he would have preferred to be there with Jordan alone.

"What's up?" Brody replied.

I looked up slowly, my heart playing double-dutch in my chest. Seven looked just as good today as he did the day he left me for dead in the park. I swallowed a pool of spit. "How's it going?"

"Fine, fine. I can't complain."

The bastard barely gave me a second look. He was all gaga over Jordan. I waited for him to do a double take or for a flicker of recognition to cross his face. I got nothing. Pissed didn't begin to describe what I was feeling. This asshole was really tripping.

"You know you sort of look familiar to me. Have we met?" I prodded.

"Uh, I don't think so." Seven waved me off like I was a nuisance.

He wouldn't know because he didn't even look at me. I snapped my finger in front of his face trying to reel him back in. It wasn't that I was feeling some kinda way about the way he was looking at Jordan. It was the way he was not looking at me, like I was shit on a stick.

"Lacy can you fix my guest a drink? You make the best cocktails in Atlanta."

"Sure. Does anybody else want anything while I'm in the kitchen?" It took everything in me not to launch myself off that sofa and cut that bastard to the white meat.

"We are good babe," Brody said as he winked at me.

"I'll be right back. Jordan can you play that track I told you about? They have been talking about this song all over the radio. I want to hear what the hype is about."

"It's tight girl. K Michelle is on point with this one."

The opening bars of K's bonus track called 'Fuck You' began as the door to the kitchen area swung shut. I walked in throwing my arms in mock punches in the air. I imagined myself whipping the shit out of Seven.

"I'll be back in a minute with some lemon drops." I yelled through the doors as I grabbed the glasses I had previously prepared and lined them on a tray. I mixed the vodka and lemon juice in a strainer over ice and poured some of the mixture into each of the four glasses. At the last minute, I decided against using the tray. I carried Jordan and Brody their drinks and went back into the kitchen to get the other two.

"Hey, where's mine?" Seven complained.

"I'm not a spider fool, I only have two hands." I took the bottle of Visine from the counter and squeezed in several drops into Seven's glass. I slipped the bottle in my bra and shook the glass to mix it up. My conscious almost got the best of me. For a split second I almost changed my mind about giving it to Seven. I wasn't trying to go to jail.

I walked over to the sink and started to pour out the doctored drink when I heard Seven talking about me from the living room.

"Your friend might be in the kitchen drinking those drinks instead of making them. You want me to go see if she needs some help? I'm pretty good behind the bar, if I do say so myself."

"Hey man, chill. She will be out in a minute," Brody answered, his tone icy.

I pulled the bottle out of my bra and sprinkled a few more drops into Seven's glass. "That's for being a smart ass." I pushed open the door with my butt and carried the drinks into the living room. "Jordan, I think dinner's ready. Do you want to eat now, while it's hot?" I was all smiles as I handed Seven his drink. For a brief moment our eyes locked but recognition didn't live there. Pity.

"Yes. We don't want to wait until it gets cold. You gentlemen can go into the dining room while Lacy and I serve."

I put my drink on the table and went back into the kitchen with Jordan.

"Is that the same guy? He acts like he doesn't know you from a can of paint."

"Oh, it's him alright. I guess I didn't make as much of an impression on him as I thought I had."

"So what are we going to do? I don't want this fool staring at me all night long like I'm a piece of chocolate cake."

"He won't. I'll find a way to get rid of him. Leave that part to me."

"If you say so. I'm not sure how much more of this Brody is going to stand for."

"I hear you. You get the side dishes, I'll carry the fish."

Brody had taken a seat across from Seven and was deep in conversation when we came back into the room.

"Your face is so familiar to me. Have we met before?"

"I don't know, but you look a little familiar too. I get around. We might have bumped into each other somewhere or the other."

"Yeah. I guess."

I detected something akin to disgust in Brody's voice. Jordan sat next to Brody leaving the only available place setting left next to Seven, for me.

"That lemon drop was on point. Too bad the glass was so small to enjoy it." Seven said.

Oh no this mother fucker didn't. At this point, I didn't even want to keep up the pretense. I found out what I needed to know. Even if I didn't get sick that night at the park, this bastard would not have been in my life. He would have taken whatever he wanted from me and would have been gone. I gripped the edge of the table to keep from picking up my knife and planting it in his lap.

"Did you want me to fix you another?" I asked with the sweetest voice I could muster.

"Yeah, that would be tight. And see if you got a bigger glass. That way you won't have to keep running back and forth to the kitchen. You were just teasing a brother with that one."

I could feel Jordan staring at me as I slowly stood up. "No problem. I'll be right back."

"Do you need some help," Jordan inquired. She knew I was pissed.

"Oh, I got this. It's no biggie. Y'all go ahead and start eating while I fix up another batch." My chair bounced off the wall leaving a mark on the white walls. Kicking the chair was the only visible sign of my anger, but Seven apparently missed even that.

"Maybe you should bring him the whole bottle," Brody mumbled under his breath loud enough for me to hear when I walked passed him.

"I know right." I mumbled back.

"Jordan, did you cook all this?" Seven asked with a mouth full of food.

"I sure did."

"I don't know if it's the munchies or whether I'm hungry as hell, but this food is delish."

If Jordan responded, I didn't hear it from the kitchen. I pulled a larger glass from the cabinet and fixed Seven a generous drink. I didn't appreciate having to get up from my plate to fix him another drink so soon after I prepared the first one. I was about to leave the kitchen when I remembered the tiny bottle nestled in my bra. This time, I didn't even hesitate to squeeze off several more drops of the liquid into the glass. "Serves him right for disrespecting me in my own home," I whispered. I wasn't trying to kill the man but I did want to see him suffer. With any luck, he would shit his pants.

"I hope you don't gulp this one down like you did the first one." I said as I shoved the drink in his direction.

"Damn, baby, chill. If it didn't taste so good, I wouldn't have drunk it as fast."

I didn't believe that for a second. He was high and feigning. I could have given him warm piss and he would have been happy. I giggled loudly as I visualized myself peeing in his glass in the kitchen.

"You alright, Lacy?" Jordan asked. She was looking at me like she wanted to say something else but stopped herself.

"I'm starving. We've been going all day and this is the first thing I've put in my mouth all day."

"I know that's right."

"It really is good. Isn't it Brody?"

"It sure is. Who knew she could cook so well."

"Cooking ain't the only thing I'm good at." Jordan suggestively added.

"You don't have to tell me. I already know." Brody lifted up his glass and they shared a private toast. For all intents and purposes, they could have been alone. They appeared to be oblivious to anyone else in the room.

"She watches all of those reality cooking shows. She even knows most of the stuff they put in those dishes. Me, I just eat them." I just wanted to say something to make them remember they weren't alone.

Brody looked at me with a surprised look on his face. "You don't cook Lacy?" Brody asked while dabbing his mouth with a napkin.

"Yeah, I can cook but my meals are simpler."

"Well, the next time I'm going to invite you both over to my house for dinner. I can't promise you stuffed shark but it will be good."

He included me in the invitation but I was not about to go over to his place and become a third wheel. This little dinner was hard enough to swallow as it was. Jordan and Brody continued their conversation quietly while Seven continued to stuff his face. If he was at all concerned about Jordan's apparent disdain for him, I couldn't tell. The only thing he appeared to be interested in was his glass and his plate. He ate with gusto, chasing crumbs around his plate until it was empty. He dropped his fork on his plate.

"That shit was good," he said burping loudly while rubbing his belly.

I didn't know if I was more embarrassed about the fact that I had invited him or that he was too uncouth to notice he was a pig.

"Damn, boy. Say excuse me." I snapped.

"Oh, I'm sorry. I wasn't trying to be rude. In some cultures, burping is considered a compliment to the chief."

"A simple thank you would have sufficed in this one." I was so irritated I didn't know what to do. Jordan was giving me the evil eye while Brody gave me questioning stares. It was definitely awkward, to say the least.

Seven finally woke up and saw what was happening in front of him. "I see where this is going. I guess it's going to be me and you shorty. What's your name again?"

"Annoyed."

Jordan cleared her throat loudly. "Lacy can you help me clear the table. I hope you guys saved room for desert."

Begrudgingly, I followed Jordan into the kitchen with the dishes.

Jordan whispered, "Honey, this is going from bad to worse. What are we going to do?"

"I know. I'm thinking. I thought dude was going to take one look at me and leave. I didn't count on his not knowing who the fuck I was. It's a good thing I didn't like his ass like that or I would have to cut him."

"Hey, we don't have to go there. It's not that serious."

I begged to differ. Jordan wasn't disrespected, I was. Not only didn't he remember my face from a few months before, he couldn't remember my name after hearing it about twenty times in a row. Fuck him. "Don't worry about it. I'm about to get rid of this fool. Why don't you and Brody go out and sit by the pool?"

"I don't know about that. You know how your temper gets. We might do better if we tell Brody to ask him to leave."

"I'm not dragging Brody into this. I will get rid of Seven in a non-violent way. I promise." I crossed my fingers behind my back. If the Visine didn't work, I was willing to do what I had to do to get him out of our home.

Jordan still didn't look convinced but she took my suggestion and led Brody to the patio leaving me alone with the asshole.

"You think I can get something else to drink? What did you call it?"

"It's a lemon drop. Are you always this obnoxious? Or are you making a special effort to impress me?"

"Damn, I just asked for a drink. It ain't like your girl can't afford it. Her uppity ass invited me over here and shit and she ain't doing nothing but ignoring me. I might as well drink up all her liquor."

"Did it occur to you that she might be ignoring you because you came in her house high as hell reeking of weed and shit?"

"You can smell it?" He asked as if he were surprised.

"How can I help it? It's all in your clothes."

"I can share. I brought some with me." He started fumbling in his pockets as if he was about to light up right there in our house.

"Naw. We ain't trying to do that up in here."

"Y'all too fancy for a little weed? Ain't nothing wrong with it. It's natural, grows in the ground. In some states it's legal."

I was flabbergasted. Who was this fool talking to me? He may have looked good on the outside but inside, where it really mattered, he sucked.

"I don't have a problem with weed. I have a problem with obnoxious jerks."

"Who you calling obnoxious?" He asked as he attempted to stand up.

"Do you see anybody else in the room?" Things were heating up fast in the living room as Seven looked at me probably for the first time since entering my house.

"You look kind of familiar to me."

"You have been in my house for about forty-five minutes and you're just noticing that?"

"Damn, where do I know you from?" He started to sit back down but abruptly stood up. A scowl crossed his face as his eyes widened.

"Let's just say we bumped into each other before. Six degrees of separation."

"Yeah, yeah. Hey, do you know where the bathroom is?"

"It's down the hall, second door on the right." I wanted to laugh so hard it hurt.

"Thanks." Seven stumbled off clutching his stomach. He looked as if he was trying to walk up straight but as he got closer to the bathroom he was clearly bent over.

I picked up the stereo's remote and turned on my new anthem, *You Got The Right One*. I removed the rest of the dishes from the table and loaded up the dishwasher, smiling the entire time.

I could see Jordan on the patio and she looked like she was really enjoying herself. As a couple, they looked good together. I couldn't help feeling a little envious of what they had. I was ready to experience what it was like to have a relationship with someone I actually liked instead of someone I feared or loathed. I never made love, I only experienced sex. Bad sex at that. I wanted that fantasy love that I saw on television or read about in books. I knew that it had to exist. All I had to do was find it.

I rapped on the bathroom door. "Are you okay in there?" I could hear Seven grunting through the door.

"Yeah."

I walked away with my hand covering my mouth. He was getting the ultimate fuck you and I loved it. Served him right for leaving me for dead. I walked outside on the balcony.

"Everything alright in there?' Jordan asked.

"Yeah, it's good."

"What did you do with dude? Kick him out?"

"Not yet. He's in the bathroom."

Brody snorted. His dislike for Seven was written all over his face. "He's probably in there getting high. Y'all are lucky I'm trying to be nice today or I would have really clowned that nigga for showing up here high. That ain't cool."

"Who you telling? I feel stupid for asking him over here. Trust me, as soon as he gets out the bathroom, I'm telling him to leave."

Seven staggered down the hall, still clutching his stomach. Keeping a straight face, I put down my drink and went inside to see if he was okay.

"Are you sure you are alright?" I asked with fake concern.

"My stomach hurts. I think I need to go."

"You don't look so good. You think you should go to the hospital or something?"

"Can't go to any hospital. They might test me for drugs and try to hold a nigga up." He might have been a little wacky in the head but he wasn't stupid.

"Well, okay. I hope you feel better." I was practically walking his ass out the door but he kept grabbing on the wall for support.

"It just hurts so bad..." Seven began to sweat as he slumped against the wall as if he couldn't walk another step. I started to panic.

"I think you need to go to a hospital." I was trying to act like I gave a damn about him. Going to the hospital was the last thing I wanted him to do. I didn't want them to give him something to make him feel better. I wanted the fucker to suffer just like I did.

"I just need to get home." He tried to push away from the wall with great difficulty.

"Do you think you should drive?" He obviously didn't think it through. He could barely hold his head up.

"Is everything okay?" Brody had snuck up behind us.

I had to think quickly. Brody could mess everything up. Ever the Good Samaritan, he would call nine-one-one quicker than I could bat an eye. "Everything is fine. Seven isn't feeling well. I'm going to drive him home." This had not been in my plans but under the circumstances I felt like it was the only thing that I could do.

"You are?" Brody and Seven asked at the same time. If they were having a difficult time believing it, imagine how I felt when my mouth started talking before engaging my brain.

"Yes, give me your keys." I held my hand out to Seven.

"Must have been something I ate," Seven mumbled as he pulled his keys from his pocket.

"I beg your pardon," Jordan said as she brought up the rear of our little posse.

"He didn't mean that Jordan. The man is delusional. I'm going to take him home."

"You are?" Jordan's mouth hung open like a drive thru.

"Why is that so hard for either of you to believe? Brody don't stand around gawking, get the door. Jordan can you grab my purse for me?" I pulled Seven off the wall trying to support his weight. He wasn't a big guy, but he was solid. We both almost fell over.

"I got him. You get the door." Brody said.

I was so thankful for Brody's offer of assistance, I could have kissed him. He helped Seven to the car while I waited on Jordan. She stopped me as I was walking out the door. "Are you sure about this? How will you get home?"

"I can catch a cab if necessary. Don't worry about me. I'll be okay."

"You got your knife?"

"Always. Why do you think I asked you to get my purse?" I turned to follow Brody out the door.

"You're not going to do anything to him are you?"

"Look at him. Even I'm not that cold-blooded."

"All right. Don't make me come looking for you," Jordan warned.

She might have said it jokingly, but I knew she was serious. We had become pretty close and it made me feel good to know that she cared.

"I'll call you just as soon as I drop him off."

"You do that."

CHAPTER SEVEN
JORDAN BREE

I rested my back against the wall as I tried to force myself to calm down. Part of me wanted to pop a Xanax, the other part of me wanted to drink a fifth of Vodka. Even though I knew they weren't the answer, I still considered them. I felt like I was in an emotional vortex free falling in unknown territory without a life line. I wasn't used to not being in control of my emotions and I didn't know what to do about it.

"Get yourself together girl." I scolded myself. I pushed my body off the wall and went into the kitchen to clean up. To my surprise, Lacy had already beaten me to it. I assumed she did it while Brody and I were out on the terrace. I smiled because Lacy hated washing dishes. I froze when I heard the front door shut.

"Jordan?" Brody called from the foyer.

My breath caught in my throat. "In the kitchen." My voice sounded strange even to my own ears. My heart was pounding with anticipation. Now that we were alone, I wasn't sure how to act.

"Dinner was delightful. I feel like I gained five pounds."

"There's still desert," I said as I turned around holding the chocolate cake we had picked up earlier.

"As good as it looks, I couldn't eat another bite if I tried."

"It's a seven-layer cake. Lacy picked it out. We weren't sure if you even ate dessert. I told Lacy you were too concerned about working out to waste calories on sweets."

"Normally, I don't, but I've been known to make exceptions." Brody winked at me. My nerves were starting to get the best of me.

"Do you want something else to drink? A beer maybe?"

"I'll take a beer if you got one. I was going to bring some wine…"

The air in the room seemed thicker to me. Alive with unspoken emotions. *Did he feel it too? Or was it just me?*

"What did you think about Seven?" I asked as I handed him a beer and took one for myself.

"I feel sorry for dude. I'd hate to be the one riding in the car with Lacy right about now."

I laughed. "Yeah, she's pretty pissed off at him."

"I don't blame her. First, he shows up high as hell. Then, he acts like he doesn't even know who she is. I'll bet she is cussing his ass out as we speak."

"Her mouth can be vicious. I remember when we first met, I thought I was going to have to kill her." I was joking about it as if I didn't actually try to do it. In truth, had it not been for Brody's intervention, Lacy would have been fertilizer.

"You don't have to tell me about it. I saved her life and she was giving me straight attitude the entire time." Brody said laughing.

I didn't want to talk about Lacy. She was gone and I wanted to take advantage of it. However, I didn't know how to move the conversation to a more intimate level. "Do you want to go back in the living room? Or out on the terrace?"

"I'm just a guest. I'll go wherever you tell me to go."

Was that a sexual innuendo? Was he saying take me, I'm yours? Or was I fucking tripping? "You do know you only get to play the guest card once right? After that…"

Brody stepped closer. "What?"

I had a knot in my throat the size of a quarter. "I, uh…" I tightened my grip on my beer scared I was going to drop it.

"Go ahead. Say it." He whispered. He was standing less than two inches away but it felt like an entire football field. I wanted to wrap myself up in him.

"Then you have to help yourself."

He inched closer. "So I have to wait for next time?"

I couldn't think. He was too close. He wasn't close enough. I willed my feet to close the distance between us, but I felt like I was paralyzed. His cologne teased my nostrils. "You smell good," I said with a whimper.

"I'll bet you taste good."

Damn. How should I respond to that? I could almost feel his lips on my body as an involuntary shudder coursed through me. To be so frozen on the outside,

I was hotter than fish grease on the inside. "I guess there's only one way to find out." I closed my eyes in anticipating.

"Open your eyes," Brody demanded.

My lids snapped open as I locked eyes with him. "Okay."

"I need for you to see me."

See him? I saw him alright. Every night before I went to bed, I saw him. I laughed uncomfortably. I was sure my desire was written all over my face. His lips loomed closer, mere milometers from mine. My pulse quickened. He gave me permission to look and I took full advantage of it. "I see you." I was incapable of independent thought. If he commanded it, I would have said the pledge of allegiance backwards and I couldn't remember all those words if I had to do them that way.

"What do you see?" His eyes burned with an intensity I had never noticed before.

"Huh?"

"What do you see when you look at me." He stepped closer, a breath away. We were recycling the same air.

"I, uh."

"You said that before. Let me help you. Can you see how much I want you?"

My knees shook. Who was this man standing in front of me? The first time we slept together, I practically raped him. I opened my mouth but no words came out. I nodded my head yes. I could see it.

"Can you see how hard—"

My eyes shot to his crotch. My cheeks felt like they were on fire. My breathing ragged. I wanted to turn down the air. It was so hot in there.

"...it is for me to be around you?"

"Is it hot in here to you?" I couldn't even lift my hand to fan myself. I almost wanted to stick my tongue out to lap up the air like a puppy sticking its head out the window.

"Oh it's hot alright. Too bad I didn't bring my swimming trunks. We could take a dip in the pool."

Who the hell needed swimming trunks? We were both grown. "Too bad."

"Any other suggestions?" Brody lightly ran his beer bottle down my arm. He couldn't have gotten more of a reaction from me if he used a defibrillator. My panties were sopping wet. Was this what seduction felt like?

"Umm, that feels good." My head rolled on my neck as my eyes closed again.

"Keep them open."

"Why?" I gushed as I forced my lids back open.

He whispered in my ear, "I told you."

"I can't." I felt like I had stuck my finger in a light socket. I was trembling.

"Yes, you can. You can do anything you want to do. Don't you believe that?"

"Yes." This man was mind fucking me. A Jedi mind trick.

"Did I tell you how sexy that white dress is?" His lips were still so close to my ear it was difficult for me to concentrate on his words. He stood directly in front of me. His foot in between mine.

I shook my head as blood thumped around in my veins. I felt like I could feel each cell colliding as they moved. I wanted him to touch me.

"You didn't exactly give me the tour."

Tour? Of what? Our eyes locked again. "You have already seen it."

"I was referring to your apartment." Brody said chuckling with a knowing smile on his face.

My head snapped back breaking the spell he had spun on me. My mind has skipped straight to the gutter as I envisioned him undressing me. Oops, my bad. He acted as if he was impervious to the sexual tension in the air. Two could play this game. "Oh. I thought you wanted to see something else."

I didn't miss the way his Adam's apple bobbled. "Are you trying to entice me, Miss Bree?"

I leaned forward and tickled his ear with my lips. "Yes, I believe I am."

"What about Lacy?" He whispered. His voice dropped down low. If he were an animal, he would be a sleek panther.

"Who?" It sounded more like a moan of pleasure to my ears than an actual word.

"Where's your bedroom? I would like to see that."

I didn't trust myself to speak again as I pointed to the stairs. My sitting room was on the first floor but my actual bed was up the stairs. Brody was standing in front of me like a wall of flesh. "You gotta move first."

Brody stepped aside, his arm brushing against mine, sending electrical currents through my blood. It tingled down to my toes. Brody followed close behind me doging my steps.

"Nice. This is almost like two apartments in one."

I wasn't thinking about the apartment or the space. I only had one thing on my mind. My bedroom looked like something from the old plantation days. I had the dark cherry wood poster bed draped in a white canopy. White satin pillows lined the bed. A dark wood trunk sat at the foot of the bed covered with a white mink throw rug. My dresser covered one wall. My makeup stand covered the other.

"You know you were wrong for wearing that dress don't you?"

"You didn't like it?" My heart sank.

"Your nipples were sticking out all night. How did you expect me to concentrate with all that sitting next to me?"

"I hadn't noticed?"

"You can't feel your nipples poking out like raisins?" His eyes had a look of wonder.

"Not unless I touch them."

"Do it." Brody instructed his tone commanding again.

"Do what?" I feigned ignorance. I had never openly played with myself before. It was a definite turn on for me.

"Touch your nipples. I want you to feel what I see."

"Like this?" I asked as I brushed my hands over the front of my dress. As turned on as I was, I was sure it would feel better if he did it.

"No." Brody folded his arms across his chest.

"Show me."

Brody's eyebrow lifted. "You don't want to play?"

"I would love to play. Just show me how. Remember, I was a virgin when we met. If there is something you want me to know, you have to teach me."

"Damn girl. You are so fucking sexy without any lessons from me," Brody growled deep in his throat. I basked in his complimentary words.

Brody pulled me close to him and spun me around. The bottom of my dress flared from the sudden movement. The Marilyn Monroe like design was made for twirling. I was putting Kenya Moore to shame. Brody untied the straps and spun me back around. His eyes glued to my now bare bosom. "Like this." He grabbed one breast in his hand and squeezed it. He used his other hand and fingered the nipple sending tingles all throughout my body. "Do you like that?"

"Yes," I couldn't have said more if I tried.

He lowered his head and gently kissed the tip. I inhaled sharply as the sensations flowed through me.

"Can I make love to you?"

Again, I could only nod. I had no experience at making love. I barely knew how to fuck.

He picked me up so that I could look him directly in his eyes. Without having any prior knowledge, I recognized the look of passion in his eyes. I could only hope he saw the same fire in mine. I wanted him so badly, I ached inside.

"Hang on," he grunted. I wrapped my arms and legs around him as he carried me across the room pinning me against the wall. I loved the feel of his rock hard muscles against my bare chest. Brody shook his head as if he were in some sort of internal dispute. "If we do this again, it's going to be different."

If, what the fuck did he mean if... "Okay."

"I'm a man who happens to care a lot about you."

He was wasting time. Telling me something I already knew. "I know you do Brody." I would have agreed to anything, my desire for him was so great.

"I'm not some battery operated dildo you can pull out when you need it and tuck back in the drawer when you don't. You can't just turn me off like that."

Dildo? I never thought of him that way. He might have me confused. "I, uh…"

"If we do this again, I'm claiming ownership?"

My heart was beating riotously in my chest. "Of what?" I whispered even though I already knew the answer. The question was, was I ready for that?

"You," he grunted as he kissed me, allowing all of his passion into the merging of our lips. I opened my mouth and allowed his tongue to enter and it felt like tiny fireworks were going off all over my body, busting capillaries. Mingled with those fireworks were warning bells signaling danger. *Ownership? Like a slave? Fuck was that supposed to mean?* I had to know. "Wait, what does that mean?" I asked pushing back from his luscious lips.

"You are mine." For him, he acted like it was so simply, but I was still confused as to what that meant after his loins were sated.

"Yours? I don't want to be like cattle, branded like sheep." None of that sounded sexy to me.

Brody sighed. "Girl, stop bugging. Ain't nobody trying to have no slave. I'm just saying you gonna stop introducing me like your friend and tell folks I'm your man. Can you do that?"

That sounded easy. Brody was a catch. Sexy as all outdoors. Kind, considerate. Yeah, I could do that. "Yes, I can."

Brody dipped his head and suckled my breast. The feeling was euphoric and I wanted more. Like a starving woman I clutched his head forcing him to continue his invasion. My clit was bouncing to the beat of his desire. I moaned loudly.

"You like that baby?"

"Yes, yes I do," my girls were on fire as he flicked his tongue over them. Brody pulled me away from the wall and carried me over to the bed where he took off the rest of my clothes. I shimmied to the center of the king-sized bed in anticipation of what was to come.

Slowly, without breaking eye contact with me, Brody began taking off his clothes. This experience was so much different from our first and last encounter. That time, I didn't take the time to admire his body. It was all about fulfilling my needs. I knew right away, this time was going to be different as I waited for his final article of clothing to be dropped ceremoniously to the floor. I gasped at the size of his penis as it stared at me.

"That's all for you," Brody said as he rubbed his hand over his shaft. For some reason, seeing the effect I had on him, aroused me more. I crawled to the edge of the bed and took him in my mouth.

"Ahh." Brody's eyes rolled up in his head. His fingers balled into tight fists as I slobbered over his knob. I wasn't sure what I was doing but he appeared to be enjoying it. His pleasure was satisfying to me. I loved the way he felt in my hands.

Brody gently pushed me back on the bed. "That's enough of that."

I felt like a kid whose sucker had been ripped from her mouth. I pouted.

"I like it."

"I like it too, but you are about to end it before we even get started. Open your legs."

I did as he instructed. Normally, I didn't like it when people told me what to do. This time was different.

Brody knelt on the bed between my legs. His eyes covering every inch of my body like a silken blanket, warming me with the intensity of his gaze. "You are so beautiful to me." His dick jumped with his words arousing me further.

I admired his body too, starting with his bald head, down his muscular chest as I followed the narrow trail of hairs that led to his glorious manhood. *Was he naturally hairless on the chest? Or would I have to fight him for my wax?* Either way, I wouldn't care. He was so sexy, it was shameful. "Please," I moaned. I felt like I was window shopping at the mall with no money.

"You don't have to beg for me baby. I'm all yours." He lowered his face between my thighs and I almost shot off the bed. As good as it felt to have him taste me, I was on sensory overload.

"I can't," I moaned.

Brody instantly pulled back. My juices dripping from his lips. His eyes filled with alarm and concern. "What's wrong?"

"I feel like I'm about to explode," I breathlessly exclaimed as my head thrashed back and forth.

Brody slid up my body until his face was even with mines, his chest barely touching as he held himself over me. "Honey, that's what's supposed to happen. Don't fight it, roll with it." He dipped inside of me igniting a fuse of desire. Our concurrent moans were smothered with a kiss as he moved deeper inside of me.

I got lost in the rhythm as he dove deeper inside of me. My hips lifted off the bed meeting his thrusts. "Oh, God," I moaned.

"Yes," Brody answered back as his tempo increased. I gave up trying to keep eye contact. My stupid pupils were all over the place as I tried to match his stride. It was like we were trying to merge as one. As we came in symphonic harmony, I felt our souls unite.

"Unbelievable." Brody kissed both of my eyelids.

"Yes it was. Can we do it again?"

"We sure can. But I'm gonna need to rest a minute. You are trying to kill me as it is." Brody rolled over and pulled me on top of him. I sighed as I rested my head on his chest. His heart was beating as fast as mine.

"Okay. Me too." I kissed the side of his mouth and closed my eyes letting his beating heart lull me to sleep. I wanted so badly to tell him that I loved him. He said I belonged to him. Did that mean he belonged to me? I had so much more to learn but for now, sleep was calling me.

CHAPTER EIGHT
BRODY MASON

I was basking in a glow of what could only be described as love. This young girl had completely stolen my heart and I did not want it back. But with this love, came serious responsibility. She was naïve about matters of the heart and I couldn't dismiss the bipolar diagnosis given to her by her former doctor. The fact that I hadn't seen any psychotic behavior, since the first time we slept together, worried me. 'Would she be a basket case when she woke from her nap?' was the question that kept me from falling asleep. I loved her too much to be the source of pain for her. I would leave her alone before I did that.

"How long was I out?"

"Not too long. I enjoyed watching you sleep."

"Dag. I hope I wasn't snoring," she said as her eyes appeared to sparkle.

"A gentleman never tells," I teased. She seemed normal. I took a deep breath as Jordan playfully punched me on my chest.

"I do not snore." She giggled rather loudly. It was such an infectious laugh, I couldn't help but join her.

"Hey, that's not how you are supposed to treat your man." Rocking her gently in my arms Jordan attempted to pull away. I understood right away what I had said that made her pull away from me. She already told me she was inexperienced. I couldn't make jokes about what she did or didn't know.

"I was only kidding sweetheart. You can play with me any way you like. Even love taps." I felt her stiffen in my arms again. Damn, at the rate I was going, I would talk myself out of the relationship before we had given it half a chance. Jordan began to shake in my arms and it was like my worst fears were being confirmed.

"What's the matter?" She was trembling as I rolled her over to her side so I could look her in the face.

"I don't know anything about how love feels. I'm such a mess aren't I?"

"Are you kidding me? You are perfect in every way. I don't know a man alive who wouldn't kill to be in my shoes."

Jordon cocked her head to the side as a surprised expression crossed her face. "What makes me so special or different from any other girl?" She seemed hurt.

I hesitated before I answered her making sure I ordered my words before I misspoke. "The same naivety you seemed ashamed of makes you that much more endearing. A lot of times, relationships sour before they have a chance to develop because one or both parties bring excess emotional baggage with them into the relationship. The fact that you have none makes this transition so much easier."

"How can you say I have no emotional baggage? Did you forget about the four years I spent in the insane asylum? Don't try to placate me Brody, I don't like it."

"You are mixing apples and oranges Jordan. I'm talking about relationship baggage. It's different and more complicated."

"But you can't ignore what I have been through. Like it or not, it's a part of me."

"Who said anything about not liking it? Can you hold up for a second and let me explain myself before this gets all twisted out of shape."

"I don't want to talk about it. I need to take a shower before Lacy gets home." Jordan backed out of the bed with the sheet wrapped around her body leaving me cold and naked. If she noticed, I couldn't tell. She refused to meet my eyes. Despite all my caution and care, I managed to put my foot in my mouth.

"Jordan, wait." I followed her into the bathroom just as she was stepping into a shower clearly built for two or more. Without waiting to be invited, I slipped inside with her.

"What are you doing in here?"

"Can't I get clean too?

"I've got other bathrooms," she said pouting.

"We can conserve water this way and give back to Mother Earth." It sounded stupid, but I said the first thing that came to my mind.

"Mother Earth can kiss my ass and so can you."

From the look on her face, I could tell she was just as shocked by her comment as I was.

"Turn around and I will." She did not crack a smile. I was trying to keep things light between us and I was losing the battle. Jordan was staring me down like she hated me. I grabbed her shower puff and the soap and began working them in my hands.

"What are you doing? I need those."

"Can I wash you?" I dropped down on my knees with water pelting my back and started washing her feet. She resisted when I tried to lift her foot but she eventually gave in. I took my time washing and massaging her feet working my way up her ankles to her knees. I applied more soap to the puff and started working on her legs. "Spread them for me." I didn't dare look up. Water was pouring down my face, but I could still see the object of my desires. As I washed her legs, I gently massaged them. In spite of the water running in my eyes, I was enjoying myself.

"You shouldn't be doing this?" Jordan's voice was shaky.

"Why not? Everybody needs a little pampering."

I lifted my knee and propped her foot up on it giving me better access to her pleasure pot. I put down the puff and soaped my hands. Jordan jumped as I touched her down there. "Relax baby," I cooed.

"You dropped the puff."

"I don't need it for this." I heard Jordan suck in a deep breath causing me to smile. She wasn't the only one being affected by our closeness, my dick was screaming for attention. Jordan slumped back against the shower walls letting it support her as I cleansed her vaginal lips. I looked up, seeking permission to taste her again. Jordan nodded her head in answer to my silent question.

"Jesus," she swore as she slid down the wall landing on the floor next to me which was pretty impressive since I was still holding onto one of her legs.

"Did I hurt you?"

"God, no. I don't think I can handle that type of pleasure. It's like my whole body is on fire and I can't control my limbs."

I threw back my head laughing. Jordan frowned. "I don't like it when you laugh at me."

"Honey, I wasn't laughing at you. Never that. I laugh when I'm happy. You make me happy, damn near woozy."

"You make me happy too," she whispered. She never looked as beautiful to me as she did in this vulnerable moment.

"Shall we finish our shower?"

"Ours? I thought it was my shower." Jordan giggled bringing light to the entire room.

"You gonna let a brother sit here with water dripping from his balls? Without the benefit of soap? Woman have you no mercy?"

"Get up boy, you didn't get my back."

***

"I don't know about you, but I'm hungry again." We were back in the living room listening to music.

"We still have some dessert. I could put some coffee on too."

"That would be good. What are you going to do about your hair? I didn't mean for it to get wet."

"I'll blow dry it later. It takes forever to dry naturally."

"If you let me, after dessert I'll dry it for you. That's the least I could do since I was partially responsible for it being wet."

"You would do that for me? You have no idea what you are getting yourself into." Jordan had changed from the dress she was wearing to a jeaned shorts set. On her head, she wore a green towel tied in a turban. She looked like an Egyptian Queen to me.

"You can teach me. I'm willing to do that and so much more," I honestly admitted.

Jordan sat staring at me for a couple of seconds before she went in the kitchen to prepare our snack. I had never done a woman's hair before but how difficult could it be. If I could work my way around with a hammer without breaking my damn fingers, how hard could wielding a hair dryer be?

"Do you take cream and sugar?"

"I can fix it. Remember, I'm not a guest anymore."

"In order for that to apply, you are going to have to leave and come back. It's after the second visit that you're no longer a guest."

"Oh. Then I'll take two sugars with a splash of cream."

Jordan had just brought in the tray carrying our coffee and cake when we heard the front door open. She sat down heavily beside me. I grabbed her hand and held it. She seemed nervous and I didn't know why.

"It's okay," I whispered. She clutched my hand tighter for several beats and let it go.

Lacy's heels clacked loudly on the hardwood floors. "Hello, hello," she shouted as she entered the living room.

Jordan stood up, "Is everything okay?" She nervously played with the towel and tugged at her shorts.

"Yeah. It's cool." Lacy looked us up and down suspiciously.

"We were just having dessert," I said as I took a sip of my coffee.

"No shit."

"I can make you some coffee if you like or maybe some tea," Jordan gushed.

"I ain't no guest. I know where everything is." Lacy tossed her bag on the coffee table and took a seat in the arm chair.

"This cake is good. You will have to tell me where you got it from." Jordan's nervousness was contagious.

"Y'all fucked didn't you?"

The cake flew out of my mouth like a projectile as I began to cough. Jordan sat back down and started pounding me on the back as Lacy laughed hysterically.

"It's not funny," Jordan admonished even though she sounded like she was trying to hold in her own laughter.

"What's funny is you two trying to pretend like you didn't. I ain't mad at you. If I had a dick handy, I would be working it out my own self."

"Must you always be so crude? You are trying to kill Brody with your choice of words. You should be careful. You don't want to give him the wrong impression, do you?"

"What? Last time I checked, we were all adults here. I don't know why you are trying to front. The fact that your hair is jacked means it was good." Lacy was tickling her own self.

Although I would have preferred not to have been present while all this transpired, at least Jordan didn't have to go through the hazing by herself. "If you must know it was great." I got up to clean up the mess I had made.

"I'll get it," Jordan said. Her cheeks were red as she pushed me to the side. She went in the kitchen and came back with some 409 cleaner that she used to wipe down the wall. I was embarrassed by my actions.

Lacy said, "See what you did? You got Jordan to blush."

"I got her to blush. You are the one asking personal questions."

"Touché. And now that we have exposed the elephant in the room, we can talk about why I wanted to speak with you. I need your help trying to locate my sister. I haven't seen her in a couple of years and I need to know if she's okay. I can pay you, but I don't want you to tell her where I am if you find her."

Jordan came back in the room and sat back beside me. "Am I allowed to ask questions?"

"Of who?" Lacy warily asked.

"Family members maybe? Friends?"

Lacy and Jordan exchanged glances. There was more to this story and something told me I didn't want to hear it.

"It's kind of of complicated Brody." Jordan grabbed my hand.

"If I can't ask any questions, how am I supposed to find her?" I had no problem with helping Lacy find her sister but I wasn't about to do it blindly.

"I thought you could use your resources to check her social security number or see if she has a driver's license."

"How long has it been since you last saw your sister?"

"It's been about two, maybe three, years."

"Can I ask where you last saw her?"

Lacy began fidgeting in her chair obviously uncomfortable with the question. "Um ..."

"Lacy, you are going to have to give me something to work with if you want good results otherwise we will be spinning our wheels in the wrong direction. I'm all about helping you, but you have to work with me."

Lacy hung her head down. "Batesville. We lived in Batesville, Mississippi."

"See, that was easy. Who is we?"

Lacy stood up. "Never mind. This ain't such a good idea after all."

I stood up as well. "It's okay. You don't have to tell me that for now. How old is your sister?"

"She would be twenty-three right now."

"Would be?" Red flags were going up inside my head. The words 'would be' left the door wide open for a lot of possibilities.

"Lacy, I think you should tell him," Jordan pleaded.

Lacy eyes grew wide with what looked like fear. She shook her head no. "I can't."

I was at a loss on what to do. To begin this search without knowing the particulars would be foolish.

What if I found something that I was compelled to report about? What would I do? And what would it do to Jordan's and my relationship?

"Do you want me to tell him?"

Lacy didn't answer, she just walked out of the room leaving Jordan and me sitting there.

Jordan pulled me back to the sofa. "Let me go make sure she's okay."

"Sure, take your time." I went into the kitchen and poured myself a drink. One thing that was absolutely clear to me was that whatever happened had to be traumatic for Lacy not to want to talk about it. There wasn't anything that I knew about that she wouldn't talk about. For something to render her speechless, it had to be deep. Needless to say, I was very curious to find out what it was.

Jordan came back to join me a few minutes later. She sat next to me and rested her head on my lap.

"Is she okay?" I asked as I smoothed back the wild hairs on her head. She had removed the towel but her hair was still a little damp. I didn't even think she realized that she would leave a wet mark in my lap when she removed her head. I didn't even care how it would look.

"Yeah, she's okay. She just needed some time."

"What do you want me to do?"

"Find her sister, if you can. She may even be dead."

"Dead? Was she sick?"

"No. Not that I'm aware of. There was a man. He might have done something to her. At least that is Lacy's fear."

"Why couldn't she tell me that?" I already knew the answer before she told it to me.

"The guy that told her this was bad news. He used to abuse Lacy and her sister. He's the lowest scum on the face of the earth, abusing children who couldn't fend for themselves."

"Fucking pervert. I'll find that bastard and we will have a come to Jesus meeting."

"He might already be in a meeting but it won't be with Jesus."

My head snapped back. "What kind of meeting? You mean the cops got him? I gotta go to jail to see him?"

"He might be a little lower." Jordan sat up straight.

"Whoa, as in under the dirt? She killed him?"

"She doesn't know, but she sure as hell tried. He was bad Brody. Very bad. He was screwing them both and sometimes he made her watch him take her sister. She flipped out when he told her he killed her sister."

"Damn baby. Are you sure you want to get involved in this? What if she did kill him? Then we both become accessories after the fact."

"You know what? I don't need you to help her. I hope she did kill the bastard. That's my girl and I got her back and you can see your way out of here!" Jordan stood up pointing to the door. Her face could have been carved in granite.

My heart sank. I wasn't ready to lose her over this. "Wait, babe. I didn't say I wasn't going to help. I was just making sure you understood what it could mean. What's the guy's name?"

"Karl Wester. He's a low down, rat faced, fat, slimy, cock sucker."

"Tell me how you really feel." Jordan walked into my arms and I realized I was just as committed to finding the fucker as she was.

"Are you going to help us?"

"Yes baby. I'll do what I can. I'm going to need Lacy to fill in the blanks for me. Do you think you can get her to come out and speak with me?"

"I'll see what I can do. She was crying when I left."

CHAPTER NINE
LACY BATES

For the first time, in a long time, I was scared and I didn't know what to do about it. I understood why Jordan told Brody about my past, however, it didn't make me feel better. I wanted him to like me for me. Not because he felt sorry for me. I could feel sorry for my own self. As much as the situation sucked, I needed his help. I wanted a normal life and this was my only chance to get it.

"Are you going to talk to him? He's still here."

"I'll talk to him. I just don't feel like doing it right now."

"When then?" Jordan pressed.

"Damn. When I feel like it. Okay?" Pressure was the last thing I needed. I didn't respond well to pressure.

"You don't have to jump down my throat. I, I mean we, only want to help."

"If you want to help so damn much then leave me alone. I can't think right now." I pulled a pillow over my head hoping Jordan would get the message and leave my room. I never had a problem with her respecting my boundaries before. I hoped this time wouldn't be any different.

"Fine. But remember this was your idea. I'll go right back in there and tell him to forget about it, if that's what you want me to do."

Leave it to Jordan to try and flip the script. "Great. Tell him. I don't give a fuck."

"Damn it, Lacy. Get your narrow ass off the bed and go talk to him. You asked me to bring him here and I did. Now handle your business, I'll be in my room."

I sat up throwing my pillow off the bed. "You are going to just leave him in the living room?"

"No, you are leaving him in the living room. I'm going to blow dry my hair." Jordan slammed my door.

I was conflicted. I didn't really think that Jordan would be so rude as to leave Brody all alone in the living room, but then again, I had pissed her off. Still, it wasn't fair to Brody. Especially if he only wanted to help me. I used my adjoining bathroom to wash my face and pulled my hair into a ponytail. I put on a pair of sweatpants and a tee shirt. I regretted trying to do two big things in one night. First, dealing with Seven and second was reliving moments from my past.

I walked into the living room and sat down on the couch with Brody. "What do you want to know?" My shoulders were stiff and tight. I was coiled so tightly, I felt like I was about to snap a tendon.

"Can you get me something to write on? I have had a couple of drinks and I don't want to forget anything important."

"Well God Damn. Whoever heard of a reporter without a pen and paper?"

"I didn't come over here as a reporter. I came as your friend."

He had a point, but I was a little too irritated to acknowledge it. I had no idea where we had paper and a pen. We were an electronic household and did everything on the computer. "Shit, Brody. I don't know where no pen is. Can you use my laptop and email yourself the notes?"

"Yeah, that would work." Despite his outer calm, I could tell, I was pissing him off.

"Fine." I knew I was acting like a little brat. Hated myself for doing it, but I felt like I was incapable of stopping it. The last thing I wanted him to do was to tell me to go fuck myself. He knew enough about me to be dangerous. I would hate to have to kill him. I passed him the laptop and flopped down in the chair.

"I know this is difficult for you but I need to know a little bit more about this man."

"You have no idea how hard this is. I've spent the last few years trying so hard to forget him."

"You might be right, but I have a very vivid imagination. When was the last time you saw him?"

"Two and a-half years ago."

"What did he look like?"

"A short fat fucker."

"I'm not that sure I know what a fucker looks like. We can come back to that part of the description later. How old is he?"

"I don't know. Early forties maybe. He was slinging it with my mother. She's around that age."

"Mother? I don't recall you ever mentioning her."

"Like I fucking tell you everything. Come on man, get real. If you hadn't did me that solid, we wouldn't even be talking today."

"You ain't lying. I wouldn't be fucking with you either."

I couldn't even say anything at first. His comment was so unexpected, I had to laugh. "Okay. I deserved that. I'm popping off at the wrong person."

"Right. So what about your mother?"

"She won't be of any help. She didn't help me or my sister back then."

"Did she know?"

"Hell yeah, she knew. She was in denial, but she had to know. We were scared to death of that man and she continued to allow him to stay there."

"Lacy, please don't take what I'm about to say the wrong way. I don't know what the circumstances were and I'm not making any assumptions, but sometimes children hate what they don't know without any basis. Especially when it comes to our mothers and fathers."

"We had plenty of basis." Lacy stood up and turned around lifting her shirt. Thirty round brown spots dotted her lower back.

"What is that? Please don't tell me that's an iron pattern."

"It is. He made me get the iron, fill it with water and turn on the steam. He held it over my back while he fucked me. He knew not to put it directly on me, but it was so freakin' hot, he might as well have."

"Fuck. You showed this to your mother and she didn't lay that motherfucker out?"

I shrugged. "My sister had worse and our mother didn't do anything."

"That's crazy to me. What about the authorities? Your school?"

"Man, you ever tried to tell an adult something when they are not ready to hear it? If I showed them my back then they would have taken me from my sister and she was the only thing that was keeping me sane."

"But you could have stood together. Then—"

"You are talking a lot of should have, could have, would haves. None of that bullshit matters now!"

"I know. I just can't believe he was allowed to do that to you."

"He did worse. He started sleeping with my sister when she was fifteen. He started with me at twelve. He told me he would kill my sister if I ever told. He told her the same thing."

"Your mom didn't do anything about that? Where was she when all this was going on?"

"At work or at the store. She would leave us there with him at night while she worked. He was nice enough to us while she was there, but the minute she was gone, it was on like popcorn."

"Did this happen every night?"

"Pretty much."

"I can't wait to find the fucker. I'm going to make sure he doesn't put his hands on anyone else."

"Brody, I appreciate your outrage. I used to get mad every time I thought about it, but at the end of the day getting mad didn't change a damn thing. My sister got mad. Told a DFAC worker, who actually came to the house and gave it the good housekeeper's seal of approval. Bunch of bureaucrats, they didn't care."

"My God, Lacy, you had all the evidence right there. All you had to do was show them your back."

"Karl said he wasn't afraid of dying. He would kill me before I could close my mouth. He was a sick fuck. I believed him. As miserable as it was, it was still my life. I wasn't ready to die."

"Okay. So what happened when your sister disappeared?"

"She changed. I know it was harder on her than it was on me. In the beginning, he only used me to punish her, or if she was on her period. She thought she failed me." Tears were running from my eyes like a faucet. I couldn't have stopped them if I tried. Brody handed me some tissue. I was so involved in my memories, I didn't even hear him leave the room and come back.

"That wasn't your sister's job to protect you."

"I fucking know that, Brody!" I was sorry the moment I said it. I twisted the tissue to shreds.

"So what happened?" Brody went on, never missing a beat. He was a consummate professional.

"After the DFAC deal, London stopped fighting back. Karl liked it when we fought. He liked to see the fear on our faces. He liked to see us cry or make us beg for mercy. London didn't do any of that. One night, he beat her so badly she couldn't move off the floor. He carried her out that night and I never saw her again. He told my mother that she ran away. He told me she was dead."

Brody said, "If you don't mind, I think I need another drink."

"Bring the whole damn bottle. I need one too."

Brody came back with a bottle of Patron, the ice bucket and two glasses. We didn't talk as we prepared our drinks. The silence was awkward. Now that I had ripped the scabs off my wounds, I was ready for the Band-Aids, the feel better pill.

"So, how did you get away?" Brody asked as he stirred his drink with his finger.

My voice dropped. "My sister kept a straight razor under her pillow. I cut him with it, emptied his pockets and ran. I caught the Mega Bus to Atlanta. Fucker didn't have much money. I was too young to get a hotel room, even if I could afford it. So I stayed on the street until I met Mrs. Gates, from the group home Jordan and I met at. Mrs. Gates was volunteering at a soup kitchen. She offered me a way off the streets. Few people know how nice she really is."

"Wow. I guess I owe the woman an apology. I thought she was being a hard ass for nothing."

"She was a hard ass, with a heart," I said laughing. I hadn't thought much about Mrs. Gates since I left the home but I did owe her a visit. It was so funny how objective I could be now that I was on the outside looking in.

"Does you sister have any friends that she trusts?"

"None that she would go to if she needed anything. We didn't associate with many people our age. Wester forbid us to have friends. We pretty much stayed to ourselves for the most part."

"I bet he did. If you think of someone who may have known more about her, let me know."

"Okay. There was this one chick. I think she still lives near the area. Used to work at the casino in

Tunica. I can't remember her name right now, but I'll keep thinking about it."

"Good. If you do, we might just take a trip down there. Matter of fact, we might take a trip anyway."

"I can't go back there Brody."

"It's going to be okay. You won't be Lacy Bates when we go back. Let me handle that part."

Brody picked up my laptop, his fingers posed over the keys. "Let's list our objectives. Finding out about your sister is our number one priority. What else?"

"I need to find out if anyone is looking for me. Jordan wants to travel and I can't even get a freaking passport until I know what's up with that."

"I can get you a passport. A whole new identity if you need it. That's not a problem."

"It's that simple?"

"It is if you know the right people. I've got some connections. People that I've done favors for in the past. Is there anything else?"

"For now, that's enough. It's been so hard keeping this all inside. The doctors say I'm bipolar. I think it's stress."

"That's possible. Once we get this all settled you might want to get a second opinion. In the meantime, I wouldn't recommend changing what you are doing. I'm no doctor, but whatever you are doing appears to be working."

"I'm tired now. Are you staying the night?" I could tell by the look on Brody's face he didn't have a clue.

"Uh…"

"Just go upstairs and get in the bed. I doubt she'll kick you out."

"I don't think I'm going to take that chance. I would hate to fuck up what we have going." Brody stood up carrying the ice bucket.

"Wait right here. You have been drinking. I can't let anything happen to you. If all else fails, the sofa is very comfortable."

CHAPTER TEN
JORDAN BREE

Lacy was sitting at the kitchen table when I came downstairs for coffee. She was holding her head with her hands and basically looked like shit. Dark brown circles lined her eyes. Her irises' were red and the lids appeared to be swollen. "Damn, did you get any sleep last night?" I plucked a cup from the rack hanging on the wall and poured me a cup from the pot Lacy had already brewed.

"A little bit. I kept waking up and shit. Did Brody go home?"

"Yeah, he left as soon as the sun came up."

"Did y'all have a good time?" Lacy rocked back in forth in her chair like she was riding something. It was a good thing she still had her sense of humor or I would be crying for her. It hurt my heart that she had to go through so much in her young life.

"We both fell asleep. Thank you."

"Sure you did." She said nodding her head playfully.

I wasn't going to try to convince her otherwise because she was going to believe what she wanted to anyway. Had the night gone any differently we may have ended up fucking like rabbits, but both of us were mentally drained so we only slept. "Whatever negro. You should put some ice on those eyes. You are looking like a raccoon this morning."

Lacy brought her hand up to her eyes as she touched her puffy lids. "I guess it's going to be a MAC day after all."

"Hey, you never did tell me what happened last night with Seven. How did you get home?"

"I caught a cab."

"And that's it? You ain't going to tell me anymore?"

"Dag, aren't you the nosy one."

"Excuse me? I know you ain't calling me nosy after the way you have been grilling me about Brody. I think I have a right to know about Seven especially since you lied to him when you said you were me."

"So, I lied. It didn't hurt you any. You promptly ignored his ass when he got here."

"What was I supposed to do?"

"You could have at least pretended to have a conversation with the man. Humph, all y'all did was talk to each other."

"We included you in the conversations. Besides, what was I supposed to say to the man? I don't know him from a can of paint. He came over here fucked up, smelling to the high heavens like a weed farmer. He was late for dinner and I don't do late. And he came with both arms swinging at the same length."

"His arms swinging? What the hell are you talking about?"

"When your arms are swinging at the same length, it means you don't have shit in them. If he were a gentleman, coming to a girl's house or guy's for that matter, for the first time, it is customary to bring something. Hell, he could have plucked a dandelion from the curb for all I cared. But something, damn."

"Well, maybe he isn't up on his social graces. I didn't see Brody carrying nothing in his hands." Lacy's head was rolling around on her neck like a bobble doll.

"That's because you told him not to. But I want to understand why the fuck we are arguing about this. You don't like that fool do you?"

"No, I couldn't give two fucks about his country ass."

"Then what's the big deal? Why are you acting like you care about him?" I had let my coffee get cold so I poured it out in the sink and fixed another cup.

"If you must know, I guess I'm feeling a little guilty."

The hairs stood up on my arms and the back of my neck. There was nothing about that statement that I liked. "Why? You didn't owe that fool anything. Including a good time."

"He deserved everything he got."

"Oh, shit. What did you do?" My mind was already racing ahead thinking of ways I was going to fix whatever it was that Lacy had done. She had every reason in the world to be mad at the prick, including the way he showed up at the house and appeared to not have known who she was.

"I put some Visine in his drink."

"Lacy, No! Is that why his stomach was all fucked up?"

Lacy's head dropped so I couldn't see her facial expressions as she nodded her head.

I was outdone. "Why would you risk doing something to him like that, over here of all places? You could have dropped him anywhere. Are you trying to get both of us locked up? Do you have some sort of captivity wish that includes both of us?" I was beyond pissed. This was probably the most reckless thing that Lacy had ever done and it made absolutely no sense to me. The fact that she did it right under my nose made me even madder. Brody and I sat there like boo-boo the fools while Seven was being poisoned.

"I didn't mean to do it," she whimpered.

I was dumbstruck. "Fuck you mean you didn't mean to do it? The intent was clearly there or you wouldn't have had the Visine in the kitchen in the first place."

"No, that's not what I'm trying to say. You talking all fast has got me tripping over my words. I only meant to cause him some discomfort. I wanted to embarrass him like he did me. You know, like maybe make him shit his pants or something like that." Lacy snickered as there was something remotely humorous about this situation.

"So what the fuck happened?" This was not how I envisioned my day starting. Rather than basking in the afterglow of great sex, I was thrust into a fight or flight situation.

"You were there. He was being obnoxious."

"Lacy you can't just keep going around town dropping bodies like a hooker drops her drawers. For Christ's sake, use your head."

"I was using my head. Besides, there is no way he could prove I did anything to make him sick."

"You weren't the one cooking Lacy. Of course you would be in the clear. But me, I'm ass out in this."

"No you're not. I begged him to go to the hospital but he wouldn't go. He said he had been using drugs and he didn't want any trouble with the police. For all we know, the drugs he took caused him to get sick."

"So, is he dead?" My heart was hammering inside my chest.

"He wasn't when I left."

I gave up on the coffee and grabbed the bottle of scotch. "You are going to make an alcoholic out of me yet."

"Don't blame me because you are reaching for a bottle at eight o'clock in the morning."

"I swear, if I didn't love your ass, I would drop kick you in the face right now."

"I love you too," Lacy mumbled.

"How do we fix this? Should I get dressed just in case the cops are on their way over here? I would hate to go to jail wearing this." I had on a red silk robe covering my nakedness.

"No. Stop saying that. There is no connection between us and Seven."

I could not believe we were having this conversation. "Hello? What about the Facebook connect? The fucking doorman saw him come in here and someone may have seen you leave with him last night. Hell, Brody practically carried his ass out of here. If those aren't connections I don't know what is."

Lacy waved away my arguments. "I accidently dropped coffee on his laptop after I formatted his hard drive. Wink, wink."

"Are you serious? You went into his house?"

"How else was I supposed to get his ass out of the car? Remember, he wasn't walking all that good on his own."

"Fuck. Just because you wiped out his computer it doesn't mean the records are gone. It's the worldwide web fool. All you have to do is log onto another computer and BAM, it's all there! Not to mention his phone. Damn near everybody with a damn smartphone has Facebook on it. You taught me that."

"I didn't think about that."

"Right. What else did you forget? For someone who is so smart this was an incredibly stupid thing to do. What about finger prints in his car or in his apartment?"

"I'm not worried about that. I don't exist in any of their databases."

"Well you should be worried. Get dressed. We need to go over there and make sure that nigga is okay."

"I don't give a shit about him." Lacy stared down at her fingers plucking crud from under her nails.

"I don't either. I'm only doing this to save your dumb ass if I can. Now get dressed!"

***

"There's his truck. Now can we go?" Lacy said when we pulled into Seven's apartment complex.

I ignored her question. "Is that the way you parked it?" The truck was clearly taking up more than one space.

Lacy shrugged. "I needed the extra room to get him out of the truck."

"Was the parking lot this deserted last night?"

"Yeah, I don't think this building is overflowing with tenants. Looks like it should have been condemned a long time ago."

"At least we have this one thing working in our favor." We were still sitting in my car, neither one of us making any attempt to get out.

"What do we do now?" For the first time, Lacy looked nervous.

"Make sure he's alive."

"And if he is?"

"Then we walk the fuck away. If he needs help, we take him to the doctor or call an ambulance."

"Uh, what if he's dead?"

"We bend over and kiss our ass's goodbye."

"Seriously?"

"No. We still call the cops. Pretend that we are concerned friends, yada yada yada. Under no circumstances will we admit to anything."

"Then why get involved at all? I'm telling you there is no way anyone can tie this back to us."

"And I told you all the ways which they can. Besides, it's the right thing to do, boo. Trust me on this. We don't need this shit coming back to bite us." I could tell she didn't want any parts of this judging by the way she walked behind me. Little did she know I wanted to do this even less than she did. I was afraid of what we would find, but we had to know. We couldn't add anything else to the list of things to be afraid of. We had enough skeletons in our closets. The last thing we needed were more bones to bury.

"Are we just going to stand here looking at the door or are you going to knock on it?" Lacy asked in her most surly voice ever.

"You are the one that should be knocking. I wasn't here last night." If the stakes weren't so high, I would have marched my ass right back to the car. Instead, I knocked on the door. Several minutes went by and I knocked again.

"Guess he ain't here." Lacy said.

"His car is here."

"He could have called a friend to pick him up or maybe an ambulance."

"I know you don't give a damn but we need to fix this."

"Fine. Give me your credit card."

"What are you going to do with it?"

"Would you just give me the damn card?"

"I have had enough of your attitude." I handed over my debit card, jamming it into her hand. Working quickly Lacy popped the lock to the door.

"Satisfied?"

"How the hell did you learn how to do that?" I asked in amazement.

"Did you really think locking your door at the home kept me out?" Lacy said laughing. She pushed open the door and walked into the apartment with me following closely on her heels. This heifer had more tricks up her sleeve than a magician.

"This place is a mess. Did you do this?" There were papers, soda cans and empty bottles of booze littering the floor. Dirty socks and underwear were flung on the sofa. The pugnent odor from them singed my nose.

"Hell no. The nigga just likes to live in filth. He was in the bathroom when I left him." Lacy walked down the hallway leaving me in the living room. I walked over to the dining room table scared to touch anything. Had I been thinking, I would have suggested wearing gloves. It would be difficult enough explaining to the police how it was that we broke into Seven's apartment. The silence of the apartment reminded me of the library.

"Did you find him?" I whispered but she didn't answer me right away.

On the coffee table, I could see where Lacy had destroyed his laptop. My gut told me we should take it with us to avoid some clumsy retrieval system finding any clues to our identity.

"Yeah, he's in the bedroom." I followed the sound of Lacy's voice with a feeling of dread in my stomach. She didn't appear to be alarmed although it hardly made sense to raise a fuss over a dead man.

"Is he okay?" I could not bring myself to ask her if he was dead as my fingers steepled in prayer.

"He's alive, if that's what you mean."

When this was over, Lacy and I were going to have to have a long talk or else I was gonna to put my foot straight up her ass. I peeked over her shoulder. Seven was lying face down on the bed. "How do you know he's alive?"

"He said so." I jumped back startled to see Seven staring back at me.

"Hey you." I said for lack of something better to say.

"How did you two get in here?" Seven mumbled as he attempted to raise his head off the pillow.

"The door was open. I guess I forgot to lock the door when I left here last night," Lacy lied.

I didn't know about her but I was ready to run like hell. "We were so worried. We wanted to make sure you were feeling alright. You certainly didn't look so good when you left."

"I feel like shit."

"Well at least you look better than you smell. You puked all over the bed." I was sure Lacy didn't need to inform him of this. I shook my head at her balls.

"I know. I couldn't make it…"

I felt sorry for Seven. "Do you want us to take you to the hospital?" I didn't mind driving him but it wouldn't be in my car. Lacy gave me a scathing look letting me know she wasn't feeling my question.

"I'm going to be alright. Just thirsty as hell." Seven rolled over on his back unleashing new aromas. I backed away from the bed.

"Go get him some water Jordan since you want to be all helpful and shit."

There was no mistaking the animosity in her voice. "I think you should be the one to get him some water since you have been here before." I wasn't about to go into the kitchen especially after seeing what the living room looked like. Even though I was no stranger to roaches, there was a lot more than six degrees of separation between us now.

"I'll get the water and then I'm ready to bounce. This smell is making me sick." Lacy stomped off.

My mind took me back to the bad days when my mother would get sick, suffering from withdrawal. There were many days where my sister and I had to clean her up and being here reminded me of those times. Instinct took over. "Lacy skip the water. He needs some Gatorade or something to replace the electrolytes in his body."

Lacy marched back into the bedroom. "Come again?"

I knew this was the last thing she wanted to hear but this brought back too many memories for me to just walk away and do nothing. It hit too close to home for me. "Work with me Lacy. It will take less than a half an hour to run down to the gas station and get this man something to drink. Water isn't going to cut it after all he's been through. You can take my car or his, I don't care which one. Just get the damn juice." I figured this was the least she could do since this was her fault. I would have gone myself but I didn't trust her to stay with him until I came back.

"I got some in the refrigerator," Seven whispered. He looked like one of the walking dead. His tongue was practically hanging out his mouth.

"Good. Lacy help me change this sheet." I started tugging on the sheet freeing it from the mattress. Lacy looked like she was about to fall out on the floor in a fit. I ignored her as I walked around to the other side of bed to get those ends too.

"This is some bullshit, Jordan. What else you gonna do, give him a bath."

Seven lifted his head off the bed and smiled.

"No, he can do that for himself. Now get the Gatorade and some sheets from his linen closet. The sooner we do this, the sooner we can go."

"How you know he got any extra sheets? Have you looked around this dump?"

I couldn't even hide my irritation. "I wish you would stop being so damn difficult and help me so we can get out of here."

As Lacy walked off I could hear her fussing. "Fine, but I still say this is some bullshit."

"Seven, I'm going to need you to get up and get in the shower. Do you think you can stand up?"

"You gonna get in there with me? I might need some support."

"You must think this is a dream buddy. Now move your ass before we leave you stinkin' in this shit." I wanted to chuckle at the hurt expression on his face. I kept expecting him to ask more questions but he didn't. I didn't volunteer any information either.

It was a good thing I had dressed down for this visit, because all of his weight fell on me as I helped him off the bed. It took everything in me not to push his ass to the floor.

"That's gonna leave a stain." Seven said as I practically dragged him to the adjoining bathroom. I couldn't tell if he actually needed me to stand up or if he was trying to cop a feel on the sly. The only thing I was certain of was that Lacy was going to owe me big time for this bullshit.

"Don't worry about it. I'm gonna send you the bill for my dry cleaning." I got him to the edge of the bathtub and he sat down on it. His breathing was rather shallow and I started to think making him shower might not be such a good idea. I leaned over and turned on the water for him.

"Don't make it scalding. I can't have you burning my balls," Seven joked.

"I'm glad you still have your sense of humor about the situation."

"You would have one too if you had a night like I did. For real man, I thought I was gonna die."

"Then you should have taken your ass to the hospital like I told you too," Lacy said when she came in the bathroom. Her face was scowled up in a tight knot as she stood with her hands behind her back.

"Is she always this angry?" Seven barely looked in her direction.

"I found the sheets." She pulled the sheets from behind her back.

"Good," I said.

"Look what else I found." She held up a brown purse and allowed it to dangle from her fingers.

"What the? I, uh…" Seven stuttered as he attempted to stand up.

I didn't make the connection. "Is that supposed to mean he has a girlfriend or something?" I was completely confused. Lacy was looking like she was about to whip someone's ass and I was very afraid it could be me.

"It's my purse. I lost it one day when some asshole left me to die in the park."

"Oh shit. You know what, I think now would be a good time for us to get the hell out of here."

"What do you mean that's your purse? You can't be the same girl from the park. Are you?" Seven's stinky ass was standing on his own now with a dazed look on his face.

"Yeah. Where the fuck is the money I had in here?"

"Girl, you had five dollars. Don't act like there was more than that.'"

"Whatever nigga. It was my five dollars and I want it back."

I was caught in the middle of a genuine shit storm. It was only going to take a few more minutes before he made the connection between what happened to him the night before and the night in the park. Karma was a bitch and it came back to bite him. This conversation had nothing to do with me and I was about to see my way out of it. I edged past Lacy who was blocking the door.

"Lacy I'm going to the car now. I suggest you come with me."

"I want my damn five dollars back."

"Is it really worth all that?"

"Damn right."

"Lacy, I know you won't believe me, but I tried to find you. I went to the address on your identification several times but you must have used a fake address. It was some type of group home. I couldn't get pass the bitch at the door."

The fire seemed to flow right out of Lacy. "You did?" Lacy was skinning and grinning now.

"Yeah, why else do you think I held on to that purse?"

I did not like where this was going at all. "Lacy, don't forget the way he was acting last night. He couldn't even remember your name. That fool was all in my face like stank on shit."

Lacy waved me off. "That's because he thought you were going to suck his dick." She never took her eyes off Seven.

"He thought what? Why the hell would he think that?"

Lacy shrugged her shoulders as if it was nothing. "How do you think I got him to come over to the apartment?"

Seven didn't say a word. He just stood there stinking and grinning.

I wanted to get mad but they were so sickening, it was kind of cute. "Ain't nobody got time for this. I'll be in the car. Don't have my ass sitting out there long either."

I could not believe what I was witnessing. Lacy and Seven appeared to be encased in a bubble of love that even the aromatic smell of vomit and maybe shit couldn't penetrate.

"Don't wait on me. I'll be there when I get there."

The only thing I could do was shake my head as I let myself out of the nasty apartment. If she thought I wasn't going to get in that ass when she got home she didn't know me very well after all.

CHAPTER ELEVEN
BRODY MASON

I was sitting in my office going over the events of the last twenty-four hours. I considered them events because each incident by itself could have effectively ruined any chance I would have at having a relationship with Jordan. It was strange, but I was beginning to categorize my life in terms of before and after meeting her. I never would have believed I would ever find someone who could change my whole perspective on life. I even found myself wondering what she would do in certain situations. This was laughable to me since she believed I had so much to teach her. While I believed it was the other way around.

Lacy was an enigma to me. She came off as this tough bitch who doesn't give a damn about anyone else but herself, yet I couldn't deny the love she had for Jordan. That fiery hatred she once had for her had manifested itself into respect and what I believed was a genuine friendship. They were both flawed and they accepted each other's imperfections. I honestly had so much to learn from both of them. For me, helping Lacy was not an option, even though the potential outcome was frightening. I wasn't much of a praying man, but this morning, I humbled myself and asked for a little help from the Man above. I believed both women were put in my path for some reason. I just had to figure out what that was.

Lacy's biggest fear was that she was being hunted by either the police or some scumbag named Karl Wester. To me, the perverted Mr. Wester posed the biggest threat. Since he had presumably lost both his girls, he has more than likely hunted for some more. I highly doubted he would stop being a pervert just because his victims were gone. I did an advanced search for him using all the information Lacy had given me. Fat scum-faced fucker was eliminated from the criteria for my search. It was always amazing to me the amount of information you could get merely by surfing the web. As long as you knew the questions to ask, the information was readily available.

I did a Google search on Mississippi crime stoppers. It was a website that contained unsolved cases in the state. It also had a link to the most wanted criminals in their data base. Thankfully, I didn't find Lacy's name listed on either of those sites. That didn't mean they weren't looking for her. It just meant she wasn't a top priority.

My ringing phone was a distraction I didn't really want right now. When I was in research mode, I tended to shut the rest of the world out to concentrate. My first impulse was to ignore the phone but I recognized Jordan's number on the caller identification. My dick got hard immediately. "Hey, sunshine. How are you doing?"

I suspected my greeting caught her off guard because she hesitated for several seconds before she spoke. I pictured her clutching the phone blushing six ways from Sunday. "Uh, hi. Are you busy?"

"Never too busy for you beautiful."

"You really know how to charm the ladies," Jordan said laughing.

"Honey, hush. I don't say that to all the ladies." I kept the rest of my thoughts to myself even though I was sure she already knew how I felt.

"Lacy got her purse back so she won't be needing that fake ID."

"Really? Should I be asking how she did it?"

"You don't want to know." Jordan said laughing.

Her laughter was like a drug to me and I craved it just like an addict needing a fix. "Lacy mentioned wanting to travel. Depending on where you two would like to go, it might not be a bad idea to at least up your ages. I would hate to see you get carded and y'all lose your damn minds." I guffawed with the visual that came to my mind.

"You are so right. That wouldn't be cool at all. Do you think you can hook both of us up then? We still need passports too."

"No problem. As long as you don't go disappearing from my life again, I got you covered."

"Why would I do that?" She answered innocently.

Unfortunately, I didn't have as much confidence as she displayed. She had already shown me how she could disappear on more than one occasion. "What are you up to today? Do you want to catch a movie later or do dinner?"

"That actually sounds good."

I breathed a sigh of relief. I was still trying to read Jordan and anticipate her moods. "Excellent. I have been doing a little research this morning. I checked with both the Tennessee and the Mississippi crime stopper's units and Lacy is not listed on their website. That doesn't mean she is in the clear but at least we know her picture isn't hanging in the post office or convenience stores."

"That's good news isn't it?"

"Yeah, it's great news. I'm still doing my preliminary research but in order to be sure, we should plan on going to Memphis. These websites claim to be updated weekly but you never know. Given the fact that she left over two years ago, they may have taken her information down, although I doubt it. I saw some cases on the site that went back to 2009 and they are still being updated."

"I'm not sure we can get Lacy to return to Mississippi." I could hear the concern in Jordan's voice.

"Lacy does not have to go with us. Uh, I was thinking more along the lines of you and me going."

"Together?" I could hear Jordan's breathing increase like she was about to have a panic attack or something.

"Hey, if you don't want to do it, it's no big deal. I could go alone. I just thought it might be fun to run around on Bourbon Street or maybe hit the casinos."

The line grew quiet and I was afraid the call had dropped. I looked at my phone and saw that we were still connected. "Hello?"

"I'm here. I was just thinking about what to wear? Does that sound superficial to you? I've never been on a trip before. I don't even have any luggage."

I was so happy I could shout. "I might have to up my luggage game too. I only have an overnight bag and a garment bag. If we stay longer than few days, I'm gonna need to get some too."

"Can we gamble too?" I could hear the excitement in her voice.

"Yeah, just let me work on getting you some identification. We can talk about it more when I get there tonight. What time do you want to get together?"

"I could, um, come over now and help you with your research."

"Are you kidding me.? If your fine ass comes over here, the last thing I'm gonna want to do is research."

"So, that means you don't want me to come?" She sounded like she was sulking.

"Girl please. My momma didn't raise no fool. I'll see you when you get here." I was grinning my ass off when I hung up the phone. I still had on the same clothes from the night before so I rushed to get in the shower. Normally, it might not have mattered to me especially since I showered before I left Jordan's house. However, if something were to jump off when Jordan got there, I wanted to be ready. It wasn't like I was going to jump her bones the second she walked in the door. However, if she put it on the table, I would be happy to sit down and eat.

***

"Why are these butterflies fluttering in my stomach?" Jordan asked me as I opened the door.

"Don't feel bad, I got them too."

"What are we going to do about it?"

"Do? I'm not complaining about it. I actually like it." I leaned in closer for a brief kiss but Jordan surprised me and drew me in for a passionate one instead. I wasn't mad about that either.

"I like this feeling better," Jordan said with a sly smile on her face as she pulled away from our embrace.

"My, my, my, I like the way you think." If she was ready to skip the main course and go straight for the dessert, I was her man. Instead, she walked over to my vision board. I felt a slight flicker of disappointment.

"What's all this?" Jordan's cute little smile had slipped into a frown.

"This is my process. Whenever I'm faced with a puzzle, I find it's easier to figure out, if I lay the pieces out in front of me. You know, sort of like that bible passage, write your vision and make it plain. This is plain for me."

"Your vision?"

"You know, what I want to accomplish. Giving Lacy her life back is my goal and mission. That's my vision, if you will. All these little pieces are parts of the puzzle to do it. I've got to find the pieces that fit and throw away those that don't."

"This actually makes sense to me in an odd sort of way. Did you do this when you were working on my case?"

I felt the hairs on my arm stand up. *Was this a trick question?* "Not in the beginning. I did towards the end when I got into the details of your case."

"Why not in the beginning?"

"Honestly?"

"Of course."

I was still uneasy. Some people couldn't handle the truth. "In the beginning, I didn't know what my vision was. I didn't know if I was rooting for you or the old lady you tangled with. You could have been some nut."

Jordan cringed. "That's fair. I'm glad you sided with me. You do know I gave that old lady fifty thousand dollars don't you?"

"You did? Wow. No, I didn't know. That's awesome. You might have changed that ladies life forever."

"I don't know about all of that. I asked my lawyer to work it out. I really felt bad for the way things turned out. I mean it was only fair even though she whipped my ass." Jordan laughed loudly.

I didn't want our day to be spent reliving her past. I wanted us to move forward with our future. "Do you know if Lacy had a Facebook page?" I was trying to draw Jordan's attention back to my board.

"I don't know. She knows about Facebook. I'm the one that is not technology savvy."

"Facebook has nothing to do with technology. We can have a crash course on it if you want. But I am really curious as to whether or not she has one. Can you call her and ask?"

"She might be a little busy."

"Busy? Doing what?"

"She's with dude."

"Seven? Please tell me she is not hooking up with that fool."

"I wish I could. When I left them they were staring into each other's eyes like they were the only ones on the planet."

"Wow. That's funny. Last night it looked like she wanted to kill him."

"If you only knew. Why is her Facebook page important?" Jordan asked.

"It might not be. But it stands to reason if she had one, her sister might have one too. They could even be friends. Or, we could find some other friends who she might be hiding out with. It's certainly worth a shot wouldn't you say?"

"Hell yeah. But why wouldn't Lacy have checked that herself?"

"She might not have thought about it. When you are too close to a situation, the easy answers are often the hardest to see." We left the board and turned on my computer. Jordan pulled her chair up close to mine making it hard for me to concentrate.

"I hope you are right. Not knowing where her sister is is tearing her up inside. Even if the news is bad, she deserves to know."

"I agree. I can't imagine how that would feel if I were in a similar situation." I logged onto my Facebook page and searched the friends tab for Lacy's name. Three names came up with private profiles.

"What about London's name?"

I tried this next but nothing came up. "Damn. I thought for sure we would hit pay dirt." I felt a pang of disappointment. I wanted to do this for Jordan.

"Yeah. I feel the same way. What do we do now?"

"It ain't over until the fat lady sings. Are you sure Lacy gave you her correct name?"

"That's a thought too. I mean she was 'running' so it's possible that she didn't."

I said, "The only way we will know for sure is to ask her. Just because we can't see a profile, doesn't mean it's not there. If she had it set to private only people listed as her friends will see it."

"Can we look at the profile Lacy created for me?"

"She didn't show it to you?"

"She showed it to me briefly yesterday. If I had seen it sooner, I would have had her take it down."

"I know that's right." I typed in Jordan's name.

"She took that damn picture one day when we went shopping. I didn't even know she had taken it."

"It's a nice picture."

"I look like a hoochie. I didn't even buy that outfit."

"You should have. You look sensational." I was practically drooling.

Jordan smacked me in the back of my head. "I can dress that way for you but I don't want the whole world seeing something like that."

"I can see your point but it's still a good picture."

"How come there isn't anything on my page like there is on your page?" Jordan said as she tried to scroll down the page.

"That's because she has it set to private. Only your friends get to see what you have posted.

"It says here I have two friends. I wonder who the hell else she's got as my friend."

"We will definitely have to call her." I said.

"Can I look at your Facebook page?" Jordan turned and looked at me with her soulful eyes. Even if I wanted to lie to her, I couldn't when she was staring at me like that.

"Uh, yeah. I don't really use it much. I used to, back in the day."

"Let me see it."

I hadn't been to the page in months. Since I was a freelance journalist, my page was wide open. "Okay but I'm giving you my disclaimer now. There ain't no telling what's going to be on my page. Folks used to post some crazy shit. When I was on here on a regular, I would clean it up a bit every now and then."

"You scared I'm gonna find out you are a player or worse, have a wife tucked away somewhere?"

"Not at all. If you will notice, it tells you right here when the last time was I logged onto Facebook. If I was truly addicted to Facebook as some people are, it would have been more recent than this." I showed her my stats.

"I like this picture of you. Do you have pictures of your family on here too?"

"To be honest, I don't remember. It's been that long. You can look through the photos if you want to. I'm gonna get myself something to drink. Do you want anything?"

"No, I'm good."

I left Jordan at the computer. Very little of my personal information was on that page but I was an open book. Anything she wanted to ask me about me, I was willing to tell her.

"I can fix you something to eat." I shouted.

"I'm good, boo."

My heart soared. She was using the same terms of endearment that I used on her. I had to stop myself from running back into the room and wrapping my arms around her. I shook my head. This woman was making me lose cool points. If she only knew how sprung I was.

"Brody Mason, you have so many near naked chicks on your page it's almost sinful. I don't think I like this very much."

"Sweetheart, I don't use Facebook like that. It comes in handy for research and sometimes for entertainment purposes."

"What do you mean entertainment?"

I had just walked back in the room and noticed the scowl on her otherwise beautiful face. "You know the funny videos and pictures. People post the wildest stuff."

"Um hum."

She didn't sound the least bit convinced which I found amusing. "You can block every last one of them near naked women if you want to. Hell, I'll even update my status to *in a relationship* if it will make you happy."

"Status?"

"You really don't mess around with Facebook do you? When you set up your page, you make up a profile and one of the questions is status. Mine says single."

"You have ninety-nine messages."

I was still waiting for her to tell me if she wanted me to change my status. My heart sank a little bit when she didn't. "I don't read those. I just delete them. If anyone really wants to get in touch with me, they will send me an email."

"Can I look at them?"

This was her test. I could tell by the way she asked the question as if she were afraid of the answer.

"I don't care. I don't have anything to hide from you."

She didn't say anything for several minutes and I almost wanted to look over her shoulder to see what she was looking at. I understood that by not doing that I was giving her the control she sought. "I can't believe some of these messages."

I laughed hard from my gut. I could only guess what she was looking at. "Are they from ladies?"

"Hell yeah. Sick."

"They seem to be confusing Facebook with blackpeoplemeet.com. It ain't just the women, its men too."

"That's all so desperate. I wish the hell I would advertise for a man over the internet. Ain't no telling what you are going to get."

"It's true. They even have a television show about that called Catfish where people meet over the internet and when they finally meet each other in person they find out one or both of them are lying their asses' off."

"I've seen that show. That's where Lacy got the idea to contact Seven. I can't believe someone could be that dumb. If I'm talking to you over a month and I don't see your real face, something is wrong. Especially if we're living in the same damn city." Jordan turned her back on the computer, a satisfied expression on her face.

"What's the matter?"

"I think I changed your status." A slow smile spread across her lips.

CHAPTER TWELVE
JORDAN BREE

I was sitting in the living room watching television when I heard Lacy come through the door. I looked at my watch. It was just after eleven at night.

"Hey," I said as she threw her keys in the basket next to the door. She walked into the living room and sat next to me on the sofa.

"Hi."

If body language had a temperature, Lacy's would be ice cold. There was nothing in her greeting that indicated she was open to conversation. The only positive was that she had sat down beside me instead of rushing to her room and closing the door. "I'm not really watching this. You can change it if you want to." I placed the remote control in between us on the sofa.

"I'm good."

She opened the door. "Are you?"

"Yeah, why did you say it like that?"

"I have just been worried about you."

"I didn't get a phone call."

She had a valid point. One which I couldn't deny or excuse. "I really didn't know if I should call you.

You know, this is the first time you have actually been out without me, with the exception of running errands. I didn't want you to feel like I was acting like your mother or something like that."

Lacy laughed and playfully tapped me on the shoulder. "Girl you better quit. We go deeper than that. Mother complex or not, I would be calling your ass if you went missing for hours."

I was trying to hear what she didn't say more than what she did. "Then you are saying I should have called?"

"Hell yeah. You didn't know what was going down over at dude's house."

"That's why I didn't call. I didn't want to interrupt you if you two were…"

"I should punch you in your throat for that. Ain't no golden arches over this pussy saying open, come on in. Fuck I look like screwing this dude who I hardly know."

She was right. I was wrong for jumping to that conclusion. "Girl, I'm sorry. The way you two were looking at each other like you were both starving, I just assumed you would eat."

"I drool when the ice cream man drives down the street but you don't see me chasing the truck, do you?"

I laughed until tears came out of my eyes just thinking about Lacy sprinting after the ice cream truck, knocking little kids out of her way. "You need to quit. I can see you now waving your dollars over your head."

"Exactly. That fool disrespected me. If he wants some of this pudding, he's gonna have to earn it."

"I feel you. Then why did you stay at his house? Please tell me you didn't drug his ass again."

Lacy laughed again. "No. His ass is safe. If you want to know the truth, I felt bad for what I did to him. He deserved some punishment, but I did go a little overboard. I damn near used the whole bottle of Visine on him. I could have killed him."

"Remind me again not to get on your bad side." I said it jokingly but I was serious. I could think of a lot of ways to die. Shitting myself to death wasn't one that I would like to have listed on my death certificate.

"I know you are not throwing shade after what you did to me. I might not hold a grudge against you for doing it, but I haven't forgotten that shit either. I have never been so scared in my life."

I was utterly ashamed of myself. "I'm sorry. I was out of line with that one. You just kept pushing all my buttons. I was trying to get you to back up off of me." Although we were making fun of what happened, Lacy was right. We were dabbling in some dangerous stuff that could have altered both of our lives.

"Only reason why I wasn't mad at you was because I deserved it."

"So, what did dude say about his computer?"

"I haven't told him yet. If he asks me about it, I'm going to swear that he did it himself. He was so out of it, he won't have a choice but to believe me."

"Damn. I would like to be that fly on the wall when he finds out. He's gonna be pissed. It was a MAC and they ain't cheap."

"Oh well."

"Before I forget, did your sister have a Facebook page?"

"Of course. You're about the only person I know that doesn't have one. Well who didn't have one?" Lacy smirked into her hand.

"Whatever, negro. Brody and I were thinking…" Lacy sat up in the chair. Suddenly I had her complete attention.

"What?"

"He was thinking that if she had a page, then she might have reached out to some of her friends for help. Or, if you had a page she might have tried to reach you on it."

"I thought of that too but I have been too afraid to look. Call me paranoid but I thought if I logged in, they might be able to find me."

"I don't think anyone is looking for you. Now if you were some big time criminal that might be true."

"How do you know this?"

"Well, I don't for sure, but Brody did check a few sites that normally list criminal searches. He said he didn't find anything about you but wanted to go there to be sure."

"Shit. I had no idea Brody would be starting on this so soon."

"What do you mean? Why would he drag his heels about this? I thought this was important to you."

"It is important. I just didn't tell him everything last night. I thought I was going to have time to speak with him again before he did anything."

I had this bad feeling I was not going to like what she said to me. "Is this going to piss me off?"

Lacy nodded her head.

"Wait, let me guess. Lacy isn't your real name."

Lacy's jaw went slack. Her eyes were like big question marks. "Lacy is my middle name."

"Why the hell wouldn't you at least tell me that?"

"I didn't really think about it. I've been going by Lacy for so long I just forgot to clarify it."

"Well, if your friends know you as Lacy then what's the big deal?"

"My last name isn't Bates."

"Of course it isn't. I should have known that too. When was the last time you saw a black Bates?"

"It's Gates."

"Gates? As in the-battle-axe Gates? Shut the fuck up!" I was practically screaming at Lacy or whoever the fuck she was supposed to be.

"Hold on, Jordan. I can understand your being a little upset, but you have to let me explain. I couldn't tell you my real last name because Mrs. Gates didn't know I was her niece."

"Shut up talking to me. You're sounding more ridiculous with every word that is coming out of your mouth. I trusted you, and I don't even know who you are." I was so angry I could have shoved all her teeth down her throat and thought nothing else about it.

"Why does that piss you off? I'm still the same person."

"It pisses me off because you are living in my house lying to me. It would have been different if you came in here the first day, and told me the truth."

"It wasn't such a big deal to me."

"What? I talked about your aunt like she had a tail."

"And I did too. I really don't know that woman like that. She thinks I'm just another wayward girl. Nothing more, nothing less."

"You had us believing that she sucked you off the streets like a Hoover vacuum. You just didn't have to lie." I was more hurt than angry.

"I'm trying to tell you, I didn't lie about that. My mother used to tell me about her sister. She said my grandparents, whom I've never met, died and left the house to my mother and her sister. My mom wanted to sell the house and split the proceeds. My aunt wanted them to keep the house in the family and live together. That didn't fit into my mother's plans, so she high tailed it out of Atlanta and moved to Mississippi. To my knowledge, they haven't spoken since. All this happened before my sister and I were born."

"Ain't nobody got time for this bullshit."

Lacy kept on talking like I hadn't objected. "Mrs. Gates kept the house and turned it into the home. Before I moved to Atlanta, I didn't know Mrs. Gates from a hole in the wall. You have to believe me on this one."

"The only thing I have to do in this life is die and pay taxes. Listening is optional, especially when all I'm hearing is bullshit." I was so angry I was shaking. I felt betrayed and devalued.

"Did you take your fucking meds today?"

I stood up. "You know what Lacy whatever the fuck your name is Gates, kiss my ass." I ran upstairs to my bedroom and threw myself down on the bed. "Oh, damn." I went from sixty to subzero in seconds. Lacy was right, I was going bat shit crazy for no reason. I sat up feeling like a complete ass. I didn't have a problem admitting when I was wrong. Sometime it took me longer than others to get to that point.

"I was right wasn't I?" Lacy asked as I walked back down the stairs.

She was still sitting on the couch channel surfing. I walked into the kitchen and grabbed my pills from my purse. I grabbed a bottle of water from the refrigerator and took my pills. I was going to have to get better with taking them. Not only was it dangerous for me, it was unfair to those I surrounded myself with. "Yes," I mumbled.

"Are we friends again?" I could hear the emotion in Lacy's voice.

"I guess so. But you have got to promise me that we won't lie to each other again. That's a huge pet peeve of mine. Trusting anyone is so hard for me. Once that trust is broken, I'm done."

"Deal. But you have got to promise me something as well."

"What?"

"Your pills. You have got to schedule them better. You can't keep flipping out on me. You can use the alarm on your phone to remind you to take them."

"Is that how you keep it together?"

"Uh, yeah."

I was still feeling antsy as I waited for the pills to do their job. "My biggest problem with taking these pills, other than forgetting them, is that I feel like it dulls my thinking. I feel like I am less in control and I hate that feeling. I want to believe I don't need them, but situations like this, tell me that I do." I was almost ready to accept total responsibility for this latest breakdown until I replayed Lacy's words in my head. My antenna went up a notch.

"Maybe you need to see Doctor Maxwell again. He can always adjust your dosage or change the medication all together. It's not rocket science, everyone is different. You just have to find out what works for you."

Lacy had a point. I was so busy trying to deny I had a problem that I wasn't looking for more viable options to dealing with it. "I'm going to call him in the morning.

"Good."

"So what is your real name?"

"Kristal Lacy Gates."

"Like the damn drink? Your mother named you after booze?" I didn't know why but that was hilarious to me.

"Now you know why I go by Lacy."

"So we are going to be completely honest with each other from this point on?" It was clear Lacy was caught off guard by my question. She started fidgeting with her shirt.

"Yeah, sure."

"Then tell me again about Mrs. Gates. How did that come about?"

Lacy took a deep breath and blew it out through her mouth. She looked as if she was wagering a war within herself. "Promise me you aren't going to flip the fuck out?"

"I'm not going to make any such promise. I do agree to listen." This was the best that I could give her. I already knew I was going hear something else I wasn't going to like.

"Like I said before, my mom and her sister were at odds about what to do with their parent's house. Even though it happened before I was born, my mother was still pissed off about it."

I shook my head back and forth as I felt anger rise up in me. Strike one. "That's not what I'm talking about and you know it."

"What?" Lacy's face was a stoic mask.

"Honesty remember?"

"I'm not sure what you want me to say."

I slammed my hand down on the arm of the sofa. "How about starting with the fact that you are not bipolar? I think that's a good a place to start as any."

Shock, shame, guilt and maybe remorse. Those were the emotions I identified on Lacy's face. "How did you know?"

"I'm glad you didn't continue to lie about it. I'm still pissed the fuck off that you didn't tell me. How am I supposed to trust you after this?" My heart wasn't ready to accept the fact that I had been duped yet again.

"I know you are not going to believe this, but I was going to tell you tonight. That is, until you went ape shit on me. I was waiting on your pills to kick in."

"Your right, I don't believe you."

"It's true. I don't like being lied to any more than you do. The lie I have been living with wasn't created for you. I was living those lies before I even knew who you were."

"That may be true, but when you didn't volunteer to fix it, it became a new lie."

"Mrs. Gates suggested I play crazy to get to know you. She wanted me to keep an eye on you but when you and I started to become friends. I stopped spying on you."

"Oh, so now you are saying I'm crazy?"

"No, uh, that's not what I meant at all. You are trying to trip me up."

"Then by all means, say what you mean." I could feel my blood pressure rising by the minute.

"I don't think you are crazy. You have good sense."

"I knew you were spying on me. I just knew it!"

"It was only for a few days. I promise you."

"And I'm supposed to believe that?"

"Nothing that I say to you tonight is going to change how you're feeling right now. You have every right to be mad at me. Can we just table this discussion until tomorrow?"

"Sure." Lacy was right. There was nothing left to say at this point. Anything else she said would be analyzed and criticized seven ways till Sunday. I got up and quickly walked upstairs to my room, closing the door. I was happy that we were able to walk away from each other without the theatrics that normally accompanied a fight between friends. The way I was feeling right now, I could have easily tried to kill her. However, I wasn't no fool. Lacy carried a knife and wasn't afraid to use it. It was thoughts like this that would cause me to lose sleep at night. I got up from my bed and locked my door. This didn't bring me much comfort either since Lacy had also demonstrated her skill with picking locks.

I grabbed my phone off the night stand and called Brody.

"Hey babe."

I felt a tingle travel down my spine when I heard the warmth in his voice. Who knew that those few words were enough to soothe me? "Hi. Listen, we need to backtrack a little on this Lacy investigation."

"Why? What's wrong?"

"I found out some things about Lacy that changes the direction we should be going in."

"What kind of things?" I could hear the apprehension in his voice.

"I don't even feel like talking about this right now. I'm so mad at her I could scream."

"Don't get yourself all worked up, babe. Whatever it is, we can handle it."

I liked the way he was saying things like we and calling me babe. It made my heart wobble. I felt like Olivia Pope every time Fitz called her on the phone, all weak in the knees. "It too late about that. We got into an awful fight about it. Have you ever wondered why Lacy is always so even keeled and happy all the time, while I'm like a blithering idiot at times? What about pills, have you ever seen her take any? Or even go to the doctors for that matter? Well, you wouldn't know that part but I feel like such a fool."

"Are you saying what I think you're saying?"

"You bet your fine ass I am. I'm so pissed at her I can't stand to look at her right now."

Brody didn't miss a beat. "Do you want to come over here and chill with me tonight?"

"Ha, I'm not running from my house like I'm scared of her or something."

"Ain't nobody said anything about running. I only asked you if you wanted to come over and let me pamper you. I could run you a hot bath wash your back, give you a massage. How does that sound?"

How could I say no to all of that? My fingers flexed around the phone as I thought about all the things I would need to gather if I was going to spend the night with Brody. "I have to pack a…"

"You don't need any clothes, unless it's for tomorrow."

My breath caught in my throat as delicious images flashed through my mind. He left me no choice. "I'm on my way." I hung up the phone as I rushed around the bedroom grabbing a few essentials that I knew Brody didn't have in his home. I debated about taking a sexy nightgown, but at the last minute, changed my mind. If things went the way I thought they were going to go, I certainly wouldn't need it. My issues with Lacy seemed minor compared to the burning desire I was now suffering from. I walked past Lacy, who was still sitting in the living room and walked out the door without saying another word.

CHAPTER THIRTEEN
BRODY MASON

I walked along the short path to the wrought-iron fence and unlatched the lock. The lock clanked loudly as I pushed it closed. I was certain the noise informed everyone in the house of my presence. I strode to the front door and rang the bell. Coming to the house this time was different. There was no one on the other side expecting me. I waited for several seconds and rang the bell again. I would not be deterred. After several more seconds, the door opened.

"What are you doing here?"

I didn't expect Mrs. Gates to open the door herself. She made no attempt to open the door wider and let me in the house. "Hello, Mrs. Gates. How are you doing?" I asked as if she wasn't being rude as hell.

"What do you want?" The animosity in her voice was unmistakable.

"I would like to talk to you, if I may."

"You should have called and saved yourself the trouble of coming over here. I'm a very busy woman. I don't have time for foolishness." Without further fan fare she started to close the door.

"Wait, I am sorry for the interruption. You are right, I should have called first. If you would only hear me out, I promise to be brief." I wanted to stick my foot in the door to keep her from shutting it but I had my doubts about whether or not I would have been able to stop her from pushing me back down the stairs.

"I don't have anything to say to you, Mr. Mason. Now, would you kindly leave my property before I'm forced to call the police?"

"For what? I haven't done anything." I was starting to get angry. I could understand why she didn't like me very much. When I used my press credentials to help Lacy leave her home, it wasn't anything personal against you.

"We don't allow solicitation here. Can't you read?" She pointed to a small black and white sign that was hanging over the doorbell.

"I'm not selling anything. I just want to talk to you."

"And I told you, I have nothing to say to you. I don't appreciate your coming back here and I won't be bullied again. Now, leave."

"I'm sorry about the way things went down the last time I was here. It was never my intention to do anything to harm your operation. If you want to know the truth, I actually admire what you are doing with the house your mother left you."

Mrs. Gates eyes grew wide as her mouth dropped open. "Are you investigating me now? How dare you!"

Mrs. Gates opened the door wide enough for her to slip through while blocking my view inside. She shut the door behind her. As she stepped out on the porch, I realized how tall she was. Funny, I didn't realize it before. As she stood in front of me, I almost felt intimidated. I could only imagine how she made Jordan and Lacy feel when she stood up to them. I swallowed a big lump in my throat and took a few steps back so that we didn't swallow each other's air. "No, well, not really."

"I will not have my name tarnished and dragged through the muck by the likes of you, Mr. Mason. Whatever your angle is, I don't want to know. If those girls think they are coming back here after the way they treated me, they have another thing coming." She folded her arms across her chest defiantly.

"Mrs. Gates', I can assure you that neither of the girls, or women, wish to return to your home. They are quite happy where they are."

"Then what are you doing here? And why are you bringing up my mother's business?"

I held up my hands. "Hey, wait a minute, you really don't understand. Can we please go inside and discuss this privately?"

"You must have lost your fool mind. I'm not letting you inside there again."

"Well, can we at least go over to the bench and sit down? I promise not to take up too much of your time."

"Give me one good reason why I should do that?" She was heaving so badly, I thought she was about to hyperventilate.

"It's about your niece, Lacy."

Mrs. Gates seemed stunned. "My what?" She clutched her chest as she fell back against the door causing the screen to buckle. I stepped forward quickly and pulled her away from the door and over to the bench. She did not recoil from my touch.

"I know this is a shock to you, but Lacy Bates is your niece. Actually Lacy is her middle name. Her first name is Kristal."

"I, uh…"

"I know how you feel. We were a little stunned too. Seems she fooled us all."

"But, I don't understand—"

"Your sister had two children after she left Atlanta. Lacy is the youngest. It seems as if your sister was still angry about the disposition of this house and regularly complained about it to her children."

"I did not cheat my sister out of her birthright. We couldn't sell it because it needed so many repairs done to bring it up to code. I tried to tell her this but she wouldn't listen. Any potential profit would have been sucked up by escrow. She could have lived here with me if she wanted to."

"Mrs. Gates, that's not why I am here at all. I could really care less about whatever happened between you and your sister. What you have done for these girls inside is commendable. I sincerely mean that."

"Then why are you here?" Her eyes were accusing.

I was a little perplexed about the way this conversation was going. I expected her to deny Lacy's relationship or ask for some kind of proof, but she didn't. Instead of answering her question, I asked another one of my own. "You're not surprised by this information, are you?"

"I guess I'm not. I don't make it a habit to pick up strays off the street. Something about Lacy drew me to her. Did I know she was my niece? No, I didn't. But I'm not surprised their mother is still pissed at me. My sister and I rarely saw eye-to-eye. She wanted that fast life," Mrs. Gates said shaking her head.

"Yet she left Atlanta and moved to Alabama. That's an oxymoron. Ain't a damn thing fast about Alabama. From Alabama, she moved to Tennessee."

"To be honest with you, I didn't know where she moved to. All I knew was that she was gone. And I was happy about it too! If she had stayed here, ain't no telling what would have happened to this place. That girl was hell bent on destruction. She has my father's genes in her. Is she dead? Is that why you are here? I don't have any money. This place has mortgages too, so selling it ain't an option." Mrs. Gates was practically babbling.

"I mean you no harm, and neither does Lacy. She's an incredible woman."

"Humph. If that's the case, why are you here instead of Lacy?"

I could see her point. "Because you scare the shit out of her. Excuse my French." Mrs. Gates laughed long and hard.

"Yeah right. She didn't act all that scared when she left up out of here."

"It's true though. Lacy had a hard life. She also has some trust issues."

"Who hasn't? She ain't had no harder road than the rest of those girls in there." Mrs. Gates pointed to the house.

"I don't know their stories so I can't comment on them."

"I knew my sister was pregnant when she left here. Got herself knocked up by that preacher down at First Baptist Church. She thought he was going to leave his wife for her. I guess she was wrong."

"I don't know about that either."

"Then what the hell do you know? And why are you here? Told you I got things to do. I don't have time for any foolishness." Mrs. Gates stood up apparently recovered from the shock of finding out she was an aunt.

I stood up as well. "I know that Lacy's sister is missing, presumably dead and that Lacy is afraid to go home. That's why she came to Atlanta to find you."

"Oh, my. I'm sorry. You must think I'm a real bitch." She sat back down on the bench. It swung wildly beneath us.

"No, I don't." I wasn't being one hundred percent honest.

"What about my sister, where is she in all this mess?"

"That's what I need your help with. I could go down there and start asking a bunch of questions and possibly make things worse for Lacy. Or, you could make one call to your sister, to see if everything is all right. Lacy is worried to death about her sister."

"I don't mean any harm, Mr. Mason."

"Brody, please call me Brody."

"Brody then. My sister ain't got any love for me. She won't answer any questions I have. I'm not sure I want her back in my life like that. You don't know the kind of hell she likes to keep up. Always chasing a buck. I can't do it."

I couldn't say I blamed her with all the things I had heard about Lacy's mother. However, from what I gathered, Mrs. Gates had been taking the high road all her life. What made this situation any different? "I guess I understand. You don't know your niece, so I shouldn't expect you to be concerned about her welfare." I turned to leave.

"How dare you say that to me? You don't know my pain. Oh, you might think you know, but you don't really know what causes me to wake up in the middle of the night in a cold sweat!" Mrs. Gates started crying.

I wasn't prepared for that. I absolutely hated it when a woman cried. I couldn't take it. I was at a loss for what to do. Instinctively, I wanted to put my arms around her shoulders and tell her everything would be okay. However, Mrs. Gates' demeanor made me relunctant to risk it. If she hauled off and smacked me, she could seriously hurt me. Not that I was a punk or anything like that. I just didn't like folks hitting me unless I could hit them back. My strict upbringing wouldn't allow me to strike a woman. I thought about it for only a second before I went against my better judgment and took Mrs. Gates into my arms. Thankfully, she didn't fight me. I rocked her gently, as best I could, while she cried.

"What do you want from me?" She asked as she slowly pulled herself together.

"I just need you to make one call to your sister. That's all. Ask her how she's doing. Ask her about her daughter, London. Don't say anything about Lacy since you are not supposed to know about her."

"What makes you think she's going to tell me anything? She hates me."

"That was a long time ago. Time tends to change our perspective on things."

"You don't know my sister."

"Could you at least try?"

"What sort of trouble is Lacy in?"

Mrs. Gates' insightfully went straight to the root of the problem. "Trust me, you really don't want to know."

"I never thought I would be saying this, but, you're right. I don't want to know. Just promise me you won't drag this house and my name through the mud. I don't have much left. I can't afford to lose it."

"You have my word."

"Can I have some privacy? I really don't want my sister cussing me out in front of you. I just might have to cuss back." Mrs. Gates said smiling through her tears. She took the number from me and went inside to make the call, while I waited on the porch.

***

"Well?" I asked Mrs. Gates when she came back outside. She wasn't on the phone long so it could not have been that bad.

"I need a drink, and I don't normally drink."

"Can you leave now? I'm sure we could get one somewhere." I wasn't sure about the set up inside and whether adult supervision was required.

Mrs. Gates had her purse slung over her shoulder. I followed her lead as she walked down the stairs without letting anyone know we were leaving. So I assumed everything was okay. I rushed ahead of her and unlatched the gate for her.

"Where's your car?"

"It's the CRV over there."

"Seriously?"

"Oh come on. Don't tell me you are going to crack on my car too. What's wrong with a Honda? I don't get it."

"There's nothing wrong with a Honda. I just pictured you driving something else."

I was going to seriously have to think about upgrading my car. I couldn't have folks snickering every time I pulled up. "Where are we going?"

"There's a Mexican restaurant around the corner. I need a big margarita."

"Okay, just show me the way." Except for the directions she gave, we drove for a couple of blocks in silence. I got out of the car and opened the door for Mrs. Gates.

"I could learn to like you after all. I can't tell you when the last time a man held a door open for me."

I laughed out loud. Mrs. Gates didn't seem so mean anymore. I rushed ahead to open the door to the Mexican restaurant. If being a super gentleman was winning me brownie points, I would take them.

"We can sit at the bar. I don't feel like waiting on the waitress." Mrs. Gates said with authority.

Once again, she surprised me. I could no more picture her drinking, let alone being posted up at someone's bar. But it was obvious this wasn't her first time doing this. I took a seat next to her on the bar stool. When the bartender came over, I gave him our drink orders.

"Come here often?" I asked as I looked around the shabby bar/restaurant. It certainly wasn't my cup of tea. Although I could see why someone would come here. Especially if they didn't want to be seen. The place was practically empty. The time of day could have been a factor but somehow I doubted it.

"Heavens no. I don't normally drink. I come from a long line of drinkers and substance abusers. The thought of getting addicted to anything scares me to death."

"I hear you." I wasn't about to tell her I didn't believe this was her first rodeo. She was way too familiar. I was trying to think of a good way to lead the conversation back to her sister. I didn't want to seem like I was rushing her. I nursed my Budweiser Ice and waited for her to pick up the ball.

"You know, when my sister first left, I thought about her every hour of every day. I worried that something bad would happen to her. Darn near worried myself to death. It was awful. Some nights I would wake up crying out for her."

"I could understand that. I felt the same way when my brother went off to college." If that wasn't the dumbest thing that I had ever said, I didn't know what was. My brother going off to school couldn't even compete with her sister running away pregnant and alone.

Mrs. Gates just stared at me for several seconds. She finished her drink and signaled the bartender for another. Thankfully she didn't call me out on my blunder.

"Not knowing was the hardest thing but you know what?"

"What?" I waited for several beats for her to answer.

"Time heals all that. Every day, I thought about her less and less. Eventually, it got so I didn't think about her at all. Then you had to come over and start this shit up again."

"I'm sorry, I didn't—" I truly felt bad for dredging up old memories for her.

"None of those numbers work you know." Mrs. Gates was already slurring after she guzzled her second drink. Maybe she was a light weight after all.

"None of them? Even her work number?" I didn't try to hide my disappointment. I was counting on at least the job number being useful.

"Nope."

"What happened with the other two?"

"The cell number belongs to someone else and the home phone is disconnected."

I knocked over my beer. "Fuck. Oops, I'm sorry. I shouldn't have said that." If my mother had been there and heard me cuss in front of Mrs. Gates she would have popped me in the mouth. I knew better than to cuss in front of my elders.

"You can say it again for me. My sister is in jail." Mrs. Gates was ordering another drink.

"Oh crap, really? How did you find that out?"

"Her old job."

"Did they say what for?"

"No. I was too embarrassed to ask? Why do we do that? I feel guilty and I haven't done anything."

"Human nature, I guess. Happens to the best of us. You know if her cell number has been reassigned it could mean she's been locked down for a minute. I guess I need to go down there and see what I can find out."

"Ain't no guessing in it! You made me think about her again, so you damn sure better go and find out some answers. You don't understand. My sister is the only family I have left." Mrs. Gates began crying softly. This was a little creepy since she was wearing this crooked grimace that could almost be a leer.

"Mrs. Gates, I think maybe I should get you home." She was leaning off to the side of the stool and making me very nervous. Picking her up off the floor wouldn't be a good look for either of us. Thankfully, Mrs. Gates was an amicable drunk and allowed me to lead her back to my car.

"You gonna find my sister and bring her home?" Mrs. Gates asked hopefully.

I knew better than to make a promise that I couldn't keep. "I'm going to do my best to find out what happened to her and if there is anything that I can do for her, I will certainly try." It was the best I could offer and she seemed content with it.

CHAPTER FOURTEEN
LACY BATES

My final touch to the breakfast platter that I had prepared was a chilled glass of grape juice. Satisfied with the way my tray looked, I carried it upstairs and kicked at Jordan's door. I was a little nervous that she wouldn't answer. I put my ear next to the door to listen for movement. I didn't hear anything but I was almost positive she was inside. Before I started cooking, I went outside to make sure her car was there. Here lately, Jordan had been spending a lot of her time over at Brody's house and I missed her company. I put the tray down on the floor and knocked.

"What?" Jordan barked from behind the door.

"Can I come in?" I had my hand on the door knob waiting to turn it. If I had to slide the tray inside like Celie from the Color Purple, I would. I was sick of fighting with my best friend.

"What do you want?" Jordan was not going to make this easy on me. I fought the urge to get mad. She wasn't acting any differently that I would have under the same or similar circumstances.

"I want to stop talking to this damn door." I turned the knob and pushed it open. Bending over, I picked up the tray and backed into her room. If she was going to throw something at me, at least it wouldn't hit me in the face.

"What's all that?" Jordan sat up among all the pillow decorating her bed. She had so many pillows surrounding her I wondered how she could even sleep in there.

"I made you some breakfast," I said smiling. She didn't kick me out, so I was feeling pretty good.

"Bitch, I'm not trying to eat anything that you cooked."

I stopped short, causing the juice to slosh around the rim of the glass. The tray was heavy with select pieces from our dining flatware, but that wasn't the reason why my hands were shaking. "Bitch? Why I got to be a bitch?" She should have slapped me, and it would have felt the same. I sat the tray down on her dresser. I no longer cared if her food got cold.

"Humph. I think you already know the answer to that." Jordan wasn't even looking at me. She was examining her nails instead. As if they were growing right before her eyes.

"No, I don't. You have every right to be upset with me. You don't have to call me out my name. Especially, a bitch. Last time I called you one, you wanted to peel my cap back."

"Well that's was when I thought we were going to be friends."

"Oh, so we ain't friends now? Everything we have been through was all for nothing?" I could not believe what I was hearing. I had risked my life and my freedom for this heifer and she was ready to kick my ass out in the cold over a stupid act of omission.

"You tell me. Friends don't lie to each other."

"For crying out loud Jordan. I said I'm sorry. What do you want from me, blood? Should I slit my wrists right in front of you? Would that make you happy? Had my ass down there cooking all this shit. I even made your funky ass some grits and you know how I feel about grits!"

"Ain't nobody ask you to cook me a damn thing." Jordan glared at me with what looked like hatred in her eyes. I was done. I couldn't fix our relationship by myself. She had to want it too and it was becoming apparent to me that she didn't.

"Fine. Forget it. Can't nobody say I didn't try." I left the tray on her dresser. She could take it back to the kitchen her damn self. I was almost at the door before Jordan stopped me.

"My ass ain't funky either."

I was so hurt. I didn't have the energy or desire to say anything else to her.

"What did you do with the Visine? Because if I start shitting and gagging when I eat this shit, we are going to have a big problem."

"If you start shitting it will be because you are so full of it. And it won't be because of something I did to your food." I started laughing.

"Whatever. Hand me that tray and let me see what you have done. I hope you didn't fuck up my grits and put some cheese in it."

"I don't know what you are talking about. Cheese would have been an improvement to that mess." I put the tray on her bed and stood there while she removed the covers off of her plates. I had fixed soft scrambled eggs, bacon, hash brown, grits and toast. There was enough food on the tray for two.

"Wow, you did go all out. If I eat all of this, you will have to roll my ass to the gym."

"I brought my own fork to help you." I was smiling as I pulled a fork from my back pocket.

"Well damn. You were so sure I was going to give in, weren't you?"

"Actually, no. I just brought my fork in case you wanted me to taste test it for you. Or if I had to stab you with it."

Jordan paused with fork mid-air. A look of concern crossed her face and for a few seconds I thought she was going to change her mind about eating. A loud rumble from her stomach may have convinced her otherwise. "Like I said, if I start to shitting, I'm going to make sure the first thing I shit on is you." We both laughed as we shared the breakfast. For me, it was a feeling of relief. I was tired of walking around feeling like something was missing from my life.

"Jordan, I really am sorry. I never wanted to hurt you. Am I forgiven?" I had to know we were good before I got too comfortable with her again.

"We are good. Just don't do that shit again. Okay?"

"I won't."

We finished up the rest of our breakfast in silence. As Jordan finished off the last piece of toast, I took the tray away.

"You did good, grits and all."

"I'm going to take this down and clean up the colossal mess I made in the kitchen."

"Oh, crap Lacy. Haven't you heard of cleaning up while you cook?"

"Yes, but I wanted to make sure your food was hot when you got it. It won't take me long to get it all cleaned up."

"I'll get dressed and help you."

I smiled as I walked out of the room. I was happy things appeared to be getting back to normal.

***

"Brody wants to take a trip to Tunica."

My heart began to beat faster. It always did that any time someone mentioned home, or somewhere close to it. "When y'all thinking about going?" My easy tone did not reveal the emotional turmoil I felt inside.

"As soon as he gets our identifications back."

"What do you need identification for?" I was confused.

"Because I'm going to gamble while I'm down there silly. I have never been to a casino before. I'm not trying to get my feelings hurt by someone telling me I can't come in."

Despite the danger, I wanted to go so badly I could taste it. "How long will you be gone?" I asked as I loaded the last dish into the dishwasher.

"Depends on what we find, I guess. While Brody is out being Perry Mason, I'm going to be chilling at the casino. You could come with us you know."

I felt like a hand had grabbed my heart and was squeezing it with steel like fingers. "I don't know, Jordan. I'm scared to go back."

"I can understand that, but you don't even have to go anywhere near where you used to live if you don't want to. You can chill in the casino with me.

Besides, there is something that I need to tell you that you might not like."

Fear, mixed with dread makes an awful combination. Everything that I had eaten was coming back up. I rushed from the kitchen toward the bathroom with my hand cupped over my mouth.

"You better not be throwing up because you put some shit in my food," Jordan warned as she stood next to me, holding my hair from my face."

My stomach was acting up so badly, I couldn't even respond to her. Tears seeped from the corners of my eyes as I gave into the pain. I wanted to sink to my knees and wrap my hands around the toilet but Jordan kept me standing, barely. The dry-heaving seemed like it would go on forever when in actuality, it was only a few minutes. When I was done, I stumbled away from the toilet and went to wash my face. I was deeply embarrassed.

"Are you alright now?"

I nodded my head not wanting to speak until I had brushed my teeth and used some mouthwash. I despised showing weakness of any kind, but I could not get the image of my sister's face out of my head. After a few more moments, I pulled myself together. "I did not poison you." My throat felt like I had swallowed a handful of gravel. I coughed.

"I know. I'm sorry. I was trying to lighten the mood."

I followed Jordan back into the living room and sat down. I was tired and afraid. My chest felt like it had caved in and I was having a difficult time getting enough air

"Are you okay? You don't look so hot." Jordan patted my hand as if that would make me feel any better.

"I feel like I can't breathe." I was fighting hard not to hyperventilate. It felt like I was losing the battle.

"Put your head down below your knees and lift our arms out to the side."

"Do what?" I stared at Jordan.

"Put your head down and lift your arms." Jordan repeated rather harshly.

I did as I was told. With my face buried between my knees, I started to breathe a little easier. I sat this way for about a minute, until my arms began to get tired. "What's this supposed to do?" I asked with my arms still out at my side.

"Medically, nothing. Mentally, it gave you something else to think about besides your breathing."

If it hadn't helped, I might have punched her. "I'm glad you are finding this situation funny."

"Who said I was finding it funny? You were about to pass the fuck out. I had to think of something."

I sank back on the sofa slightly relieved. "You might as well go ahead and tell me what it is before I make myself sick again."

Jordan picked up my hand and started rubbing it. *What is it with all this hand holding shit?* I liked my news straight with no chaser. Whatever it was that she wanted to tell me wasn't going to change no matter how many times I threw up.

"Brody found out some information about your mother. It's not good."

"My mother? I thought you were going to tell me something about my sister." I exhaled, immediately feeling relieved. Although I loved my mother, and respected her for giving me life, she turned a blind eye to me and my sister when it came to her man.

"Sorry I didn't make that clear. Brody still hasn't found out anything about her. That's one of the reasons why he wants to go there to ask around."

"Well, what about my mother? Is she pissed off that I left or something?" I intended to have that honest conversation with my mother one day about the hell I lived through. Today was not that day.

"Actually, he didn't get to speak with her. Both her cell number and the home number have been disconnected. He had someone call her job. They informed him that your mother was in jail."

I slapped Jordan's hand away suddenly angry. If this was her idea of some kind of joke, the shit was not funny. "What the hell you mean my mother's in jail? For what?" My mind was racing with possibilities and all of them led back to that fucker, Karl Wester. I just knew he had to have something to do with it.

"We don't know the details, but we can assume she's been there for a minute. If both her home and cell numbers have been recycled it suggests that the bills were unpaid. Speculating on it is futile. Brody thinks the best way to get information is to actually go down there and look. He can do a search of court records and some other spy shit behind the scenes to get the real deal."

"I'm coming with you guys."

"Really? I thought you were afraid."

"That's my mother for Christ sake. Fuck you talking about Jordan?"

"Hey, don't be yelling at me. I'm just the messenger. I was just trying to make sure you had thought this through."

"Will you make up your mind? Fifteen minutes ago you said I should go with y'all and I could chill in the casino with you. What's changed?"

"You changed. You are acting like you want to beat up the whole world and shit. I don't want you to go and do something to make this shit any worse than it is."

"I'm fine. Yes, I want some answers, but I'm fine."

"And you promise not to go down there and show your ass?"

I couldn't answer her for a few seconds because I honestly didn't know how I would react once I got back to Mississippi. I survived a lot since I left there. Sometimes, I almost felt invincible. But I didn't know how well that false bravado would hold up when I was faced with my past. I left that place as a girl. I was going back as a woman. "I will do my best to behave myself. Will that suffice?"

"If that's the best you can offer, it has to be. Let me call Brody and tell him that you are coming with us."

"Okay. How are we going to get there?" I was already going over what I was going to pack and the things that I was going to need.

"I think we are driving. At least that is what we said we were going to do the other night. We talked about flying for a hot minute and changed our minds. Since we are not sure how long we are going to be there, flying is less of an option. If we drive, when we come and go is up to us. We could all take turns at the wheel if we had to. It's only about a six hour drive from here."

I didn't know why she was telling me how far the distance was to Mississippi as if I didn't know. I fucking used to live there. I might not have been driving when I left but I knew how far it was. I caught the Mega bus and that took forever and a day. I couldn't shake the feeling that I had somehow failed my mother. That was the hardest part for me to reconcile. Even though my reasons for leaving there were sound and justified, it didn't make me feel any better.

"Lacy? Are you even listening to me?"

"Huh? Damn, I guess I wasn't. What did you say?"

"I was asking you if you wanted to go get our hair done before the trip?"

Hair? Was she fucking kidding me? She calmly tells me that my mother is in jail and she wants to know if I want my hair fucking blown out? "No, you go ahead. I am too amped up to be sitting in a crowded place."

"Girl, I know how that must have sounded. I'm not trying to be insensitive. I was trying to find some way to get your mind off of it until we knew something. No one knows better than me how hard the not knowing is."

I was glad that Jordan explained herself to me. I had been there when she went through her trying time with her own mother. It was good to know that she was with me during mine. "Thanks. I think I'm going to take a short nap. My head is hurting a little bit."

"Okay, boo. Call me if you need me."

As soon as I closed the door to my room, the tears started flowing. I didn't want to really cry in front of Jordan. It was okay to shed a few tears but for this water work show I was having, I needed to be alone. I threw myself down on the bed and buried my face in my pillow. I intended to cry until I got sick or felt better. Whichever came first.

CHAPTER FIFTEEN
BRODY MASON

I glanced in my rear view mirror once more and shook my head. The mood inside the car was gloomy. It had been this way during the entire six hour drive to Mississippi. It was beginning to wear on my nerves. My mother used to say, "If you know better, you would do better." I knew better than to take a road trip with a potential fugitive, yet there I was driving the fucking bus. I could only hope that it wouldn't come back and bite me in the ass.

"Are you sure she's okay?" I turned to Jordan who had also been alarmingly subdued during the trip.

"Yeah, she'll be alright. It's a lot to deal with. I can't imagine how she's feeling."

"I get that. I would be a straight basket case if I found out that my mother was in jail too. But she ain't bugging. She looks drugged. She's been sleeping since we left. She hasn't eaten. Hell, she hasn't even got out to go to the bathroom. And you know how y'all women are, got to go to the bathroom every five minutes," I said laughing.

"Hey, watch out now. The only reason why I keep making you stop is because I don't know when I will see another restroom that I think might be clean. It's different for you guys. Y'all can go anywhere. We have to be a lot more selective where we go."

"Girl, please. You think I'm going to let you plop that fine ass in just any old spot. When you gonna learn that I got you?"

"You got me? What's that supposed to mean?" Jordan asked laughing.

"It means that I'm going to always look out for you first, babe. You are my Queen. Don't act like you don't know this." With every passing day, I was getting closer and closer to telling Jordan exactly how I felt about her. Right now, the only thing stopping me from trying to take our relationship to the next level was passed out in the back seat. I had to be the only man alive that didn't want my girl and her girlfriend too.

"I know you do. You have been a really good friend."

Did she just call me her friend? I almost slammed on the brakes. I felt like she was giving me a demotion after all the hard work I had put in. I couldn't help but to feel a little salty about it too. What else could she want from me that I haven't already given her? My fingers tightened on the steering wheel as I pressed my foot down on the gas.

When I first proposed the trip to Tunica to Jordan, I thought we were going to have a romantic little get away. I booked us a room at Gold Strike, one of the newest casinos in Tunica. Jordan upgraded us to a suite. I wasn't mad about that either because I had heard their suites had huge Jacuzzis in them. I had big plans for that Jacuzzi too. Then, she hits me with the bad news that Lacy was coming with us. Not the best way to start off our vacation, but I was willing to make the best of it. It wasn't that I had anything against Lacy. It was just hard to be romantic with a third wheel present.

"Are you pouting?" Jordan asked.

"Hell no, I'm not pouting. Men don't pout." In truth, I may have been pouting but I wasn't about to admit it.

"That's a lie. You are pouting. You got frown lines all around your mouth. I'm going to have to see what I can do to turn that frown into a smile." Jordan traced her finger around my mouth. Her touch changed everything. How could I be mad when she was touching me like that? I felt my lips slide open wide. My foot pressed harder on the gas, but I eased up when I realized what I was doing.

"Don't be making no promises that you can't keep because I will be holding you to this one."

"Oh trust me. I always deliver on my promises," she said with a seductive smile. For the moment, all was right with my world again. That is, until I looked back in the rearview mirror again. Seeing Lacy lying there so despondent was an instant buzz kill.

"I'm still worried about Lacy. Is she going to snap out of this?"

"Of course she is. She's resilient. Just give her some time."

I could only take Jordan's word for it. She knew Lacy a lot better than I did. I pulled up in front of the casino with mixed emotions. This could go either of two ways. Really, really good, or really, really bad.

I was hoping for the first one. Jordan and I got out of the car.

"Are we just going to leave her in there like that?"

"I just need to check in. You can get the bags out of the car."

"Well, I need to go in too. Remember one of the rooms is in my name."

"Oh shit. I thought I told you to cancel yours. I booked two suites instead of one."

I should have been relieved but she still didn't tell me which one of those rooms she would be sleeping in. "Don't worry about it. I'll give them a call while you check in." If it weren't for the difference in time zone, they might have charged me for the night. Fortunately, I made the call in time to cancel my reservation without incurring a fee. I wasn't balling out of control like Jordan. I could find good use for the two hundred and fifty dollars a night they charged for a hotel room during peak season.

Lacy got out of the car while I was pulling bags from the back. While the bellman was loading them on the dolly, I spoke to Lacy. "Good. You are awake. For a while you had me worried."

"I know right. I can't believe I slept the whole way." She said as she yawned loudly.

"See, y'all were talking junk about my car. I told you it would come in handy for trips. It sleeps good, doesn't it?"

"Whatever, nigger. I was so tired. I could have slept standing up on a bus."

"You are going to give my ride some props sooner or later. Mark my words." I wasn't going to let Lacy's sour face mess up my good mood. I was feeling extremely hopeful that things were going to work out better than I had anticipated.

We followed the bellman to the front desk area where Jordan had just finished checking us in. She walked over to us with a big smile on her face. "I got them," she mouthed as she pumped her fist in the air. She handed me a key. I pushed the key in my back pocket and tried to keep the frown off my face. The little envelop she handed me felt light. Like it only held one card instead of the two I had been hoping for.

"We got the Oxford Suite and the adjoining suite."

"Sweet," Lacy said. She hadn't cracked a smile in miles and it was wearing on my nerves.

"Lead the way," I followed the bellman to the elevator trying my best to mask my disappointment.

Jordan pulled my sleeve. "Wait, do we have to go to the room now?"

"We don't have to. What's up?" I was a little tired after having done all of the driving. However, I wasn't about to be a stick in the mud. Lacy acted like she didn't even hear us talking as she kept on walking.

"I don't know about you all, but I'm ready to gamble. I've been waiting for this moment most of my life."

"I think I'm going to go up to the room." Lacy replied.

"You are not! You slept all the way down here. So you had better carry your ass down to the casino. You can give us at least an hour after having slept the whole way here." Jordan demanded.

I was not about to get in the middle of that girl fight. If Lacy wanted to go to the room, I was cool with that. If she wanted to stay and hang, I was fine with that too.

"Fine. I'll go." Lacy announced like she was doing us both a favor.

"Yay." Jordan clapped as she gave the bellman her instructions for our luggage. Her enthusiasm was infectious. I loved seeing Jordan this way.

"Do you even know where you are going?" Lacy asked. She was acting like a twelve-year old that wasn't getting her way.

"I'm following the sounds from the machines. Don't you hear them calling?"

"I hear them babe," I answered. Jordan had shot out in front of us. I kept the top of her head in my eyesight as she bobbed and weaved among the people coming out of the casino.

Lacy shot me a look like she was annoyed with me. I waved it away. "You are going to have to buck up buddy. You are starting to act like a Debbie Downer." I said it in a joking manner but I was really serious.

"I'm sorry. I suck. That's why I wanted to go to the room so I wouldn't ruin it for the both of you."

"Nonsense. What would you do up there? Climb back in bed? What good will that do?"

"I don't know Brody. I just feel so yucky."

I placed my hand on Lacy's shoulder. "It doesn't make any sense to worry about it right now. Whatever happened, it's already done. We'll get to the bottom of it tomorrow."

"You think you can take me over to the jail to see my mom?"

"Let's find out what we are working with first. Then I'll be glad to take you."

Lacy smiled. "Okay. I'm ready to play."

Jordan was on a dollar slot machine when we caught up to her. "You don't want to start out with something smaller?" I asked. I loved to gamble too. I just did it on a much smaller scale.

"For what?"

"Well alrighty then. If you are going to do this, you might as well bet the max."

Jordan shooed me away. "I got this Brody. Why don't you help Lacy?"

I didn't get offended when Jordan gestured for me to leave her alone. I am the same way when I gamble. I don't like it when someone stands over my shoulder; especially if they have something to say about how much money I'm spending. "Lacy, you good?"

"I guess. I mean how difficult can it be?" Lacy put a hundred dollar bill in the machine and waited for it to accept it. She pressed the max button and the wheels started turning. The machine came to life with the first spin. Bells started ringing loudly.

"Son of a bitch! I am not believing this!" I shouted amazed by her luck.

"What's happening? Did I break it?" Lacy asked.

"Hell no, Lacy, you hit the jackpot! I think you just won Eighty-Two Thousand Dollars!"

"Are you serious? Where is the money at?" Lacy was jumping up and down and so was I. I had never been this close to a major winner like this.

"They can't have all that money coming out of the machine. Can you imagine how much change that would be? One of the attendants will have to come over here and pay you."

Jordan walked over. "No way! That's fucking fantastic." She grabbed Lacy and spun her around. "They are going to put your picture on the wall and everything."

Lacy stopped laughing. She shook her head back and forth. "I can't have my picture on the fucking wall. Are you kidding me?"

"Shit. I do believe they do want to get your information and use your photo for promotional reasons."

All the joy went out of all of our faces as we realized what this would mean for Lacy.

"Fuck that. I'm out." Lacy said as she walked away from the machine.

"What are we supposed to do with your money?" Jordan yelled to her fleeting back.

"Give it to Brody. I'll be up in the room."

I rushed over to catch up with Lacy who was moving like her drawers were on fire. "I can't take your money like that. I understand you don't want your picture on the wall, but at least let me claim the money and give it to you."

"Honestly, Brody, I want you to have it. You have been so nice to me. It's the least I can do to repay you."

"You know I appreciate it, but it isn't necessary."

"For me, it is. I'll see y'all later."

"Wait. You don't have to leave the casino. Just step off to the side while I fill out the tax papers and then we can keep on playing."

Lacy looked scared as hell and it almost broke my heart seeing her this way. She seemed to think about it for a few seconds but shook her head no.

"I might come back down later, but this is a little much right now."

"Okay then. We will come up and check on you later." I still couldn't believe how easy it was for Lacy to walk away from her money. I doubted if I could do it. It just wasn't in me.

The noise from the machine was loud, almost annoying. What was more as annoying than the sound, was all these people coming over and gawking at me as if they knew me. I probably would have felt differently if I had actually won the money. Since I had not, I felt like a fraud. "Jesus, what is taking them so long," I moaned.

"Aren't you excited? I want to win too," Jordan said as she rapidly pressed buttons on the machine next to the one that Lacy had won on.

"I can't get excited about this. I didn't win."

"You want to walk away from it too?"

"Hell no. My momma didn't raise no fool." Jordan kissed me on the cheek which instantly transformed my entire attitude. It wasn't such a big deal after all. And, it was only fair that I keep the money because the IRS would be taxing the shit out of me for it anyway.

"All right now. That's what I'm talking about."

CHAPTER SIXTEEN
LACY BATES

When I left Mississippi three years ago, I never envisioned coming back for any reason. There was nothing for me to get nostalgic about. I had no pleasant memories to reflect upon. I was just empty inside, devoid of emotion. There was only one person in the entire city of Batesville, Mississippi that I cared about. That was my sister, and I had no idea where she was. Or, if she was still alive. That is what hurt the most, the unknown. Her screams that woke me up at night, made me stronger. I didn't realize that I cared for my mother until I learned that she was in jail. I could not shake the feeling that troll, Karl Wester, was the source of her demise.

I walked over to the bar and fixed myself a drink. As much as I didn't want to admit it, I was worried about her. My mother wasn't strong. She thrived on attention, male attention. For whatever reason, she needed it to validate her. I didn't know enough about her past to speculate as to why it was so important to her. I just know that my sister and I suffered because of it. There were a string of men before Karl Wester. We used to call them 'uncles'. I was eight years old before I realized they were not related to us. Wester was the only one momma allowed to move in with us. That's when our lives changed.

I sat down on the sofa with my drink in my hand. I had yet to walk around the suite or unpack my bags. I didn't even want to look around in the quaint little gift shop that I passed on the way to the elevators. If my sister was here, she would have checked my temperature. I rarely walked past a sale sign without pausing to check it out. I did that when I didn't have money and now that I did, I could care less about it. Just like with the money from the casino. I didn't feel right taking it. I felt like I didn't earn it, even if it were only luck that gave it to me. I emptied my glass. It wasn't my intention to get drunk. I just needed something to take the edge off my emotions.

I was about to fix another drink when the door to the suite opened. Jordan and Brody filed in. I frowned. I wondered what part of I wanted to be alone did they not understand?

"Honey, are you okay?" Jordan asked as she came and stood next to me at the bar. Brody took a seat on the sofa.

"I'm fine. I just needed some time to think. It was so loud down there." I said the first things that came to my mind.

"It sure was. I got that check. You sure you won't change your mind and take it?" Brody asked.

"I'm good Brody. I meant what I said. I want you to have it."

Jordan said, "I see you have already been into the booze. Do they have anything good?"

"They got a little of everything. I suspect you have a full bar in your room too."

Brody's eyebrows shot up and a sly smile crossed his face. It was apparent that he didn't know about their sleeping arrangements. It was actually cute when I thought about it. They made a handsome couple and I was happy that Jordan had found him.

"We were thinking about getting something to eat. We came up here to see if you were hungry," Jordan said.

"Yeah. They have the best crab legs at the Horseshoe Casino next door. We could really walk to it. It's that close." Brody joined in.

"Honestly guys, I'm not hungry right now."

"Sweetie, you haven't eaten anything all day. And now you are drinking. That's a good combination for a major hangover."

Jordan's condescending tone irritated me. I was no stranger to the effects of drinking on an empty stomach. "I'll be fine. I just don't want to feel. Is that all right with you, Miss Bree?"

"It's A-Okay with me. I won't have to listen to you puking and gagging all night."

Brody laughed out loud. Jordan punched him in the arm.

"Hey, what was that for?"

"Stop encouraging her. She's going to be sick and then she will really be a pain in the ass."

As much as I wanted to get mad at Jordan for implying I was a pain in the ass, I couldn't. "Damn, Jordan why can't I just be in a bad mood?" I said laughing.

"Because, you are never in a bad mood. You are like a sister to me. When you are feeling funky, I feel obligated to feel funky too. And I do not want to feel funky right now. Feel me?" Jordan folded her arms across her chest.

"Fine. What would you have me do?"

"Maybe we should talk. There are still a lot of details I need to know before we get started tomorrow." Brody suggested.

I raised an eyebrow at him. "Details? What kind of details?" I felt like throwing my hands up in the air and shouting.

Brody rubbed his hands down the sides of his pants. "I don't know. Whatever you want to share with me. Whenever I do investigations, I like to know as much as I can about the people I'm looking for."

"I don't know what I can tell you that you don't already know." I felt like he was interrogating me and it was making me uncomfortable.

"Okay. Let me ask you some questions then to see if anything jars your memories. Jordan, can you get me a pen and pad?" Jordan grabbed the hotel pad from the desk with a pen and handed them to Brody. I refreshed my drink, already feeling uneasy. It was one thing to tell Jordan things about my life. It was something different to be discussing them with Brody. I had to keep telling myself he was doing it to help me. That's the only way that I was going to get through it.

"What's your mother's full name?"

"Luetta Gates. I don't think she had a middle name. If she did, I never knew it."

"Do you know how old she is?"

"I would guess that she's in her late thirties or early forties. She had my sister and me when she was rather young." So far the questions were relatively easy, but I knew they were going to get harder.

"Where did she work before this all happened?"

"She worked the night shift at Winchester Factory." I felt like he should already know this if he really did call my mother's job but I didn't call him out about it.

"Winchester? The gun place?"

"Yeah. I don't think they make guns. Just the bullets for them."

"Get the fuck out of here. Why would such a big ass factory set up shop in such a tiny ass town?"

"Maybe they got a tax break or some other incentive. Fuck if I know. Besides, I was born in that tiny ass town so watch your mouth." I feigned indignation when I understood completely where he was coming from.

"My bad. Why did your mom pick Batesville, of all places, to live?"

"I couldn't tell you. It was before I was born. If I had to guess, it was probably because of some man."

"Oh, I see."

I wasn't sure how I was supposed to take that. It made me feel some kind of way but not enough to fight about it. Even though I was reluctant to talk, it felt good doing something.

"My sister was born in Alabama. I was born in Batesville."

"So, as far as you know, you don't have any family in Batesville?"

"Not that I'm aware of." I was sure the uncles didn't count.

"What about Alabama? Any family there?"

"I couldn't tell you. That was before my time." I patiently answered.

"You didn't go back for visits or on holidays?"

"We didn't get to go anywhere."

"Okay, that's all right. This guy, Karl Wester, can we talk about him for a minute?"

I felt the hair stand up on the back of my neck as bile tasting fluid filled my mouth. I bolted from the sofa and ran into the bathroom. I barely made it to the toilet before I threw up.

"See, I told your ass you would get sick from drinking on an empty stomach," Jordan said as she came into the bathroom behind me.

My stomach was still heaving so I couldn't cuss her out like I wanted to. It took a few minutes, but I managed to get myself together. "My throwing up had nothing to do with the drink I had. It's that man that makes me sick. Every time I think about him, I have to fight to keep from throwing up."

"Damn, boo, I think I would have to kill a motherfucker if he made me throw up every time I thought about him."

"Believe me, I tried."

Jordan handed me a glass of water from the bathroom sink, which I greedily gulped down. She had her arm around my shoulders as she led me back into the living room. I was slightly embarrassed but Brody immediately made me feel better.

"I didn't mean to push you Lacy. I know this man brings back some horrible memories for you."

"He does. I just can't understand how one man could be so evil. I also can't understand why my mother couldn't see it."

"What did he do for a living?"

"I think he used to work over at Fitzgerald's casino. He might have gotten fired because it seemed like he was always at the house with us. Mom used to push us off on him all the time while she worked."

Neither Brody nor Jordan commented. I didn't really expect them to. After all, what could they say? They didn't know how my mother's brain worked. Or, in this case, didn't work.

"I hate to keep pushing this envelope, but when was the last time you saw Karl?"

"The second of November, three years ago."

"Good. I'm glad you can remember the actual date."

"I'll never forget it. I tried to slice off his stubby knob, but I think I only got him in the balls."

Brody jumped up, dropping the pad to the floor. Jordan and I laughed at the hurt, then confused expression on his face. "Damn. You should have warned a brother before you went there." Brody walked over to the bar and fixed himself a double shot of Patron. He threw it back and wiped his mouth with his sleeve when he was done.

"You thirsty babe?" Jordan said laughing.

"That's not funny Jordan. That's one thing men don't joke about. Their dick and their balls. That shit is sacred. You know what I mean?"

"Obviously, we don't." Jordan and I said together. It was the first laugh we had shared in a long time. It felt good too. I missed my friend and I knew she felt the same.

"All I'm saying is, if you are going to tell me some shit like that, warn a brother. Say something like you might not like this but..."

"Okay, I'll try to remember that. It's not like I make a habit out of slicing balls. Give me a break. As I was saying, I was trying to cut off his dick, but sagging balls got in the way of my knife. All I think I did was slice under his balls. As far as I know, he still has them flat fuckers. He had these fat droopy balls. Reminded me of a bag of pennies."

"Lacy, stop. You are killing me," Jordan said as she threw her head back laughing.

"I wasn't trying to be funny. It's what I remember. They were stinky too, like something had crawled up inside of him and died. And he always wanted somebody to suck on them." I started crying. I always did when I remembered that part.

Jordan stopped laughing then. There was nothing funny about what my sister and I went through. Nothing funny at all. Coming here brought all of the memories back to me. Things I hoped to forget.

"Lacy, if this is too much for you to talk about we can come back to it later. Better yet, you might want to do the same thing that I told Jordan to do when she was dealing with a lot of pain."

"What's that?" I said between sniffles. Jordan had left the room and returned with some tissues.

"Write down all those terrible experiences you want to forget. The things he did to you. The fear, the hurt, the shame, the agony, all of it. Get it down on paper and get it out of you. You will be surprised how good it will feel once you release it."

I locked eyes with Jordan. "What should I do with the paper when I'm done with it?"

"Set it on fire."

"Yeah, it will be like telling those people, places and things to catch fire or go to hell," Jordan added.

I nodded my head at Jordan as our eyes locked. I knew all too well about some of the people on her list. They were burning alright. But it didn't have anything to do with some piece of paper. "Actually Brody, it's helping me to talk about it. I haven't told anyone, not even Jordan, this part. But I'm going to warn you, it's graphic."

"Okay, I got you. Go ahead." Brody poured another shot and walked back to the sofa. He picked up his pen and pad.

"I was in the bathroom, taking a bath. I thought I was alone for a change. He came in, with his nasty-ass drawers around his ankles, holding his dick. He held it with both hands like he was holding a monster. That fucker thought he was fooling me. Bitch came in there like a fireman holding his hose. Should have come in like a fisherman clutching his worm."

"Honey, I can't. You can't tell this story like that. I'm about to pop a stich in my side," Jordan said laughing.

"I don't know any other way to tell it. I was a child the first time it happened to me. I was pretty much a child when I left. How am I supposed to handle that?"

"Baby, let her tell it any way she wants to," Brody admonished. I could tell he was caught up in my story.

"I'm sorry. I'll be quiet."

"He kicked off his drawers and climbed in the tub with me, shaking his little thang at me. I can still see them tracks in his drawers as they lay on the floor.

Every time I tried to close my eyes, he would tell me to open them back up. I wanted him to go away. I wanted him to go really badly! We were home alone. I knew there wasn't anybody there to help me." I started to get up to fix myself another drink but Jordan grabbed my glass and fixed it for me. I waited until she returned to finish my story. It wasn't much to tell, after that.

"I had this knife. I had taken it from biology class and I kept it with me at all times. Jordan, I know I told you I got it from my sister's bed, but that was a lie. I had it when I got in the tub. Maybe I knew he was coming. I don't know. Wester leaned forward and put his hands on the wall. He was right over me. His junk right there. I could smell him and I was trying so hard not to." I was crying harder now, but I had to get it out. I had to finish it.

"Take your time, Lacy." Brody said. His voice was very soft as he coached me.

"He had his hands on the wall and he was pushing his crotch in my face. He wanted me to lick them balls. That's when I thought of the pennies and the cooper smell. Now that I think about it, it was probably because I was biting my lips to keep my mouth closed. So maybe it was blood I was smelling and not really the smell of his thang. Hell, I don't know. Anyway I had the knife and I tried to cut it off. But the motherfucker jumped two feet when he saw what I had in my hands."

"Oh shit," Jordan exclaimed.

I closed my eyes and finished my story. "He fell forward and I was able to climb out between his legs. He sank to his knees screaming. He was yelling at me to help him. I told him to shut the fuck up! I didn't want to hear him anymore. I should have gone back and stabbed his ass again but I dropped the knife in the water. I was covered in blood and shaking. I washed my face, as best I could and I stepped into the shower and dried myself off. I didn't want him looking at me. And then I ran in my room, put some clothes on, took the money from my piggy bank and I left. Wait, I grabbed the fuckers money from his pocket too. Then I caught the bus to Atlanta. That's it." I exhaled loudly. It was like a huge weight had been lifted from my shoulders.

"Can we eat now? All this talk about balls is making me hungry." Jordan asked.

The room was silent for several seconds before we all started laughing. Jordan's comment was just what we needed to change the dismal mood in the room.

"Yeah, let's go." I said. Now that I had unloaded my excess baggage, I was starving too. I was feeling so good, I even wanted to try my hand at gambling again. If I won, this time, I was keeping it.

CHAPTER SEVENTEEN
JORDAN BREE

"Do you think it was such a good idea to leave Lacy alone for the night? Am I a bad friend because I would rather spend the night with you?"

"No, she seemed fine when we left her after dinner. If I thought she was in any danger, I wouldn't let you spend the night with me. I care about both of you too much for that. I know in my heart, if something were to happen to her, it would hurt you too much."

"Brody, you say the sweetest things sometimes. Where have you been all my life?" My heart was racing. I wanted to tell him then what I had been trying to deny for months. I had fallen deeply in love with Brody and the thought scared the shit out of me. I didn't know what it was like to hand my heart over to someone on a silver platter. It surprised me that I was willing to do just that, and more. I wanted to gift wrap the motherfucker too!

"I know. I'm a cornball sometimes." He leaned over and kissed me gently on the lips. We had stuffed our bellies with crab legs and were propped up in bed in our suite, which was fantastic.

"I was thinking about getting in the tub for a nice long bath. Would you care to join me?"

"I was hoping you would ask. How about I order us some room service? Maybe get some ice cold champagne?"

"I've already beaten you too it. It should be here any minute."

"When did you do it? You haven't left my sight."

"When I went to the bathroom silly. They have a phone in there. You wait on the bellman, while I get things ready in the bathroom." I jumped off the bed and skipped into the bathroom. I was the happiest I had ever been in my life. I prayed that nothing would happen to spoil this wondrous feeling.

"Okay, Miss Bree. I'm going to let you have this one. But at some point, in the very near future, you are going to have to let me start handling things my way. Don't get me wrong, I like your take charge attitude. I really do, but you have to allow me a chance to be the man that I am."

I stopped walking as I considered what he had said. I turned around and rushed back to the bed. "Honey, I'm sorry. I didn't realize I was doing that. You know that I have never been in a relationship with anyone before. Everything I'm doing and everything I've done has been purely based on... instinct. I would never intentionally do anything to undermine your manhood." I almost slipped up and said I loved him. If anyone was going to say it first, I wanted it to be him.

Brody touched my face and smiled. "I realize that. I just wanted you to know that you don't have to do everything. Hell, I got some extra money now, I can do some things. I probably can't compete on the same level as you. I don't want you to feel like you have to take care of me. That would be too much for me to deal with."

"I can see that. Thank you for telling me. I want us to always be like this. Able to talk about things."

"Me too. Now go run that bath. I feel like making love to my woman." Brody patted me on the ass as I turned away with the biggest smile on my face. My body was still sore from the nights before but there was no way I was ever going to say no to this man. Not now, not ever.

***

"Good afternoon babe. Do you plan on sleeping all day?" I leaned over and kissed Brody awake. He was sleeping so good, I almost didn't want to disturb him. I needed him to know what I had been up to while he slept.

"Afternoon? Are you kidding me? What time is it? When did you get dressed?" His naked chest was proving to be a distraction for me. I pulled the sheet up to his neck to hide it from my roving eyes.

"Yeah, it's after eleven. That means it's after twelve our time so it's technically afternoon. I have been a busy little bee while you were sleeping. After my shower, I went and rented a car. Lacy has been blowing up my phone. I don't know how long we'll be able to keep her contained."

Brody propped himself up on his elbows. "Is she okay?" His brow was wrinkled with lines.

"She's antsy. She wants to go visit her mother today. I don't know if we will be able to stop her either."

"Shit. I don't know if that's such a good idea."

"I know. But what can we do? She wanted to rent a car but she doesn't have a driver's license. I had to get one just to appease her so we can be ready to go the second you tell us it's okay."

"Let me get dressed. Ask Lacy to come have brunch with us. We can talk about what we are going to do while we eat."

I slipped off the bed before I could see Brody stand up naked. If I did, I knew I would be tempted to get in the shower with him. "Okay, do you want me to order brunch in or are we going to go down and get some from the restaurant?"

"We can eat downstairs. In fact, why don't you both meet me there in about forty-five minutes?"

"Okay. We'll meet you outside the restaurant."

I closed the door behind me and used my other key to go back into Lacy's suite. She was sitting in front of her laptop, furiously typing.

"Brody said we should meet him at the restaurant in forty-five minutes. What are you doing?"

"Working on my list."

"Oh shit. Lacy, you know dropping bodies is not the solution to your problems. I mean you do know this, right?" Lacy gave me a wicked side-eye.

"Ain't nobody said nothing about dropping any more bodies. Besides, I thought we weren't going to talk about that anymore."

"I'm just saying…"

"Well, you don't need to. Once I find out what is going on with my mother, I'm hitting the reset button."

"Really? I like that." This was the best news that I had heard all day. Lacy meant the world to me but I was not about to go down if she wasn't willing to pull it together. The shit that happened to her in the past was fucked-up and she had every reason to be upset about it; but incidents like what happened to Seven…that shit couldn't happen anymore. If it did, she was on her own. I had to start thinking about my life and where I would be five years from now. I never really thought about the future before. I was too busy trying to live in the present.

"My sister had a friend who she kept in touch with off and on. I had forgotten all about her because I didn't get to see her anymore."

"What's her name? Do you know where to find her?"

"Her name is Verlia Williams. And I found her Facebook page and sent her a message. I just hope she answers it. I can't see the activity on her page because we aren't friends."

"Did you try looking her up in the phone book? Hell, in a town as small as Batesville, she might be easier to find than you think."

"That's if she's even still in Batesville. To my knowledge, my sister hadn't seen her in years. When Wester moved in, we stopped being able to have company come over to the house. Verlia was my sister's friend from grade school, so they kept in touch. You know, like cards on holidays and birthdays. That type of stuff."

"We can ask Brody to add her name to the list of folks that he's going to check today. He's got this super spy shit program on his laptop that might give us more information than what you are getting at. Let's go on downstairs. I don't want to keep him waiting."

"You are really falling for dude hard, aren't you?"

I froze. Was I so blatantly obvious? "Yeah, I guess I am." I stood waiting for Lacy to say something critical that would make me punch her in the face.

"Good. You both deserve each other. I'm happy for you."

I let out the breath that I was holding. All was right with my world. It felt good not to have to worry about Lacy's feelings when it came to my relationship. "Thanks. I really needed to hear that from you." I hugged Lacy tight.

"No matter what happens, Jordan, I always want you to be happy."

I paused. I couldn't tell if Lacy was being melodramatic or if she was warning me that shit was about to get ugly before it got better. I hoped it was more melodramatic. While I was pretty confident that Brody had some feelings for me. I cared about him too much to allow him to get caught up in some mess. "Come on, he's waiting."

I held open the door while Lacy put on her shoes and grabbed her purse.

"Did you tell Brody that I wanted to go see my mother today?"

"Yes, I told him." I increased my pace.

Brody was waiting for us when we got off the elevator. He was wearing a pair of dark blue jeans and a light blue crew neck shirt. Normally, I hated the color blue. On him it looks good. Of course, he looked better naked. Those jeans were a close second.

"Humph, that is one fine man," I muttered.

"You ain't even lying. It's a good thing that you saw him first or honey you and I would be fighting over this one."

I stopped walking as I stared at Lacy. My fingers curled into tiny fists. "Don't play Lacy. Ain't anything funny about this." I hissed between clinched teeth.

"Girl, I know you are not balling up your fists at me. Brody is like a brother to me. You are my sister. Don't get it twisted." Lacy walked by me and went to say hello to Brody. I was ashamed of my reaction to Lacy's jest. I knew that I was going to have to apologize to her at some point. I decided I would do it when we were alone.

"Y'all ready to eat?" Brody asked.

***

Lacy put down her fork. "I still don't see what harm it will do if I go to the prison right after we eat."

"Honey, you don't even know if she is allowed visitors," I suggested. Lacy had taken it better than I thought she would but it was still early. She could turn on me and Brody at a drop of the hat.

"Jordan's right. Depending on the institution, visitation is different at each facility. Some prisons require that visitors be on a list before they are allowed to visit."

"Fine, then I will get on the list. How do I do it?"

"Well, that is one of the things I aim to find out. We don't know what the deal is being that it's such a small facility."

"Brody, I know you mean well but you are not making sense. Why can't I just go there and demand to be put on the list? The worst thing they can do is tell me no, right?"

"From my experience, inmates make the lists. Not the other way around. Most prisons run extensive background checks on individuals listed before they are allowed into the facility. Do you think your mother put you on the list?"

"Uh."

"Right. We need to be prepared for this. We don't get any second chances at it."

Well, maybe this would apply to Atlanta. Here in Batesville, Mississippi, I'm not so sure."

"I agree. It might not work like that here. Are you willing to take that chance? Are you willing to go through a background check? What if you waltz in there and they arrest you for being an accomplice? Then what?"

Jordan chimed in. "Lacy you should listen to Brody. He has way more experience with this then we do."

"I don't really care about any of this right now! All I want to do is see my mother."

"And I'm not trying to keep you away from her. Can you just give me three hours to do some checking around? Then, I will take you to the prison myself."

Lacy snorted. "What difference will three hours make?"

"It will give me time to go through the court documents to find out what the hell we are dealing with. I mean, I have my ideas about what I think may have happened. Until we know for sure, it's better to err on the side of caution. Can you do that for me?"

"Brody what am I supposed to do for three hours while you are out doing what you do?"

I said, "We can visit the spa. They have great spa packages available in the hotel. I saw them when I was looking at the room service menu."

"The spa? Jordan I could care two fucks about getting a manicure or pedicure right now. I'm not some shallow superficial bitch—"

"Oh, shit," Brody said. He reached for my hand and I pushed him away. I don't know what he thought I was going to do.

"It's a good thing that I know you weren't implying that I am, superficial, because we would most assuredly be fighting right now. It's also a good thing that I love you because you know how I feel about the word bitch."

"Jordan, I wasn't talking about you at all. I was just trying to get you both to see how badly this whole situation is fucking with me. When I left this town, I swore before God, that I would never come back. I didn't think there was anything that could make me do it. Then you tell me that my mother is in jail…it changed things for me. I promise you, I didn't even think I cared one way or another about my mother until you told me where she was. I can't help but to think it's because of me."

"I understand all that Lacy. We both do. I went through the same emotional roller coaster when dealing with my own family issues. I suggested the spa to get your mind off of it, even if it was only for just a little while. Three hours isn't going to make a damn bit of difference to what has already transpired."

"Lacy, it might not even take me three hours. Let me go to the court house and review the files. I don't know what I will find. Maybe nothing. We don't even know if your mother has been arraigned yet."

Lacy shook her head back and forth several times before she answered. "Okay, fine. I'll go to the damn spa. Will you call me Brody the moment you know something?"

"I sure will."

"Fine, let me go back to my room and get a few things. Jordan I'll meet you in the lobby."

"Okay, boo."

As soon as the door closed, Brody turned to me. "Are you sure she's going to be okay? I would hate to leave here only to rush back because she has nutted up on the staff here."

"Lacy doesn't nut up like that. She has other ways to take out her aggression." I thought about that the girl she had laid out in the street that she didn't even know. Thoughts such as those, I kept to myself.

"What about you? Are you going to be okay?"

"I'll admit that I would have preferred to go with you on your search. However, I'm afraid that if I leave with you, Lacy will be out of here shortly after that."

"I tend to agree with you. Let me get going and I'll phone you as soon as I know something."

I leaned over and gave Brody a lingering kiss.

"Umm, don't start Miss Bree."

"Later," I whispered. I grabbed my purse off the desk and went to go meet Lacy.

CHAPTER EIGHTEEN
BRODY MASON

I took about four calming breaths before I pushed open the double doors of the Batesville Police Department. The parking lot was littered with white and blue patrol cars and a few black and white ones. Judging by the number of cars in the lot, they had a sizeable force considering it was such a small town.

I walked up to the front desk where an older white gentleman was reading the newspaper. He did not look up as I approached. The adjoining waiting room was empty. On the wall was a bank of four television screens which were all off save for one. The semi-modern facility was not what I had pictured in my mind. I expected to walk into a precinct reminiscent of Andy Griffin's office, on his late sixties television sitcom, still in syndication. I almost chuckled out loud.

"Excuse me." I tapped on the desk to get the officer's attention. He clearly wasn't used to anyone interrupting him while he read.

"May I help you?" The man looked to be in his late fifties, early sixties. His broad round face was fixed with a grimace even though his words contradicted his expression.

"Yes, I sure hope so. I have a rather unusual request for assistance."

"Well, what is it?" He looked at his watch as if he had something better to do. Although there were no other officers in the immediate vicinity, I was quite sure they weren't far off.

"My name is Brody Mason, I'm a free-lance reporter."

"No comment."

"You haven't heard my request."

"I said I don't want to talk to you." I was positively perplexed by the way he immediately shut me down.

"I am so sorry. I know that you are extremely busy." I wanted to barf saying that blatant lie.

"Damn right I am." The officer practically popped his collar.

"I know you are. I just need some help with a special project."

The officer raised one brow at me. "What type of special project?" His right hand disappeared off the desk presumably into his lap. He nodded at me to continue.

"I'm working with *Lifetime*, the television station—"

"Christ, I know what *Lifetime* is. I've got a wife."

He said it like it was a prerequisite to watching the show. Again, I stifled the urge to chuckle. "Great. Have you ever seen that show *The Women That Kill?*"

"I don't know about all that. I'll have to ask the wife. I don't watch that trash."

"If she watches *Lifetime*, I'm sure she's seen it."

"Well, what's your point? I ain't got all day."

"My job is to interview inmates for the show. Find out whatever I can. And, if the producers think it's a good enough story, *Lifetime* will come here to film it."

"Oh really?"

I knew I had him when he sat up taller in his chair and pushed his paper to the side. "Yeah. I'm so sure, if they elect to come here, I could put in a good word for you. And, maybe, they will even include some cameo shots of you."

"You mean I could be on TV?" He slicked back his hair with his hands as if I were holding a camera in my left hand as we spoke.

"Absolutely. That is, if you have someone that you think fits the profile…"

"Profile? What profile? I don't know anything about any profile."

"Well, it has to be a particularly brutal crime. Not just a regular old shooting or stabbing. You know what I mean?"

"Like if they set somebody on fire or something like that?"

"Yeah. I'm sure they would be interested in something like that. But, it has to be committed by a woman. Do you know of anyone like that?"

The fire went out inside the man's eyes and he became a dim wit again. "Shucks. Ain't nobody burn nobody up. Not that I know about anyway."

"Darn. I guess that says a lot for your town and all. But that's bad for me. I guess I'll have to move on to the next town on my list." I turned as if I was going to walk away.

"No wait just a minute fella. I am sure we could find you something that the television station would be interested in."

I had a smile on my face almost a mile wide that I had to hide before I turned around. I didn't want to appear to be smug or overly confident. "Oh, that would be great."

"Does it matter how old the case is?" The man asked as her peered at me over his computer screen.

"Well, it can't be too old. Putting together these shows takes time. We don't really like to do shows with old women on them. If you know what I mean."

"We had this lady a few years back. She did an awful thing. Kind of makes me sick every time I think about it."

"You think she fits the profile?"

"I'll say. She's a sick son-of-a-bitch. Just hateful what she did."

My fingers curled over the desk. I wanted to grab his computer screen and turn it around so I could surf it myself. "What did she do?"

"Cut the man's dick clean off, pumped it full of super glue and glued the shit right to his head. Pardon my cussing. That happened about three years ago and every man in here ain't been right about it yet."

I felt queasy. "I guess not. That's pretty sick." I had no doubt he was talking about Lacy's mother. Even though the details of the attack were different than what Lacy described, the similarities were too close to ignore.

"You ain't lying a bit. She came in here just as nice as strawberry pie. But her eyes were like a soulless pit. Gave me the hives just looking at her."

"You still got her here?" I played stupid.

"Heaven's no! There wasn't a man in this building that felt safe while she was here. We shipped her ass off to County. I mean Panola County Penitentiary."

"Dag." I pretended to be disappointed.

"You think those people would have been interested in her?" He seemed surprised.

"I would think so. It's not every day you hear about a woman doing something like that. But, I would have to interview her myself to find out. Too bad she's gone."

"Iffin I was able to get you into the jail to speak with her, you think I could still get that cameo on the television show? My wife would split her side to see me on the television."

"Heck yeah. You arrange to get me in and I will do everything I can to get you a speaking part on the show, if they agree it's a good fit."

"What do you mean a good fit? You said you liked gruesome murders and stuff."

"Well, she has to cooperate too. We can't tell her story if she won't talk. Do you understand?"

"Of course I understand. I ain't stupid you know."

My jury was still out on that one.

I raised my hands in the air. "Hey, I didn't mean it like that. I meant if you could do something to make sure she will see me. She might not want to talk to me if she has other people in there with me. Do you know what I mean?"

He was a little slow on the uptake. I tried not to let my impatience show on my face. I was still trying to get back to the hotel before my three hour deadline.

"Oh, I get it. I think I can do that. Got a cousin working over at the prison. If you have a seat over there, I'll give him a call." He pointed to a seat in the empty waiting room. I tried not to let my excitement show on my face. I didn't want him to get suspicious and start asking for my credentials. I had only made up my cover story on the drive to the jail so I didn't have a single thing that could back up my lie.

"My cousin wants to know if there's a small part in it for him too?" The man said with a wink. He had his hand over the phone while he talked.

"Of course. Not as big of a part as the one you would get of course."

He spoke back into the phone for a few more seconds and was smiling when he hung up. He waved me back over to the desk as he began writing something on a piece of paper. When he was finished, he handed me the paper.

"Here's the address. When you get there ask for Nate, my cousin. He will take care of everything else. If you go now, she should be waiting for you when you get there."

"This is great. Thanks so much. What's your name so I can make sure production gets in contact with you first?"

"Ronald Anderson. Folks around here call me Ronnie. I wrote my number on that paper too." Ronnie said proudly with another wink of the eye.

"Great. I'm headed there now. Thanks again. You'll be hearing from someone soon."

"All right then."

I quickly left the station before he could say anything else to me.

***

As I entered the prison, I could not help but feel nervous. I didn't know a black man alive that wanted to walk into a prison, no matter what the circumstances. I would even go so far as to bet even black lawyers got their asses tight when they visited their clients. Mine was cinched up too. This wasn't anything like my visit to the police department. I had to empty my pockets in order to go through the metal detectors. I piled my change, phone, belt and pen in the plastic bowl they had sitting near the conveyor belt.

"Any metal on your body?"

I was confused by the question since I had just emptied my pockets. "Excuse me?"

"Ear rings, piercings in strange places? Shrapnel?"

"Uh, no." I didn't want to think about what he thought I may have pierced. I also took offense to his asking me if I had shrapnel in my body. It was like he was saying all black people had been shot.

"Go ahead through."

I walked through the metal detector and collected my things. Nate found me before I could ask for him.

"Hi, I'm Nate."

"Brody Mason," I said extending my hand to him. He looked at it for a second before he shook it.

"You really from the television station?"

"I sure am," I lied.

"I got the inmate you wanted to talk to. She doesn't look like much now. She about scared the shit out of all of us when she got here."

"Was she violent?"

"No, just the opposite. You know what they say about them quiet women. Those are the ones you have to keep your eyes on." He turned around and I followed him down a short corridor. He paused before the door. "She's in there. We got her restrained for you." I peeped through the observation window and gasped.

"Is that necessary? I don't want to antagonize her before she even starts to talk to me. You know what I mean?"

Nate snorted. "She cut off a man's dick!"

I couldn't argue with his logic but I knew of the extenuating circumstances surrounding the event that he might not be aware of. Not to mention there was a possibility she didn't do it at all. Despite everything Lacy had said, I had to keep an open mind. I could not ignore the possibility that Lacy actually did the stabbing and her mother was taking the fall. "No problem. I hope she won't decide not to cooperate because of the restraints."

Nate frowned as he thought about what I said. "Wait here a moment." He opened the door and went inside. He was in the room for several minutes before he came back out. He was twirling the handcuffs when he exited the room. "She's all yours."

To say that I was nervous would have been an understatement. I turned the knob and stepped into the room closing the door firmly behind me. Miss Gates looked up at me suspiciously. I wondered what they told her about my visit.

"Good afternoon, Miss Gates."

"My name is Luetta and I am not interested in being on television. Not for what I did. Wasn't anything to be proud of." Luetta hung her head and my heart went out to her. Looking at her, I could tell where Lacy's good looks came from. She was stunning even in prison garb.

"Luetta, I'm not from a television station. I'm a friend of your daughter, Lacy."

Her head shot up, her eyes wild. "You liar! If this is some kind of twisted joke, it isn't funny." She pounded her tiny fist on the table.

I was afraid she was going to start yelling so I pulled my chair closer to her. It was a risky move considering her alleged violent behavior. "I didn't mean to lie about that but that was the only way that I could get into see you."

"Lacy is dead. That miserable prick told me she was. Why are you really here? What do you want from me?"

"I promise you, Lacy is not dead. She's at a hotel in Tunica waiting for me to come back with some information about you. We cane as soon as we found out where you were. She wants to come see you so bad she can taste it."

Luetta didn't look the least bit convinced. "But how? I don't understand. Karl told me he killed her." Luetta's mouth opened and closed repeatedly. Her eyes were bucked and unblinking.

"For what I gathered, I think Mr. Wester was good at telling lies to you and your children. I think he controlled your kids with them. They were deafly afraid of him. He hurt them badly." I didn't want to share with Luetta all the atrocities that Lacy had told me about. I didn't see the point especially since Wester was dead already.

"I can't believe this. I should have known the bastard was lying. If he were fucking here, I would kill the bastard all over again."

"Luetta, I don't know much about your case yet. I want to help you get a lawyer. Lacy told me some of the things Wester did to her and her sister."

"I want to see her. This could all be some sick joke."

"I promise you what I am saying to you is true."

"Then bring her to me."

"I will. As soon as I can figure out how to do it, I will. I'm sure you have a lot of questions for her."

"What do you mean figure out how to do it? Why can't she sashay her ass in here the same way that you did?"

"She probably can. The question is will she help your case if she does?"

"I don't understand. What does one thing have to do with the other?"

"Did you kill Karl Wester?"

"You damn right I did and I would do it again too if he was sitting here next to me instead of you. I hope that motherfucker is roasting in hell right now."

"I feel you. I was hoping I could have gotten my hands on him too. Have you told anyone else this?"

Luetta shook her head. "I ain't said anything to nobody, until now. Ain't nothing to say."

I reached across the table and covered Luetta's hand with mine. I removed it when Nate tapped on the window reminding me we were being watched. "Please don't get angry with me. Lacy told me that she was the one to cut Wester. So, I assumed she dealt the final blow."

"Well, she didn't. The fucker was alive when I got home from work. He was in the tub, blood was everywhere. He wanted me to call for help."

I had so many questions that I wanted to ask but none of them were my place. "Lacy does see you. Do you think you could add her to your list of visitors? That is the only way they will let her come in. We will figure out the particulars of this case later once we have secured a lawyer to represent you."

Luetta was sobbing now. "No. I changed my mind. I don't want to see her anymore."

"Are you kidding me? She will lose her mind if I told her this."

"How am I supposed to face her after all this? Don't you see? I failed her, and her sister."

"It won't be pleasant, but you have to do it. I honestly don't think there is anything that I can do to keep her away."

"But you said I had to agree and put her name on the list."

"That is true. I think you owe her that much. She feels like you are here because of her."

"That's just plain stupid. If I hadn't brought that fool into our home, none of this would have happened." Luetta was clearly getting agitated and I was afraid Nate was going to see it and come into the room.

"We can't play the if game. Now, I'm not a lawyer nor do I claim to have a vast knowledge of the law. But it seems to me that what you did could be constructed as justifiable homicide. You acted on impulse after finding out that Wester molested one of your children and claimed to have killed them. The only thing the lawyer has to prove in my humble opinion is reasonable doubt. Hell, he could even plead temporary insanity. The fact that Lacy is alive and can support either of those defenses is a big plus. You have to believe that."

"I'm not sorry for what I've done."

"You don't have to be. If you get a jury trial, there is not a woman alive that wouldn't do the same thing for their children. I think it's worth a shot."

"What about London? Is she here too?" Luetta wiped away her tears as she appeared to digest all that I had said.

"I'm sorry." I didn't know what else to say. We are still looking."

"Is she dead?" Her voice rose to a shrill wail.

"We don't know yet. Lacy asked me to try to find her. That is how we found out about you. Your sister called your old job and they told her where you were."

"My sister?" Luetta pushed her chair back from the table with a surprised look on her face. She spat out the word like she had swallowed something unpleasant.

I realized this was about to get ugly and I had to nip it in the bud. "Luetta, I don't know how much time we have so we have to remain focused. I think you should talk to Lacy. She has more answers than I do."

"Why did you have to go and involve my sister in this mess?"

"We thought she might have pieces to the puzzle. When Lacy left home, she went to your sister. Your sister didn't know who she was, but she took her in and cared for her."

"Ain't that fucking special. I take it she knows what a fucked up job I did raising my girls."

I couldn't think of anything to say about that so I just nodded.

"That's just great. Now I'll have to hear her mouth too."

"Your sister loves you very much. She begged me to come and help you."

"She did?"

"Yes. She did. So, will you add Lacy to the list?"

"I'll think about it."

"Have you met with an attorney yet?" I felt like I was playing chess and was getting my ass kicked. For every move I made forward, I was taking two steps backward.

"I'm waiting for them to appoint one to me. With me not working, I can't afford one and truth be told, I deserve to be punished for what I did."

"Please don't say that. I would have done the same thing if it happened to my child. Let us worry about the lawyer and your defense. Just leave that part to us. We will be here working for you on the outside. Now will you agree to talk to your daughter?"

"I said I will think about it damn it."

"Okay, no pressure. Well, maybe a little pressure because I have to go back to the hotel and look Lacy in the face. You know your child. She is going to want some answers and no ain't the one she is going to want to hear."

"Fine. I'll add her to the list. Anything else?"

"Great. I only need to know two more things for now. After I leave here today, I doubt they will allow me to talk with you like this again. Do you have any idea where London would go if she was running away from home?"

Luetta shook her head no as fresh tears washed her face. I wasn't really expecting her to know but I had to ask. "Do you really think Wester killed her knowing what you know now?"

"Yes, I do. He was a twisted fuck. I can't believe I didn't see it." My heart sank. Her saying it didn't necessarily make it true. After all, she thought Lacy was dead as well.

"I haven't given up hope yet. Don't you give up yet either. I am going to leave now before they come in and make me. Please don't tell them this was all a rouse to see you. We'll work on getting you a lawyer and you should expect Lacy to come visit you soon." I stood up to leave.

"Thank you."

I didn't know what she was thanking me for. I hadn't done anything yet. I knocked on the door and Nate opened it.

"Everything alright?"

"Yeah, looks good. I'll be in touch. Take good care of her. She just might be your ticket to fame." I said after shaking his hand goodbye.

"Yes, sir." Nate said smiling.

My mind was going a hundred miles a minute. I almost called Jordan to tell her the news then changed my mind. This type of news was better served in person. I had one more stop to make before heading back to the hotel. I wanted to stop by the local newspaper to see what kind of press coverage there was of the Wester incident. In particular, I wanted to see if there was anyone that spoke out on Wester's behalf.

***

"Son of a bitch," I said as I pushed away from the stack of papers in disgust. I didn't like it when I wasted my time and this trip to *The Panolian* newsroom was just that. I could have saved myself a trip if I had bothered to check it out on line. I pushed back my chair and stacked up the newspapers that I had been perusing to return them. My displeasure was written all over my face.

The kindly old lady who had helped me find the back issues of the paper looked up as I approached her desk. "Did you find what you were looking for young man? We don't get many people coming into the building these days. Most times people look at the paper on line. Hell, I can't remember when was the last time we had somebody come in here."

I wasn't in the mood to talk. I just wanted to get back to the hotel and let Lacy know what I had found out. "Not really. Thanks for your time."

"It's no problem at all. I was more than happy to help you. It's about time some of these big time papers recognize our city."

I had told the woman that I was doing a story on small town cities for the Atlanta Journal Constitution. Of course, I had opened myself up for a full dialogue about the values of small town living versus big city living which I couldn't care less about. This paper was a damn joke when it came to reporting. Instead of a newspaper story with details of each crime, crimes in general were reported blog style with no details. "Thank you for your time."

"And we don't have all that crime they have over there in Memphis. They can keep that mess over there too. We don't need it here. I'll tell you this is a nice place to raise your family."

"I'm sure it is. Is there any other newspaper in the city?"

"Humph. We don't need any other paper. Town ain't that big. Paper only goes to print twice a week. See this here pile of papers? We are about six months behind getting the stories printed. I took sick and couldn't keep up with the work. Had to have my gall bladder removed. Painful, it was downright painful."

"I'm sure it was." I was looking at the door like it was the gateway to heaven. The woman kept on talking.

"Besides, town folks don't look to us to report the news. They get that from the Memphis paper. We keep the social calendar mostly."

"Ah, that explains a lot. Thanks again."

"What exactly are you looking for? If you don't mind my asking? I don't want you going away from here mad."

I felt a surge of panic. I hadn't really thought my cover story all the way through. I didn't think I needed to. "Uh, we're doing a story on teenage runaways. In Atlanta, the number of missing children is staggering." I thought I did pretty well for my lie on the fly.

"You don't say. Do you think they will turn up here?" The older lady's face seemed to light up expectantly as she appeared to try to connect the dots.

"No, um, I'm not really sure."

"Then what you come out here for? Ain't making any sense."

This woman was a lot sharper than I had given her credit for. "Uh, we wanted to know if smaller towns processed information on missing children different than larger cities." I could feel myself sweating and I hoped that the lady didn't notice.

"How do they do it in Atlanta?"

I was the one that was supposed to be asking the questions and it felt like this old lady was grilling me. "Typically, children have to be missing for twenty-four hours before they can be listed as 'missing.' By that time, they are more than likely already out of state." This wasn't necessarily true. Atlanta did have emergency response mechanisms. such as amber alerts, which would alert authorities immediately especially in cases of child abductions.

"Around here, we pretty much do it by word of mouth. If one of ours gets missing, we call damn near everybody in town to see if they have seen them."

"Well, that's assuming they haven't already left town, isn't it?"

The woman shrugged her shoulders. "I ain't saying its right, that's just the way we do things."

It appeared as if I hurt the lady's feelings. "Pardon my manners. I don't even know your name."

"It's Andrea. Andrea Tanner."

"Mrs. Tanner—"

"Miss. It's Miss Tanner. Never did find the right one, if you know what I mean."

"I understand."

"Have you found the right one, Mr. uh?"

This conversation had just slipped to the left. "I'm sorry, just call me Brody. Yes, I have been lucky enough to find the right one. I'm thinking about asking her to marry me real soon as a matter of fact." I surprised myself with my confession. Saying it out loud actually made me feel good. I smiled.

"That's good. That's real good. Young people today don't know anything about marriage. They want to live together instead of making a commitment to each other. I wish I had married. You better make that lady a priority. Life ain't promised to you." Miss Tanner had a faraway expression on her face.

"I am sorry to cut this conversation short. I really have something I need to do right now." I rushed out of the office before she could say another thing. My desire to have Jordan as my wife had just become a priority.

CHAPTER NINETEEN
LACY BATES

As much as I appreciated what Jordan and Brody were trying to do, they were taking entirely too long to do it. I couldn't continue to sit around waiting for something to happen. Not if I wanted to stay sane in the process. The not knowing was driving me nuts. I picked up my purse from the nightstand and slung it over my shoulder. The last thing I felt like doing right now was to sit in a damn spa like I didn't have a care in the world.

I caught the elevator downstairs to the lobby where I was supposed to meet Jordan. Needless to say, she was not there. The lobby was a beehive of activity which was a stark difference from when we had checked in the night before. Since it was Friday, it seemed like a lot of people were checking in for the weekend. This only added to my irritability. I walked over to the gift shop to get out of the way of people getting on and off the elevators.

"Fuck is Jordan doing?" I said out loud as I looked at my watch. She had said we were meeting in fifteen minute and it had been more like twenty-five. I looked in my purse for my phone but I must have left it in my room. I turned back around and walked back to the elevator. I didn't want to knock on Jordan's door because they might have gotten into something and I didn't want to be the one to interrupt them.

I opened the door to my room and I saw my phone next to the keys to the rental car Jordan had gotten. My hand hesitated for only a fraction of a second before I scooped up the keys and put them in my purse. I tiptoed over to the door and looked out the peep-hole to see if anyone was in the hall. When I didn't see anyone, I quietly snuck out of my room to the elevator. Nervously, I stabbed at the down button silently praying that I could get to the car before I ran into Brody and Jordan. The tiny bing announcing the elevator's arrival sounded more like a gong as I rushed into the elevator and closed the door.

I felt like Lady Luck was riding my coat tails. First the huge win in the casino. Now this. I backed out of the parking space as fast as I could without hitting anything. I didn't take my first full breath until after I had cleared the lot. Now that I had gotten away from the hotel, I wasn't sure what to do. Everything Brody and Jordan said about going to the jail made sense. However, my heart said I had to go and see for myself if it were true.

Part of me was ashamed of my actions. This was exactly the type of impulsiveness that Jordan frowned upon. I knew she would be mad when she discovered that I had left with her car. But if anyone would understand my behavior, it would be her. I was banking on it. Jordan's family hurt her immensely. She wanted more than anything, to find out why her family treated her so badly. It was literally tearing her apart. In the end, I had to give her the space to handle it by herself. As hard as that was to do for me, I knew it was necessary. This is how I felt right now. I couldn't let someone else fix this for me. I had to do it myself.

I stopped at a traffic light as anxiety tickled my heart. Without thinking about it, I was driving back to the place that tormented my dreams. Even though I knew that it was no longer occupied by the people that meant the most to me, I had to see it. Behind those doors, our nightmares became realities. I had to know if it still had the power to haunt me.

The streets from Tunica to Batesville were practically desolate. Cotton fields lined both sides of the rural country roads. I always told myself that one day I would stop and actually pick some of that cotton. Today was not that day. I was on stolen time. I turned on the radio and tried to find the blues station from Memphis. Normally, I didn't care for the blues. I didn't want to listen to someone else's pain when I had so much of my own. Today, it somehow felt appropriate. Listening to someone else's pain almost took my mind off my own.

As I raced down highway fifty-five, I tried not to think about what I would do when I saw the house. It wasn't like I still had the key on a ring somewhere and I could just walk in. I only hoped it would be enough, just to look at it again. Why I thought the house was to blame was a mystery to me. The walls couldn't provide the answers that I sought but something was urging me to follow this through.

This stretch of road was practically void of all cars going in the same direction as me. I pressed down on the gas and the car surged forward. The drive time from the casino to my old house was approximately fifty minutes. I needed to make it in twenty. Time was of the essence. I knew it would be impossible for me to get there and back before Jordan realized I was gone. However, the quicker I got there, the quicker I could go back. As I exited off highway fifty-five, I eased off the gas pedal. My apprehension grew as I drove the last few miles to town.

My senses were on high alert. I expectantly scanned the streets hoping for a glimpse of my sister. It wouldn't be the first time I had done this exercise. Every time I left home, I searched for her. The only difference between then and now was this time I was doing it by car. Before, I had to rely on my own two feet. I was hopeful that having wheels would make a difference and allow me to broaden my search.

The town was busier than I had imagined for a Friday afternoon. This congestion both irritated and excited me. The more people there were, the more likely I would see my sister. It might have been a foolish notion, but it was all that I had. My stomach was a flutter with nervous energy as I scanned the crowds looking for familiar faces. I wanted to find someone who knew me or my family. I debated about whether or not to park the car and walk amongst these strangers but that would mean spending time I didn't have to waste. I continued driving through town without any luck recognizing a familiar face. "How is that possible to live somewhere most of your life and not recognize a soul?" I mutter aloud. It made me realize just how cut off from society we really were.

Our house was several blocks south of town. My apprehension grew the closer I got to our old neighborhood. The flutters in my stomach grew exponentially with each minute that passed.

I turned on my street barely going the posted speed. The back of my shirt was sticking to my skin like I had dipped it in water. Sweat was dripping from my brow as my knuckles tightened on the steering wheel. "What am I doing here?" I asked out loud. My heart was pounding rapidly against my chest. I could see our house and it brought tears to my eyes. I stopped about five hundred feet from it and pushed open the car door holding my head outside. Everything I had for breakfast came back out. The vomit choked me with its intensity. I cried as I wretched, barely managing to hold onto the wheel. Had I let go of the wheel, I would have surely fallen out of the car.

I knew I was going to feel some kind of way about coming back home but I never expected this. When I stopped retching, I felt slightly better but not much. I pulled myself back inside the car and looked through my purse for a tissue. I found a crumpled up napkin and used it to wipe my face and mouth. "This was a very bad idea," I said to myself. I closed the door when my insides stopped quivering and when I was sure that I was done. My eyes were being drawn to that house. I expected to see some tangible evidence of the crimes that had been committed inside, like crime scene tape or boarded up windows but there was nothing like that present.

The house was clearly vacant. The yard was a complete mess. Over grown weeds and trash littered the once immaculate yard. When we lived there, we couldn't get away from yard work. I think we were the only girls in the neighborhood that had to cut the grass and trim the bushes. At the time, I hated having to do it. However, I often times felt a sense of pride when I compared it to the neighboring yards which were cared for by boys. Maybe, had our lives been different, my sister and I could have opened our own landscaping business. It was something we talked about during the late hours of the night. It kept us from talking about other things, like what happened when my mother left us alone.

Surprisingly, there wasn't anyone milling around on our block. It's like they were all hiding inside their homes waiting for me to leave. Part of me wanted to get out of the car and march up to my next door neighbor's house and knock on it. I wanted to ask them if they had any idea of the horrors we sustained in that house. I wanted to know if they had seen my sister or what happened to my mother. In the end, I didn't do any of that. I started the car and drove off slowly. Different ideas of what ifs were floating around in my head. Going there was a complete waste of time. I had opened up a whole can of misery that I didn't want to eat. Jordan and Brody were going to be all over my ass and the only thing that I could do was take it. I decided to hightail it back to the hotel. I turned the car around and headed back through the center of town.

As I approached downtown, I couldn't help but gawk again at the people walking the streets. Hoping against hope to see someone who may have known me. I was stopped at a light when my phone rang scaring the shit out of me. Instinctively I reached for the phone and mashed the gas. When I realized what

I had done, I slammed on the brakes. The phone slipped from the seat and fell to the floor. I had almost run a red light. I put the car in reverse. As I was backing up the car, I noticed the blue flashing lights behind me.

"Oh, shit." My chest heaved. I was so preoccupied looking in front of me I didn't see the police cruiser slip up behind me. "Are you kidding me?" I moaned. This couldn't have happened at a worse possible moment. I reached down and grabbed my phone to silence it as I put the car in park. My heart rate plummeted. This was not good. I was going to fucking jail in a town I abhorred.

The officer got out the car and cautiously approached my vehicle. He stopped next to my window. I was numb. I raised my hands up over my head. The officer tapped on the window. Tears were already forming in my eyes. I lowered the window.

"Good afternoon officer," I said in the bravest voice I could muster.

"Driver's license and registration." The officer said. His hand rested on the butt of his pistol making me even more nervous than I was when I saw those flashing blue lights. The people on the street started to cluster together in groups.

"Is there something wrong?" I feigned ignorance.

"Driver's license and registration," he repeated a little more gruffly.

"Can I put my hands down?"

"Don't try anything funny young lady," he curtly stated.

I slowly put my hands down as I tried to think of something that would get me out of this situation. I reached for my purse and began riffling through it as if my license were actually tucked inside. "Oh sweet Jesus. I can't find my wallet. I must have left it at the hotel."

"It's against the law to drive a motor vehicle without a license."

Duh, did he really just say that to me? "I, uh, didn't say I didn't have a license. I just don't have it on me." This was Mayberry fucking RFD, why was this cop being such a fucking hard ass?

"Same difference. Where is your registration? Did you leave that at the hotel too?"

Sweat dripped from under my arms. I reached for the glove box hoping that at least Jordan had put the proper paperwork in there. "It's a rental Officer. I'm not sure it's in the glove box or not."

"Hell, I know it's a rental. You have got out-of-state license plates. And a big ass Avis Rental sticker on the back."

Figures, it would be just my luck to get a wise-ass cop to pull me over. "Sorry, Sir. I'm a little nervous." I managed to open the glove box but it was empty of any paperwork. Next I checked the center console but it was empty as well. Knowing the neat freak in Jordan, she gathered up all the paperwork and took it inside the hotel. My tears started rolling down my face. I hung my head to try to hide them from the officer. I didn't have anything clever to say. I was going to jail and I knew it.

"Where you headed?" the officer asked. He was patting his pen against his ticket book.

"I am going back to my hotel Officer." For a split second, I felt hopeful that he would let me off with a warning.

"You were about to run that red light." He pointed at the traffic signal.

"But I didn't Officer. See, my phone rang and it startled me. I hit the gas by mistake but I stopped right away."

"You were texting too?"

"Huh?" This wise-ass was actually a dumb ass.

"I asked you if you were texting too? You city folks don't know how to just drive. You want to do multiple things at one time. It's against the law down here."

I wanted to tell him that it was against the law everywhere. Even in the bush of the jungle, I was quite sure it would be illegal there too. "But I wasn't texting. My phone was on the seat. I running a little late for meeting my friends at the casino."

"So, you were speeding too?" The officer flipped open his pad.

"Don't be ridiculous. I was stopped at a red light." I didn't mean to call him ridiculous, it just slipped out.

"Who you calling ridiculous? Get out of the car and place your hands on the roof."

My heart started to beat faster. I didn't want to get out of the car and be on display for the whole town to see. I could even here the shop door bells tinkle as people working in the stores filed out onto the sidewalk. "Officer, I wasn't trying to be disrespectful. I was just trying to get you to understand—"

"So, now you think I'm stupid too." He reached for his gun again.

"No, no. Not at all."

"Then get out of the car. I'm not going to tell you again." This Barney Fife looking son of a bitch was working my nerves.

As I opened the door and prepared to step out of the car, my phone rang again. The shrill sounding bell scared both me and the officer. He looked around wildly as he drew his weapon. This situation had just gone from bad to worse. The last thing I wanted was to be facing the barrel of a pistol from an incompetent white officer on the red-neck side of town. "Oh, shit." I exclaimed as I reached back to turn off the phone.

"Put your hands where I can see them!" The officer shouted. The crowd was growing increasingly larger and moved in closer.

"I was just trying to turn off my phone.

"Get the fuck out of the car now!"

Something inside of me snapped. Instead of stepping out the car, I turned the car over and threw it out of gear. My foot was pressed to the floor. As panic took over my senses. All I could think about was getting away.

"Shit!" The officer exclaimed as he raced back to his car to give chase.

I was splitting my attention between my rear view mirror and what was in front of me. Suddenly it seemed as if every car in Batesville was on the road, and in my way. "Where did all these cars come from?"

The cop turned on his siren as he quickly gave chase. My heart was pounding in my chest. As I maneuvered through the small downtown streets. I knew I needed to get back to the expressway if I had any hopes of getting away. I pounded on the steering wheel in frustration at this stupid move I made. Either way it went, it wasn't going to end well.

I glanced back in my rear view mirror and I saw that the officer was using his radio, I assumed to call for back up. "Fuck, fuck, fuck." The tears that had been practically blinding me before, had dried. The only thing I could think about now was getting away. I knew that running from the cops was never a good idea but there was something in that cop's voice that sent me over the edge. He reminded me of Wester, and that triggered a fight or flight situation to me.

The officer used the speaker in his cruiser "pull over now!" This motherfucker was still yelling at me and it did not make me want to do as he asked. In fact, it only made me drive faster. I rushed through two traffic lights before I cleared downtown. As I left behind the shabby town, I pressed my foot harder to the floor. The tiny sports car accelerated easily but the patrol car was close behind me.

I reached over and grabbed my phone and entered my passcode. I had to do it three times before I put in the right numbers. I pressed recent calls and redialed Jordan. She answered on the first ring.

"Lacy, where the fuck are you? I've been looking all over for you."

I glanced back in the mirror and the cop was trying to come up on the left side of my car. I swerved over into his lane, blocking him. He ripped the wheel to the right and drove off the black top for a quarter of a mile.

"Jordan—"

"I've walked this entire casino. I've been back to the—"

"Jordan—"

"…and the spa—"

I screamed, "Will you shut the fuck up and listen to me?" The cop had regained control of his car and was attempting to come up on the right side of me, riding down the wrong side of the highway. I countered and cut him off again.

"Who the hell are you yelling at? And what is that noise?"

"It's the fucking cops. I got one chasing me!"

"Cops? Oh, Lord, Lacy, what have you done?"

"I think I'm going to need a lawyer." I was trying to remain calm despite the blood racing through my veins.

"Oh, no! Where are you?"

"Route 61. If I can lose the cop, I'll be back…"

"You are running from the police? Bitch, are you crazy?"

If I weren't travelling at ninety plus miles an hour, I might have laughed. Jordan didn't say bitch often and when she did, she was mad. I glanced back into the rear view mirror and I noticed the cop had fallen back some. For some reason, this excited me. I pressed harder on the accelerator but I was already pushing the car to its limit. Wind and dirt from the road was rushing through my open window as I crossed the state line. My hair kept whipping in my face, obscuring my vision. I wanted to roll up the window but in between holding the phone and the wheel, I had run out of hands.

"Jordan, I can't let them arrest me, I don't have a license."

"Oh, God! Lacy, please stop the car. This cannot end well." I could tell that Jordan was crying. As much as I didn't want to be the source of her pain, I couldn't think about that right now.

I glanced back in the rear view mirror again. The police seemed to have given up the chase and I was beginning to think I had a chance at getting away. "It's going to be ok—" I cruised through the red light only a few miles from the casino.

Suddenly, out of nowhere, another car smashed into the driver's side of my car. I felt the vehicle leave the road in a series of rolls. I screamed as I attempted to gain control of the vehicle. I stomped on the brakes repeatedly as the car careened out of control. I saw the ground several times as the vehicle flipped.

"Lacy!" I heard Jordan yell before the phone flew out of my hands. My body was tossed from one side of the car to the other as the car struck the pavement and tipped over again. I loss count of the amount of times the vehicle rolled. I could not understand where the other car came from. I didn't know what hit me but it felt like an armored tank.

I let go of the useless steering wheel and tried to protect my head from the flying shards of glass from the windows and windshield as I was tossed about like a pellet in a pinball machine. My biggest fear was of being ejected from the car or possibly being decapitated. My head crashed into the roof of the car and pain exploded in my head. I could feel something wet rolling down my face and I instantly knew it wasn't sweat. It was blood. I held my hands up in front of my face as the car came to a stop upside down. They were covered in blood.

"Oh, God!" I exclaimed. My phone landed next to me but I was in so much pain, I could not pick it up. I passed out from the pain and the smoke that filled the inside of the car. I wasn't ejected from the car but that might have been better than burning to death.

CHAPTER TWENTY
BRODY MASON

Guys like Wester didn't get to be creeps way overnight. Chances were they had a history of abuse. Before I went back to the hotel to face the girls, I wanted to know more about Karl Wester. In the back of my head, I was still holding out hope that I would find out some more information about London as well. I drove to the Fitzgerald casino with these thoughts on my mind. Fitzgerald's was only a hop, skip and a jump from our hotel.

After finding a parking spot at the casino, I asked the security guard for directions. "Excuse me, sir. Could you direct me to the employment office?"

"We don't have an employment office. If you are looking for a job, you will have to contact corporate or an agency."

I cleared my throat. "I'm not actually looking for a job. I was hoping to get some information about one of your co-workers." I reached in my pocket and pulled out a hundred dollar bill and palmed it.

The security guy's eyes followed the money as he offered to shake my hand. I was well aware of the cameras placed strategically around the casino. By shaking his hand, the exchange of money would not be as noticeable. "What kind of information?"

"It's regarding a former employee. Do you know of someone that would be willing to help me?"

The guard stood there for several seconds sizing me up. He had palmed my money, so I didn't know what else to do but stand there and wait. I looked around the casino. A fair amount of people crowded around the tables and a swarm of people at the slot machines. It felt like an eternity before he answered me.

"Go up the stairs to the rewards center. Ask for Michelle Scott. Tall lady with dreads. Tell her Robert said you need a player's card. Just so you know, she likes green too." The guard winked at me.

"Thanks." I nodded with understanding. I didn't expect their cooperation to come freely. I casually walked through the casino so as not to draw attention to myself. The last thing I wanted to do was attract negative vibes. If I appeared to be in any way suspicious, no one would want to talk to me no matter how much money I possessed. I knew enough about casinos to know that their employees were under constant scrutiny. Being around all that money was too tempting not to corrupt the average person. In a town like Tunica, jobs were not plentiful. If one was fired from one casino they would more than likely be banned from the rest of them.

Instead of going directly to the rewards desk, I went to the men's room first. I had been running all afternoon and this was the first chance I took to relieve myself. Instead of using the urinal, I chose the only stall in the small bathroom on the second floor. Inside the stall, I withdrew my license and two hundred dollar bills. I folded up the money to be the exact size of my license and stuck both of them in my back pocket.

Finding Miss Scott was easy. She was the only woman working at the rewards desk. She was indeed a talk drink of water, with a majestic looking face. She smiled as I walked up to the counter. "It's a great day at Fitzgerald's. How may I help you?" Her eyes lit up with her smile. She was truly a beautiful woman who seemed to enjoy smiling.

"Hi there. Robert told me I needed a player's card."

Miss Scott paused for half a second before her professional demeanor took over. "May I see your driver's license?"

She accepted the license and the money without blinking an eye. She was such a consummate professional. I couldn't help but to admire her composure. "Is this your first player's card?"

"Why yes. I was seeking some information on a former employee." I leaned in closer to the desk as if I was telling her my personal information.

"Yes, of course. And that name would be?" Her fingers continued to type information from my license into the computer. She worked fast, without looking up from her screen.

"Karl Wester."

Miss Scott's fingers stopped moving at once. Her beautiful countenance marred by a snarl. "Is the information on your driver's license correct?" She snarled at me. I could feel my chances of getting information from her slipping from my fingertips as easily as the three hundred dollars I had paid for information.

"Yes, it is. If it makes you feel better, he's no friend of mine."

Miss Scott's face relaxed as she handed me my license, minus the money. She attacked a bungee cord to the card and handed it to me. "The hotel lobby is through the archway. Someone will be there to assist you in about five minutes."

"Thanks so much." I replied as I headed to the lobby. Judging from the reaction to Wester's name, Miss Scott wasn't that fond of him either. I was slightly disappointed that she wouldn't be the one that I spoke to. The lobby was empty when I arrived. Without knowing what else to do, I wandered over to the literature rack and plucked a few pamphlets from it. I took my pamphlets over to the bank of seats and sat down. The overstuffed chairs were extremely comfortable. I pretended to be immersed in those pamphlets when Miss Scott came and sat down next to me several minutes later.

I looked up in surprise. "Oh, wow. I'm so glad it was you that came."

"Why are you so surprised?" Her eyes were practically dancing with merriment.

"Because you said someone would be here to assist me. I assumed you meant to pawn me off on someone else."

"Not when I accepted your generous offer. I don't have much time. How may I assist you?"

"I was hoping to find out some information on a former employee."

"Yes, that bastard Karl."

"Obviously, you are not his biggest fan. Neither am I. I didn't know the man myself, but from what I'm hearing, he wasn't a very nice man."

"All I have to say on that is good riddance that he's dead. What do you want to know about him?"

"How long ago has it been since he's worked here?"

"He's been gone for little over a year."

"How long had he been employed?"

"Before I say anything else, what is this all about? I'm not trying to lose my job over that dip-shit."

"Miss Scott, I can assure you that anything you tell me will remain strictly confidential. I'm trying to help a friend."

"A lady friend?"

"You could say that. Her mother has been accused of killing him. I'm trying to learn something about the man to help with her mother's defense." I decided to be completely honest with Miss Scott rather than lie to her as I had originally planned to do.

Miss Scott clapped her hands together. "In that case, what do you want to know? I despised the bastard."

I could not believe my luck. "I take it he was fired? May I ask why?"

"He was fired alright. He was the day supervisor and he harassed practically every female on the staff. He used his position to obtain sexual favors. Some of the women got roughed up pretty badly too. He fucked with the wrong one and they got his ass."

"I can't say that this information surprises me one bit. I hear he liked his ladies younger." I didn't want to come right out and admit any of the things Lacy had told me in confidence.

"That's what I heard too. I'm glad he's gone. I would have popped a cap in his ass if he had tried anything with me. Of course, I was probably too old for him," Miss Scott said laughing.

"You may be a little older than the girls he was seeking but I can assure you, you are no less pretty." I sincerely meant the compliment. Miss Scott appeared to blush.

"Aren't you the charmer? I can get you a list of the girls he accosted and their contact information, if you think it will help."

"Indeed it would. Thanks so much."

"I wish I could stay here and talk to you longer but I only have a fifteen minute break. I need to get back before someone comes looking for me."

"Thank you so much for your time. I do have one more question? Have you ever heard of a girl who I think worked here by the name of Verlia Williams?"

"I don't recall anyone by that name, but I could be mistaken. We have a large staff and I don't know everyone. If you give me your number, I could do some checking and get back to you."

"That would be wonderful." I grabbed a matchbook from the table and scribbled my name and number inside of it and passed it to her. She looked around quickly before she accepted it.

"I hope you can get the lady off. That bastard was bad news."

"Thanks again. I'm going to do my best."

I waited a few minutes until after Miss Scott left before I walked out the front door. I didn't want to risk going back through the casino so I exited through the hotel entrance. It was a short walk to the casino parking lot. All in all, I was happy with the information that I had obtained today. I couldn't wait to get back to the hotel to tell Jordan and Lacy what I had found.

CHAPTER TWENTY-ONE
JORDAN BREE

I was completely beside myself with worry. It had been over a half an hour since Lacy's frantic phone call to me and Brody appeared to be missing in action as well. I alternatively kept dialing both of their numbers as I paced the floor of my suite. My mind was not my best friend because I imagined myself losing both of them at once. The thought was simply too much for me to bear. I had been disappointed by people my entire life. For the first time that I could remember, I wanted to trust someone other than myself. I wanted to love. It scared me stupid to think I could lose either one of the people who inspired my life and gave me a reason to live.

Rushing to the window, I couldn't stop myself from looking out of it again even though I couldn't possibly decipher any faces from that distance. The only thing I could possibly see would have been flashing lights or emergency vehicles. Neither of those would be a welcomed sight as far as I was concerned. I rushed back to the desk to grab my phone. I had dialed their numbers so many times, my battery was wearing down. I retrieved my charging cord and plugged in my phone. It gave me something else to think about for approximately two seconds.

"What the fuck!" I shouted. I was trying not to panic but I was losing the fight. I knew nothing good would come from losing my cool. At the end of the day, it wouldn't change a thing. I turned on the television hoping to find something to occupy my thoughts. I purposely avoided the news channels. If Lacy really did have an accident, I didn't want to see it on the television. I flipped through the channels hoping to find a light-hearted comedy. Something that would keep me from doing what I really wanted to do, which was cry. I settled on an old episode of The Jeffersons. If anyone could make me laugh, it should have been George. Unfortunately, he wasn't providing enough of a distraction from the wicked images my brain had been conjuring.

The thing that bothered me most as I walked back and forth was the feeling of helplessness. I was stranded at a hotel, in a strange city, while the people I loved were missing. To make matters even worse, I was pretty sure that one of those people was hurt.

I could not get the sound of Lacy's scream out of my head. It was so loud and long, until it suddenly stopped. Beyond the screams, was the undeniable sound of metal crunching. Without a doubt, she hit something. This also presented another problem. Lacy took the rental car and crashed it. With all the money I had, I wouldn't be able to make that go away. Especially, if the police were involved. This is what hurt me the most, the fact that I couldn't fix this and make it go away.

I went over to the window again as I struggled to hold back my tears. I wasn't concerned about paying for the car. That was trivial and a mere bump in the road for us. My thoughts were more dismal. What would I do if she didn't survive the crash? Or worse, ended up in jail? I reached for my phone again and sent Lacy a text begging her to please call me back.

"Oh, God." I muttered aloud as another scenario played out in my head. It was something else that I hadn't considered. Lacy had been carrying altered identification. If she were arrested, Brody might also become implicated in this mess. My heart felt like it was about to break in two. It seemed like I had damaged two innocent lives by bringing them to Mississippi in a feeble attempt to fix things. The only reason why Brody had gotten involved in Lacy's situation in the first place was because of me. If I hadn't been so selfish and wanted to have Lacy with me, none of this would have happened.

It was just too much, I couldn't take it. I alternated from being angry with Lacy, to feeling scared. I reached for my purse to pop one of my pills. The last thing I needed right now was for me to sink into a depression. It would definitely complicate things and not in a good way.

I started pacing the room again. This was not good. Random thoughts were flowing through my mind and I was in a quandary about what to do about most of them. Legally, I probably should have notified the rental car company about the possibility of an accident, but there was no way I was going to rat out my friend! I didn't even think I could form my lips to say that Lacy had done anything wrong.

The only good thing that had come out of this entire ordeal this morning was my willingness to admit to Brody that I was hopelessly in love with him. I couldn't wait for him to come back so I could tell him. I was going to throw myself into his arms and shower him with kisses. There was nothing that I wanted more than to see his beautiful face. Out of everything bad that had happened to me in life, if it were designed to bring him to me, it was worth it. Just thinking about Brody, brought a temporary smile to my face and my heart. He was truly a God send to me.

I glanced up at the clock on the wall and frowned. I wasn't trying to time his movements but Brody was late. He had said he would be gone no more than three hours, yet it was pressing up on five and I still hadn't heard anything from him. Since we met, he had never given me any cause for worry. That is, until now. At this point, I wasn't sure if it was all in my mind or if I had a legitimate reason for concern. "This shit sucks." I walked over to the bar and poured myself a drink. If the drugs didn't help me to relax, I was sure the combination of drugs and alcohol would. I wasn't looking to get drunk. I just wanted something to take the edge off.

I grabbed my phone again and sent Brody a text to call me. Although I didn't tell him that I thought Lacy was in trouble, I did write that it was important. With that done, the only thing I could do was wait and pray.

Getting to my knees was such a humbling experience to me. It had been so long since I prayed, it wasn't surprising to me that prayer wasn't the first thing I thought to do. Growing up, I stayed on my knees for my family. I prayed for the souls of my siblings who were immersed in a street life designed to kill them off one by one. I prayed that one day my mother would give a fuck about someone other than herself. I prayed for acceptance from my peers. All of those prayers went unanswered. Even though I prayed unselfishly at the time, I was hoping this time things would be different.

"Heavenly Father, I know that you have not forgotten about me even though it may have appeared as if I had forgotten you. While I didn't believe it at the time, I realize now that you have been carrying me all this time. I thank you Father for the love and favor you have shown me. Father, I ask that you forgive me for doubting your love. I hate to ask this Father, but I need your help. It's not for me Lord that I'm asking. I need you to wrap your arms around my friends and loved ones. Lord, I know that I've done some things that you would not approve of. I thought I needed to do these things to survive Father and I was wrong. I believe the same can be said of my friend, Lacy. You know Lacy has had a hard life, Father. She did the things she needed to do to make it another day. Even though some of those things were bad, Father, you know her heart. Can you please cover her with your loving arms and protect her? I am not about to make any promises to you that I don't intend to keep, such as going to church every day. I do promise to keep you first, in everything I do. I promise to pray more and think of you in all my decisions. I can only pray that will be enough. Father, I want to thank you for sending Brody to me. He has shown me the wonders of love which allowed me to see you again. Can you please watch over him too and bring him back to me? These and all the blessing I ask in the name of the Father, Son and the Holy Spirit. Amen."

I was a little wobbly on my feet when I stood up. I wasn't sure if it were from the combination of the drugs and the alcohol or the cleansing of prayer. Whatever the reason, I felt more a peace with whatever was about to come. I lay down across the bed to wait.

CHAPTER TWENTY-TWO
BRODY MASON

The light was blinding. It was so intense. It felt as if it were burning my skin. I instinctively turned my head away from the light. The movement caused intense pain to shoot through my neck, back and arms. "Son of a bitch!" I attempted to raise my hand to shield my face from the light and couldn't. I was confused. Something was terribly wrong and I couldn't figure out what it was.

"Mr. Mason?" A male voice said.

I heard someone calling me and it frightened me. My mind had to be playing tricks on me. I struggled to open my eyes but no matter how hard I tried I couldn't see. As my heart thundered inside my chest, I understood. I was dead and Jesus or one of his assistants was doing roll call.

"Mr. Mason?" The voice said again a little more firm.

I wasn't trying to be rude, but I wasn't ready to speak with anyone on that side. I had too much stuff to finish on this side. If I was dead, then it would mean that my affair with Jordan was over before it had really had a chance to begin. My heart raced faster at the unfairness of it all. It seemed like I had spent my whole life looking for her and the minute I found her, she was taken from me. I tried again to move. I wondered what would happen if I bargained with God. Hell, at this point, I was even willing to strike a deal with the devil, just for a chance to get back to Jordan.

Sadness, the likes of which I hadn't known before filled me. Just thinking about not being able to see her smile again caused me anguish. It just wasn't fair. I tried to sit up but it felt like a huge weight was sitting in the middle of my chest. I grunted in frustration.

"Mr. Mason," a stern voice commanded my attention.

"What?" I barked back just as aggressively. If brownie points were given for kindness, I would be fucked today. I was ornery as a bee, ready to sting the first thing that crossed my path.

"Do you know where you are Mr. Mason?"

"I'm in hell. I'm in complete hell."

The voice chuckled. "You most definitely are not in hell. Are you in any pain?"

This man was laughing but I didn't find a damn thing funny. Perhaps they were used to this type of reaction from people who believed their time had come too soon. I tried to move my head again to no avail which only frustrated me more. If heaven was like this, it was highly over-rated. So far, there wasn't anything glorious about it except maybe the glorified heat lamp that was shining in my face. I was a black man and the last thing I needed was a tan.

"Oh, God!" My reality became crystal clear. I wasn't in heaven at all. I really was in hell. This made more sense to me. Why else would I have been allowed to find love for the very first time, and then lose it unexpectedly?

"Mr. Mason?"

"If I'm dead, will you give me five fucking seconds of peace to get used to it?" I felt like I was robbed. To think I spent most of my life trying to do the right thing and I got shipped straight to hell on a technicality.

"Mr. Mason, you are not dead." The man chuckled again.

"It's bullshit. It's all bullshit."

"Did you hear what I said, Mr. Mason? You are not dead. I am doctor Bell and you are in the hospital."

"What the what? If I'm not dead, why is it hot as hell in here? And how come I can't see your face? Am I blind?" The thought of never seeing Jordan's beautiful face again was painful, but I would deal with it if only I could hold her again.

"Oh, I'm sorry. Let me move this light from your face. You have been in an accident and you are in the hospital."

"I'm really not dead?" I felt like I was in a bad episode of Punked.

"I can assure you, you most certainly aren't dead. Although in the morning you may wish you were. You have a slight concussion and I'm afraid your left leg is broken in two places."

"But I'm not dead?" Relief was finally sinking in. I had another chance.

"No, you are not."

"Why can't I see?"

"Don't worry about that. You had a small gash on your forehead with some swelling that we bandaged up. In a few days, we will remove the bandage and you should be as good as new."

"Can I go now?" I was anxious to get back to Jordan, even if I had to crawl on my stomach.

"Not quite yet. I would like to keep you for a day or two for observation. You took quite a hit."

"How long have I been here?"

"I'm not quite sure? You were here when I came on duty at five o'clock."

"Is it morning or is it night? I have to know. My girl will be worried sick about me."

"Morning. The end of my shift actually."

I groaned. Jordan was going to be pissed. "How come I can't move?"

"We had to restraint you. You were thrashing around a bit. We didn't want you to injure yourself further."

"What kind of accident did I have? I don't remember a thing." So far, I was taking this man's word for everything. He had yet to tell me anything that I could identify with.

"You were involved in a car accident."

"Oh, wow. Did anyone else get hurt?"

"There was a young lady brought in too. I'm sorry, I don't know her condition."

"Doctor Bell, I really need to call my girl and let her know where I am. She's probably going out of her mind with worry."

"I'll have the nurse come in and contact her for you. For now, I would like for you to try to get some more rest. I'll be back this evening to check on you."

"I have to tell you man, when I woke up, I thought I was in heaven. Then, with that light and all, I thought I was in hell."

Doctor Bell chuckled again. "I heard you. It's the drugs. I'll be honest with you too, it's the only comic relief us doctors get listening to drug induced dreams and fantasies. People say the darnest things with a little Propofol and trauma."

I laughed. "Thanks doctor, for everything. Don't forget about calling my lady. You do not want to hear her mouth if she gets fired up."

***

I knew Jordan was there before she even reached out to touch me. I smelled her. Her scent gently shook me awake. I smiled. "Hey baby." My mouth was a little dry, but I didn't care. My baby was with me.

"How did you know I was here?" Her voice quivered so I could tell she was trying to hold back tears.

"My head may be a little fucked up right now, but there ain't anything wrong with my nose." Even though I knew she was troubled, it felt good knowing she cared enough about me to try to hold back for me.

"What are you trying to say? You telling me I stink?" She joked.

"Never that baby. Never that."

"I was so worried about you. I didn't know what was going on?"

"I'm sorry sweetheart. If there was anything that I could have done to save you that, I would have. I had them phone you as soon as I woke up."

"Are you okay? Why do they have that bandage over your eyes?"

"I'm fine. Only a few broken bones. The doctor told me he would take off the bandage tomorrow. It's to prevent swelling."

"Thank God. I prayed for you." Jordan softly admitted.

"You did?" I was truly surprised that she said this. After all she had been through I wouldn't think she was a praying woman.

"I just knew something wasn't right. I got down on my knees and prayed."

Suddenly, I was happy Jordan couldn't see my eyes. Even though I knew there was nothing wrong with men who periodically cried, I still didn't want her to see me doing it. "I have my own confession to make."

"Oh, yeah?"

"When they first woke me up I thought I was dead and my biggest regret was that I didn't tell you that I loved you the last time I saw you." I waited for her to say something but the room was completely silent. So silent, she could have left the room.

"Are you still here?" I asked quietly.

My heart was beating very fast. The fact that she didn't say anything could only mean one thing. She didn't love me and this thought was almost too much for me to handle. I turned my head away from the sound of her voice.

"I was thinking the same thing. I asked God to bring you back to me so I could tell you. Where do you hurt? I want to get in bed with you."

"You want to get in my hospital bed?" I wanted to shout out loud. I felt like Charlie Brown when the little red-head girl said he was cute.

"Yes, I do. What else did you break? I can see the traction on your leg." I felt Jordan coming closer and it was like a spot light shining on me. I was smiling from ear to ear. I felt her grab my hand and gently squeeze it.

"My leg. I guess I'll have to learn to walk with crutches for a bit. Hell, you might even have to drive us home."

"That's not a problem. We could even fly home if necessary."

"I know that's right. I'm pretty damn sure I trashed my car too. So flying would certainly be a good option." Even though I could not see Jordan, I was happy enough just to hear her voice.

"I was so worried about you. What happened?"

"I wish I could tell you. I was driving along. The next thing I know I woke up here."

"Are you going to let me get in there with you?"

I could imagine her standing there with her hand on her hips and I wanted nothing more than to move over and let her do it. "Get in where you can fit in. I can't really move right now with this thing on my leg. Doctor said it is broken in two places. I think my right side should be good."

"Okay. Let me know if I hurt you."

"You know you got my heart racing and my blood pressure up, right? What are you going to do when the nurse comes in and sees my dick all hard like it is right now?"

"Do you want me to move?"

"Not on your life. I've been missing this all night."

Jordan pressed her face against mine. "I'll hide your dick for you. What I want to know is how you are going to make love to me with your leg in a cast?"

"Trust and believe, I will have it figured out by the time I get out of here," I said laughing.

"Did the doctor say how long you would have to stay?"

"I think he will let me go home tomorrow, or the next day at the latest."

Jordan started kissing my exposed neck and face. I could feel the wetness of her face and knew that she had been crying and it hurt my heart that those tears were for me.

"Is there anything that you want me to do for you? Do you want me to bring you anything?"

"I'm not sure where my clothes are or if I have anything to wear home. I would hate to leave this hospital with my ass hanging in the wind."

"I know that's right. That's my ass and I don't do sharing."

We shared a laugh for a few seconds and to me, all was right with the universe. Jordan's admission of love took a tremendous weight off my heart. I was looking forward to getting out of the hospital and starting our lives together. "What did you do with Lacy? Is she out in the waiting room?"

I felt Jordan tense up and pull away from me slightly. I wasn't ready to let her go so I held on. I assumed they had another little rift. These girls were like sisters, so I wasn't worried about them patching it up.

"I don't know? She took the rental car and went somewhere. I've been calling her all day and night, but she doesn't answer her phone. I swear, between the two of you, I think I have aged ten years."

"What do you mean she took the rental car? To do what?" I felt the beginnings of a headache coming on that was penetrating the painkillers that I had been given.

"She took off right after you did. She called me and said the cops were chasing her. Then I heard this horrendous crashing sound…"

"Oh, shit. I've got to get out of here." I pushed Jordan away as I struggled to get up.

"And do what? You have a bandage over your fucking eyes and you can't walk."

"I can't just lay here! Oh no, it can't be."

"What? What are you thinking?"

"The doctor…he said there was a woman brought in—" I didn't have to push Jordan away this time. She got out of the bed right away.

"You don't mean…"

"We have to at least check it out. I mean you do." I pressed the button to call the nurse. I didn't care what they said. I was getting out of that hospital.

CHAPTER TWENTY-THREE
JORDAN BREE

I didn't stop to think about what I was going to say or do when I left Brody's room. I was acting strictly on my gut instincts. I knew Lacy was in that hospital and I was determined to find her. I purposefully walked up to the information desk and waited patiently for someone to return to the desk to help me. After about a minute, an elderly white woman returned to the desk wearing a white volunteer's cap. I was counting on the fact that she wasn't a regular hospital employee.

"Hello. May I help you?" the volunteer asked.

"I hope so. I got a call from my sister that she was involved in an accident but the call was disconnected before I could find out where they had taken her. I have to find her. I'm just sick with worry."

"Oh, dear. I can imagine. What is your sister's name?"

I froze, undecided which name I should tell the lady. A small frown appeared on the volunteer's face. "Lacy Bates." I could only pray that Lacy had used the identification Brody had provided for her instead of the one with her real name on it.

After a few heart wrenching seconds the woman said, "Oh, good, she's here. She's on the third floor, room 403."

"Thank you so much for your help."

As I walked over to the elevator, I doubted if anyone could tell how nervous and afraid I was. I anxiously stabbed the button summoning the elevator. When the doors opened, I had to stop myself from running full tilt inside and allowing the other passengers to get off first. The hospital wasn't very big, but from what I could see, it appeared to be active. This could definitely play in my favor.

I didn't have a plan as I got off the elevator, except to know that Lacy was alright. I followed the signs posted on the wall to Lacy's room. When I saw the police officer sitting outside of her room, I stopped. I shouldn't have been surprised, but I was. Given the ease of which I was given information on Lacy's whereabouts, I allowed myself to think she had managed to get out of her predicament. The young white officer looked up and locked eyes with me. He licked his lips and I smiled appreciatively. If flirting was something that I could do to get in to see Lacy, I had no problem doing it. The officer stood up as I got closer. I attempted to walk into Lacy's room as if he wasn't even there.

"Excuse me, Miss, you can't go in there." The officer turned red as he looked me up and down. He acted as if I was a piece of meat and he was starving.

"Oh, I'm sorry. I didn't see you sitting here. My mind…" I tapped my head to indicate that my head wasn't on straight.

"It's okay. You didn't know," the officer said as he stood back off to the side.

I stood there undecidedly for a few seconds. "I don't understand. Someone from the hospital called me and told me my sister was here, in this room?"

The officer looked confused. "I'm not aware of any phone call Miss."

It took everything I had not to push past him. I did what every red-blooded girl in the world would do when faced with a similar situation. I started crying. Crying on demand was an art form and I, was a Vincent Van Gogh. "My mother's going to kill me if something happened to my sister on my watch. It's all my fault that she is here." I took a seat in the officer's chair and covered my face with my hands. For good measure, I turned up the volume.

"Miss, you can't be out here like this. I am going to have to ask you to move along."

I wailed louder. "What am I going to tell my mother?"

"I, uh,"

"She is going to kill me. It's all my fault. I might as well kill myself..."

"Wait, now that isn't necessary." The officer put his hand on my shaking shoulders.

"You don't know my mother. My sister can be a brat but she's the apple of my mother's eye. If I could just see my sister, just once, that's all I need..."

"I can't let you do that. I could lose my job."

I looked up at him with tears still streaming down my face. "What do you think I will do? I can't sneak her out of here, not with you standing guard. What harm could it do if you let me in there for five minutes?"

"Well..."

I was standing so close to him, I could see the acne in his pores. "You can search me, if you want. I just want to see her."

The officer's face grew redder as his eyes roamed my body once again. Despite the anguish I had suffered through all night, I knew I still looked good. I held my arms out to my side and turned around for him to frisk me.

He may have hesitated for a second, but not much longer than that. I heard him release a heavy sigh as his hands freely roamed my body. He spent entirely too much time doing it, but I bit my tongue to keep from saying anything about it. When he was finished, I turned around. "Satisfied?"

The officer nodded his head and stepped away from the door. "Five minutes."

My heart was racing as I pushed open the heavy door, terrified of what I would see. Lacy was propped up in the bed with her arms folded across her chest and her eyes closed. She was so still, she could have been dead. "Oh, Lacy!" I quickly crossed the room. I was afraid to touch her.

Lacy opened her eyes. "I fucked things up, didn't I?"

There was no point lying about that. "Are you hurt?"

"No, they said I was lucky. The car flipped several times. I might have a concussion."

"If you weren't in so much trouble, I would choke the shit out of you. I've been scared shitless all night. First you then Brody. I swear y'all are trying to kill me."

"Brody? What happened to him?"

"There is an officer outside your door. I don't know how much time I have."

"What happened to Brody?"

"What were you thinking boo?" I ignored all her questions about Brody.

"I wasn't thinking. I got tired of sitting around and not doing anything. I thought if I could go to town, I could see someone that would know who I was."

"Dumb, just plain dumb. We are going to get you a lawyer. Remind me to kick your ass when you get out of this mess."

Lacy nodded her head.

"Did you tell them anything?"

"No, they got my name from my purse but I haven't said anything to anyone."

"Good, don't. I'll get to work on the lawyer right away."

"Where is Brody?"

I could not avoid her question any longer. "He's in the hospital too. I think he was in the other car involved in your accident. It hasn't been confirmed yet, but it's a good chance he was."

"Oh, shit. Is he hurt? I didn't even see what hit me."

"His leg is broken and he has a concussion too. Other than that, he's okay."

"I am so sorry. I never thought any of this would happen."

There was no need for me to beat Lacy up. I was sure she felt as bad about the situation as I did. "We'll fix it. Just stay quiet until we find you a lawyer. My guess is they are going to transport you to jail the minute you are released."

"Okay. Please tell Brody I'm sorry."

I nodded my head. There was nothing else left to say. My mind was rushing ahead. "I'm going to go before I get kicked out. I love you girl and everything is going to be okay. Be strong."

"I'm so sorry, Jordan. You know I'm hard-headed. I just didn't think this whole thing through. I wish I could take it all back, but I can't."

"I know boo. I know. Promise me you won't nut up between now and the time you speak with your lawyer! Okay?"

"I'll be good this time. I don't have a choice."

I kissed Lacy on her cheek and backed away from the bed before the officer could come into the room and separate us. The last thing I wanted to do was piss him off after he had been so kind as to let me in to see her. "I told the officer I was your sister."

"It doesn't matter what you said to him. I'm not talking to anyone unless you send them to me."

"Good. I think Brody may know a good lawyer in Atlanta. Don't worry about a thing. I am going to take him home but I will be back as soon as I get Brody settled."

"Okay, I'll be here." Lacy attempted a smile but it didn't reach her eyes and I could tell she was scared.

"It's going to be okay, just don't drop the soap."

"Bit—"

***

We were back in my apartment in Atlanta. Brody's bandage was off is head and he was adjusting well to his crutches. "I think your attorney friend is here?"

Brody walked into the kitchen, his crutches tapping loudly on the floor. "Finally. This waiting is driving me nuts. In between the waiting and these damn crutches, I feel like I'm going nuts. I don't like you doing all the leg work either."

"I know sweetheart. It's been hard on me too. Hopefully, your friend has some good news for us." I gave Brody a kiss on the lips before I went to answer the door. In spite of the grim circumstances, I had to believe we were making progress. Brody's friend had been in Tunica for over a week meeting with Lacy and her mother. Despite our pleas for information, he hadn't told us anything and we were anxious for a report. I opened the door and stumbled back in surprise. "Oh my goodness! Max! What are you doing here?" I asked as I wrapped my arms around his neck and gave him a big kiss on the cheek.

"Hi, Jordan. It's so good to see you." Max walked into the apartment looking around.

"Brody, come here." I shouted.

Max turned with what looked like a strained smile on his face. His smile turned into a frown when he saw Brody on crutches.

"Hey, man. It's good to see you," Brody exclaimed as he gave Max dap.

"What happened to you? Jordan beat you up?" Max laughed.

"Naw, man. I had a little fender bender, that's all and part of the reason why we wanted to see you."

I turned to Brody as I tried to mask my scowl. "You knew about this and didn't tell me?"

Brody looked properly chastised. "I'm sorry babe. I didn't know if he was going to come, so I didn't want to get your hopes up."

Max wore a satisfied expression on his face. "Just because I'm here doesn't mean I'm all in. Where is Ricardo?"

"He should be here any minute," Brody said.

I was at a loss for words. It didn't make me feel good to know that Brody had been keeping secrets from me. He of all people should know how I felt about secrets.

"Before you blow a gasket Jordan, not telling you was not my idea. Involving Max was Ricardo's idea. He suggested we keep a tight circle around it until we knew which way we were going."

I looked between Brody and Max. Both of these men had played a significant role in getting me out of the mental institution. I had love for both of them. In the end, I had to respect their decisions. I nodded my head as the door buzzed. I turned away from those men and went to answer the door.

"Hi, thanks for coming. My name is Jordan." I held the door open for Ricardo after we shook hands.

"I'm Ricardo Mosby. Nice to meet you. Is everybody here?"

"Yes, we are in the living room. Follow me." I showed Ricardo to the living room and took a seat on the sofa near Brody. Ricardo walked over and gave Brody a hug.

"Good to see you, man. It's been a long time."

"I know. We've got to do better keeping in touch. Brody and I are frat brothers." Ricardo said to all of us.

I continued the introductions even though this wasn't my party. "Ricardo, this is Lawrence Maxwell. He likes to go by Max."

"We have talked over the phone. It's nice to put a face to the name. Are we ready to get down to work?" He looked around at all of our faces as we collectively nodded our heads.

"I guess someone needs to bring me up to speed with what we are all doing here. Brody was very vague over the phone." Max said.

Brody spoke up. "I'm sorry about that. I was advised to keep it tight until we all got together. Lacy asked my help to find information about her sister whom she believed to be dead. During that search, we found out that Lacy's mother was in jail for the murder of the man who had abused both Lacy and her sister, London, for years. We went to Mississippi for more information and that's when things got ugly. To make a long story short, Lacy took Jordan's rental car and got arrested."

"Don't forget the car chase with the police and the accident that broke your leg," I added glumly.

"Yeah, that happened too."

"Wow. Y'all have been busy haven't you?" Max said laughing.

"You ain't lying."

Ricardo spoke up. "Brody asked me to look into their cases and although it's a long shot. I think both cases can be resolved concurrently."

I smiled, "Good. I'm getting a little tired of waiting. I keep thinking about Lacy being in a cell and it's tearing me up inside."

Brody added. "I know how you feel. It's keeping me up at night too. That and this damn cast. I can't wait for them to take it off."

"When I talked to her last night, she seemed to be in good spirits. I just need to see her face. Then I will know if it's all a front or not."

Max frowned. "I can appreciate how you both feel. Don't get me wrong, I like Lacy, but where do I fit into any of this?"

I had forgotten what an asshole Max could be. But, I had to agree with him. I didn't know why they had called him in either.

Ricardo never missed a beat. "Lacy's mental health could play a very big factor in her case."

"Lacy was never my patient. I haven't a clue as to her mental state."

My heart sank. If Max found out that Lacy didn't even have bipolar disorder, he would really come unglued.

"I realize that. However, you are the closest professional that she's been in contact with over the last twelve months." Brody argued.

"What about her doctor? Why didn't you call on him or her?" Max stood up and started pacing the floor. I didn't dare open my mouth and it sounded as if Brody was going to do the same.

"We haven't been able to locate them." Ricardo said after he cleared his throat.

"You do realize what you are asking me to do is both unethical and illegal. I could lose my license for this."

Ricardo seemed unperturbed. "I'm not asking you to do anything unethical or illegal. All we want you to do is come to Mississippi with us and examine both Lacy and her mother and give us your professional opinion as to their mental states. If, after speaking with both of them you don't feel there is some basis for my argument of temporary insanity or justifiable homicide, you walk away with your fee. No harm done."

"Why me? Why can't you find someone local in Mississippi?"

"Honestly, this wasn't my decision. It was my boy, Brody's. He has a lot of respect for you. He told me you cared about more than money. If it were up to me, I'd pay out the ass for a local." Ricardo tossed some plane tickets on the coffee table and shrugged his shoulders.

Brody said, "Max, Lacy tried to kill the man to get away. He told her he killed her sister in cold blood. Lacy's mom came home and found dude bleeding in the bathroom. She put two and two together and she snapped. Plain and simple. It's a clear cut case, man. Don't you want to see for yourself? Just go see for yourself, man. No strings attached."

Max looked like he was stunned. I knew there was still some bad blood between Max and Brody so I had no idea how this was going to turn out. I did the only thing left that I knew how to do, I prayed.

CHAPTER TWENTY-FOUR
LACY BATES

I didn't so much find my mother, as she found me. We were being escorted from our cells for free time in the quad. I was still getting use to my surroundings and still nervous about being around the other women. As was my habit when I was nervous or afraid, I walked with my head down. As if people couldn't see me if our eyes didn't connect. The ritual started with the unlocking of the cells. Two by two we fell in line until everyone was out on the tier. As I walked pass my mother she said, "Hold your head up." She used to say it to me all the time so hearing it again surprised me. I don't think she said it because she knew it was me. I really do believe she said it out of habit.

Our eyes locked and I could tell she was just as shocked as I was to see her. For a second, I was excited and I almost broke the line to give her a hug. She shook her head no and I remembered where the fuck I was. I kept walking with my head held high until we had reached the quad. I walked over to the far side of the yard to be alone. Being on the yard was the scariest part about being in jail to me. Since I had been there, I had seen at least seven fights in under a week. Part of me understood the aggression these ladies felt. The other part of me was terrified I would be next. I wasn't afraid of a scrap between me and someone else. I could handle myself well thanks to my sister. It was these quad fights where four or five fuckers jumped the unsuspecting girl that scared the piss out of me.

My mother walked up to me and sat on the bench next to me. We stared at each other for a few seconds, neither of us breaking the silence. "He told me you were dead." my mother said.

"Is that why you killed him?" She nodded her head without taking her eyes off me.

"I tried to kill him too. I'm glad he's gone. He used to hurt us."

Tears ran down my mother's face. "What are you doing here?"

"I came looking for you." It was true even though I didn't know it at the time. I might have tried to tell myself I didn't care about her but the moment I found out she was in jail I couldn't rest.

"Is London okay too?" There was no denying the hopeful expression on my mother's face. It tore at my heart strings with its familiarity. I wore the same expression.

"I don't think so. He told me she was dead. When I couldn't find her, I believed him."

"You friend, Mr. Mason, told me you were alive. I guess I didn't really believe it until I saw you walking down the tier. I thought I had lost you both."

"You met Brody?" I was surprised by his reach.

"Yes, he came to see me a couple of days ago."

"What did he say?" Despite the conditions of our make shift reunion, I couldn't help but to feel hopeful that things were going to be okay.

"He told me not to speak with anyone until he sent someone to speak with me. I sure as hell didn't expect him to send you. However did you manage it?"

I shook my head. "Brody didn't send me. I managed to do this shit all by myself. Although it didn't turn out exactly as I had hoped it would."

"What happened to your eye?"

"I was in a car accident."

"When did you learn how to drive?"

"I've known how to drive for years. Problem is I never got a license. That's why I'm here."

"Baby, I can't protect you in here."

All of my bitterness and anger came back in a flash as if it had never left. "You didn't do such a hot job out there either." My mother recoiled as if I had slapped her. In essence, maybe I had.

"Lacy, I—"

"It's too late for that mother. It won't change anything. And honestly, I don't want to dwell on it. I know that I sound bitter now, but I have honestly moved past the hurt and the pain. I just needed to tell you that for my own sanity. There was a time when my sister and I really needed you, and you weren't there. That's the ugly truth of the matter."

"I'm sorry. I failed you two. I should have known what was happening but I guess I didn't want to see it."

"I won't argue with you there. We tried to tell you but you weren't listening. I used to stay up late at night trying to figure out how I could make you see. I still don't understand it."

"I thought I needed him to survive. He used to tell me I did all the time. I didn't realize I was sleeping with the enemy."

"What made you wake up?"

"When I came home and found him bleeding in your tub. I couldn't deny it any longer. He wanted me to help him. He begged me to call nine-one-one. I made him tell me why he was in your bathroom bleeding. That's when he told me he killed you both. I lost it and I cut off his dick."

"You did what?" I shouted. I was so happy I could have kissed her. She finished what I was trying to do and I loved it.

"I sure did and then I took the super glue from your room and filled his pee hole with it. I got it nice and firm and I stuck it to his forehead. I wanted everyone to know what a dick head he really was."

I rolled over on my side laughing. It almost made everything that we had been through worth it. My only regret was that I didn't get to see it myself. I laughed so hard, I cried. The bell sounded ending our yard time.

"We will talk tomorrow or at dinner," my mother whispered as she went to get into her place in line.

I was still laughing after I entered my cell. Short of finding my sister, my mother had delivered the best news I had ever heard. I finally felt vindicated and the feeling was wondrous.

CHAPTER TWENTY-FIVE
JORDAN BREE

Max was sitting in the restaurant having a cup of coffee and reading the newspaper when I walked in. I was hoping he was an early riser and I was pleased to see that he was, especially since he could have ordered room service and called it a day. I wanted to speak to him alone before he went to the prison to visit Lacy. I owed him that much. I felt like I never gave him the closure he deserved.

"Good morning Max. You are up bright and early." I put my cup of coffee on the table and took the seat next to him.

Max smiled, "Force of habit. I never was one to loll around in bed when day light was burning. What are you doing up so early?"

"Most days, I'm an early bird too. This morning I got up to speak with you. We haven't had a moment alone and I wanted to see how you were doing."

"Me? I'm fine. Why wouldn't I be?" Max gazed at me suspiciously over the rim of his cup.

"I don't know. I guess I'm feeling a little guilty for not staying in touch with you. I owe you so much. I didn't want you to think I had forgotten all that you did for me."

"Nonsense. You made your choice. I mean, uh…" Max turned bright red, which was hard for a black man to do. Even the tips of his ears were red.

"Max, it was never about a choice for me. As my doctor, I never looked at you as anything other than a professional. Perhaps if we had met under different circumstances, things might have been different."

"You don't owe me any explanations Jordan. I'm a foolish old man with a childish fantasy. I'm man enough to admit it to you."

"You need to quit. There ain't a thing about you that is old and you know it. The reason I chose Brody over you, has little to do with age. I could have just as easily fallen for you, had the situation been different. I opened up to you on a professional level whereas with Brody, it was more personal. Please don't hold that against me or Brody."

"Trust me. If I held a grudge, I wouldn't be here right now."

"That's good to know. So, what are you doing these days now that the hospital is closed?"

"I have a small practice which pays the bills. I can't complain."

I signaled for the waiter to refresh our coffees. We waited in silence until he had refreshed both of our cups. Something about the air was different. I didn't feel all the tension between us which was present before we spoke.

"After this is over, I really wish you would consider taking Lacy on as a client. She has a lot of repressed hostility. She needs someone she can trust to talk to other than me."

"That would be entirely up to Lacy. If she needs me, I don't have a problem working her into my schedule. This will have to be her choice. I'm done talking to patients whose only interest in seeing me is through a court order."

"It makes a difference?"

"Sure it does. If someone comes to see me willingly they are more likely to listen to suggestions. Those that don't are only there to satisfy the requirements of the court. When they leave, they are just as nutty as the day they come to me. I didn't get in this business for that. I legitimately want to help people understand mental illness."

"That's one of the things I love about you Max." I saw hope blossom in his eyes for a brief second before he looked away. I could only pray time would heal him from his infatuation with me.

"How much has Lacy told you about the man her mother is accused of killing?"

"Pretty much all of it I think. You never know with Lacy. She and I got into a huge argument when I found out that she was related to Mrs. Gates, from the home."

"Are you shitting me? That would have thrown me for a loop too. I remember all the not so kind things she used to say about her."

"Yeah, we were both mean to her. When this is all over, I'm going to visit her. I may even donate some money to her home to help spruce things up around there."

"That would be really nice of you Jordan."

"It's the least I can do. I'm just sorry I didn't think about it sooner."

"Better late than never."

TINA BROOKS MCKINNEY

"I guess. Mrs. Gates' was related to Lacy. When Lacy ran away from home, she fled to her mother's sister. They hadn't spoken in years. Mrs. Gates took her in because she thought she was homeless. Who knew the witch had a good side after all."

"You did not just call that woman a witch. Shame on you Jordan Bree!"

"I said it with love," I said laughing. It was good to laugh with Max again.

"What else do I need to know?"

I thought about it for several seconds before I answered him. I was walking a thin line of confidence. I didn't want Lacy to feel like I had betrayed her trust, but I needed Max to understand the horrors Lacy had to deal with growing up. In time Lacy may have told him all on her own. I just wanted her out of jail sooner, rather than later.

"Lacy and her sister were abused throughout their childhood. She probably won't show it to you, but her entire back is marked with iron burns from Karl Wester. He was a sadistic son-of-a-bitch who liked to sleep with children. He even made them watch each other as he raped them."

"Damn. You know, you hear about this shit on television and you shake your head. It's different when you find out it has happened to someone you know."

"I know, right. When Lacy told me, I wanted to kill the bastard myself. When London disappeared, Lacy thought her sister had left her. She felt abandoned. Wester told her she was dead and she went ape shit. She tried to kill him and then ran away to Atlanta."

Max cocked his head and smiled at me. "You really love her, don't you?"

"I really do. She's the only family I have left." I felt close to tears when I said this because it was coming from my heart.

"And Brody?"

"I intend to marry him. He completes me."

Max cringed. "I guess you can't ask for anything better than that. We better get moving. Lacy's arraignment is in a few hours. I want to make sure I speak with her before it begins."

I reached across the table and squeezed Max's hand. "Thanks for helping with this Max. It really means so much to me."

"It's going to be okay. I have a good feeling about it now."

***

Brody was just stepping out of the shower when I let myself back into the room. "Hey, beautiful. Where have you been? I was about to come looking for you."

"I wanted to talk to Max before the hearing." Brody winced but otherwise continued to dry himself off.

"Is he okay?" Brody was trying to act nonchalant but I knew him better than that.

"He's good. I just wanted to see where his head was at."

"Good idea. We don't need any surprises. Ricardo is going to move forward as the attorney for Lacy's mother. He thinks if he can get Lacy to testify to the abuse, the judge might reduce her sentence to manslaughter."

"Brody, no! Lacy will die if her mother has to stay in jail."

"Honey, manslaughter is a hell of a lot better than death by lethal injection. He might even been able to get it reduced to justifiable homicide, but don't get your hopes up."

I walked over to my closet and pulled out the drab blue suit I had purchased for Lacy to wear to court and laid it over the bed. "Lacy is going to die when she sees this cheap-ass suit. I'm glad I'm not going to be there to see her face when she sees it."

"She is not going to be happy, but we can't have her going in there looking like a million dollars. Perception is everything. We need her to look the part of a runaway who came home when she found out her mother was in trouble."

"That should be easy because it's true."

CHAPTER TWENTY-SIX
LACY BATES

I was truly scared as I sat in the quad for what I hoped would be my last time. My mother came up and sat beside me.

"Today's the big day huh?"

I nodded my head glumly. "Yup."

"Why the sad face then?"

"I don't know. Nerves, I guess."

"You will be fine. All you have to remember is to keep calm and don't let your mouth write a check your ass can't cash."

I chuckled a little bit. The only good thing that had come out of this entire situation was the relationship I was building with my mother. It wasn't something that I ever expected to happen. "I know. I promised Max that I would be on my best behavior."

"He seems like a nice guy. He's very easy to talk to."

"He is a nice guy. I don't know why I never saw that before."

"You never did tell me how you guys met."

"It's sort of a long story and when you get out of here, I promise to tell you all of it."

"About that—" Luetta started but didn't finish.

I could almost hear bells going off in my head. "What? Have you heard something?" My fingers tightened together in a tiny ball and I began rocking back and forth.

"Hey, remember you are going to remain calm. No matter what you hear or how you feel, you have to remain calm on the outside."

"What were you going to say?"

"I don't want you making any plans for me. My faith is not certain and there is a very real possibility that I won't be walking out of here. You have to face that."

As much as I wanted to mask the emotions, I was feeling I couldn't. I wanted to just sit there and cry even though this wasn't the time and the place for it. "Don't say that."

"It's the truth, Lacy. Regardless of my reasons, I killed a man and I am going to be punished for it."

"He deserved to die for what he did!" I said between pinched lips.

"I agree with you. I have absolutely no remorse for what I've done. That is why I'm okay with whatever happens to me because of it. I just don't want you to go in a downward spiral if things don't turn out the way you want them to."

I understood the logic in my mother's words however, my heart wasn't ready to accept them. I wanted to believe that justice had prevailed and Wester got what was coming to him. "You can't go into this with a defeated mindset. If you give up before the fight has even started then Wester wins."

"Who said anything about giving up? I'm going to fight this with all my heart."

"Good. That's what I want to hear." I felt slightly better knowing that she wasn't giving up.

"But, if I don't win. I don't want you spending a fortune on my defense fighting for an appeal. Nor do I want to be spending eight or nine years on death row. I need you to promise me you won't do that to me. I want you to just let me go."

I looked at my mother with what I know was a horrified expression on my face. "Are you kidding me? You ain't on life support with no hope of recovery. I can't just walk away especially since I am the reason you are in this hell hole in the first place."

"You are not the reason why I'm here. I'm the reason!" Luetta shouted which caused a momentary stillness on the quad as the other inmates braced themselves for what they may have thought would be another fight.

"Keep your voice down," I hissed.

Luetta lowered her head. "Promise me or I'll scream bloody murder."

I could not believe she would do that. Not only would she ruin my chances of getting out of here today, she would make it harder for herself. "Fine, I promise. But things aren't going to go that way. You'll see. You don't know what we are working with. You have the best criminal attorney money can buy."

"I have no doubts about that. Ricardo seems very competent. But don't forget where we are. We are in the dirty south. Things happen a little bit differently down here."

My heart sank. She was right. Things were different in the south. "They can fuck with your case if they want to. But they will have the biggest shit storm coming their way and it won't come from me."

"What do you mean?"

"I'm talking about my friend Brody. He will write a story on your case that will make the entire world sit up and take notice. He did the same thing for my friend Jordan who you haven't met yet. I'll do what you ask me to do but you have to promise me something in return."

"What's that?"

"Don't give up on me! I'll see you on the other side."

"Okay, baby. I won't give up."

The guard shouted, "Time!" We all had to file back in line to go inside. I smiled at my mother one more time before I took my place in line. My mother smiled back at me.

***

When I entered the court room, I was actually shaking. My handcuffs were jangling against my wrists. This was my first experience with the legal system and I didn't know what to expect. Even though Ricardo had prepped me, it didn't do anything to alleviate my fears. Added to my discomfort was the hideous suit and shoes that Jordan had brought for me to wear.

I took my seat next to Ricardo and he leaned over and whispered in my ear. "Try to relax. Do not let any emotions show on your face. Okay?"

I was so nervous, I couldn't even answer him if I tried, so I just nodded my head.

"All rise," the bailiff said.

I struggled to stand but my legs acted like they didn't remember what their purpose was. Ricardo pulled me to me feet. "You got this kid. Buck up."

I was glad he was so confident. I looked over my shoulder at Jordan and Brody and they nodded back at me. I gave them a small smile and turned back around to face the judge. Jordan's eyes were red so I could tell that she had been crying. I didn't blame her, I felt like crying too.

"In the matter of state versus Lacy Bates. Am I to understand you have waived the right to a jury trial?"

Ricardo and I stood up and addressed the court. "Your honor before you read the charges, may I approach the bench?" Ricardo said.

"I would like for your client to answer the question first." Judge stated.

"Yes I do," I said.

"You may approach."

Ricardo grabbed my file off the table and approached the bench. I knew what he was going to say so I was not worried. He was going to try to get the judge to dismiss before judgment, all references to failure to stop and evading the police on the grounds of temporary insanity. He had already settled with the rental car company, so that was not an issue. I glanced over my shoulder at Jordan and she appeared to be ready to jump right out of her chair. "It's okay," I mouthed.

Ricardo and the judge talked for several minutes. It was a very terse exchange but I couldn't hear a word of it and neither could the rest of the people sitting in the courtroom. On the surface, it didn't look as if things were going in my favor. Through it all, I remained standing even though my Payless shoes were trying to cut off the circulation to my toes.

Finally, Ricardo returned to his seat. His face was rock solid and didn't give me any indication of what was about to happen. I closed my eyes for a brief moment as I fought back the tears I knew were coming.

"The court will have a fifteen minute recess while I review these documents," the judge said as he banged his gavel.

"All rise," the bailiff shouted.

We continued to stand until the judge had left the room. I could hear Brody and Jordan talking but I was too afraid to look at them. Instead I turned to Ricardo. "Well?"

"We wait. I think I presented a pretty good argument. Of course, I pissed him off but he will get over it."

"What do you mean you pissed him off?" I felt a surge of panic coming. I didn't know Ricardo but I had placed a lot of blind faith in him because he was a friend of Brody's.

"I don't think he likes niggers being in his courtroom trying to tell him how to do his job. Don't worry, it's going to be okay."

"I'm glad you're feeling all confident because I can honestly tell you I am not."

"Trust me, if this doesn't work, I have got some more tricks up my sleeve. The fact that your mother is still in jail works in your favor. I also believe it will work in hers."

CHAPTER TWENTY-SEVEN
LUETTA GATES

I waited until Lacy had left the room before I spoke. "You must think I'm a terrible person. I've made such a mess of things." We were sitting in the interview room at the Panola County Courthouse waiting for a verdict. I wasn't wearing prison garb today. Lacy had brought me a simple black dress. She had even managed to get my unruly hair into an acceptable french roll. I could really use a perm and a little color to tame my unruly locks. I also wasn't ready to embrace the strands of gray that were sprouting up on my head since I had been locked up. With the exception of the shackle on my left arm, we looked like normal people.

Max shifted in his chair. "I'm not here to judge you Miss Gates." Max was looking very handsome in a black suit with a skinny red tie. His head was glistening as if he had just oiled it before entering the room. I wanted to tell him how nice he looked but I was afraid.

Even though I didn't know him very well, I could tell he was uncomfortable. I couldn't help but wonder if it was me or the courtroom setting that had him wound up tighter than an old fashioned clock.

"You can tell me, I can take it. I think this place is making me emotionally stronger." Even as I said this, I thought about the many nights I cried myself to sleep. During the day, I wore this hard mask to hide my fear, but at night that cold exterior shell folded like a deck of cards.

Max shifted in his seat again. "I think you are doing remarkably well given the circumstances. Life behind bars has to be hard."

I shook my head angrily. I wasn't talking about prison life. I was referring to my life in general. "This ain't a big deal. I would do it again if I had to. I almost destroyed both of my girls. Lacy probably hates me and I have no idea what happened to London. How will they ever forgive me?"

"I can't speak about London, but Lacy loves you. She may harbor some resentment for a little while, but I think she has already forgiven you, especially knowing you did stand up for her."

I felt a stirring of hope. If I had to go through the rest of my life with her hating me, then they might as well kill me. "How do you know this? Did she tell you?"

"Well, she didn't come right out and say it, but I can tell. Why else would she make these weekly trips with me? She doesn't have to. She could have just walked away."

I felt my little flicker of hope diminish a bit. "That doesn't mean she has forgiven me. She might be doing it because she thinks she has to."

"You obviously don't know your daughter very well. She doesn't do anything unless she wants to," Max insisted.

"So you know her pretty well? Are you two dating?" I was slightly envious of my child. I wanted her to have all the things in life I didn't have, including the love of a good man; however, not this particular good man.

"Heaven's no! Lacy is too young for me. We are good friends." Max shifted some more in his seat.

"Humph, I've never known a man who was satisfied with just being friends with an attractive woman. Y'all have ulterior motives." I picked at the seam of my shirt so I didn't have to look him in the face.

"Believe me. It's possible. Maybe you have just been meeting the wrong type of man."

"Ain't no maybe in it. I mean what kind of woman am I, that I attract pedophiles and infidels?"

"Woman quit. Most sex offenders don't wear signs on their foreheads. Stop being so hard on yourself."

"How come I didn't see what was happening to my own children? This is the question that nags me at night. I alternate between being mad at Wester and being mad at myself. Some days I can't make myself look in the mirror. Wester wasn't the first asshole I had gotten involved with either. The girls father wasn't shit either. Therefore, I have to be doing something wrong."

"Was he a molester too?" Deep creases appeared on Max's forehead as if he were troubled.

"Not at all. He was a man of the church."

"They seem to be the worst ones sometime."

"This guy was married and was the pastor." I sounded stupid for just saying it. I fell for his bullshit like a ton of bricks.

"That is one message that shouldn't be sent; especially coming from a clergy man. I don't mean any harm, but it's things like this that keep me away from church."

"You don't believe in God?" I was more than a little surprised by his admission.

"I absolutely do! It's these people masquerading as God's messengers that I have a problem with. I have a major issue with the pastor being more interested in what you can do for him than the other way around. You have some pastors living in mansions while his congregation is struggling to keep a roof over their heads. Where is the church when Sally Joe's lights are being cut off? Or, when sister Buhlia can't put food on her table because her less than minimum wage job doesn't stretch far enough to keep up with inflation?"

"Wow, tell me how you really feel. I feel like I struck a nerve with you."

"Yes, you did. Because these same people do without so that these pastors can continue flossing. These pastors feed on people. To me, they are no better than parasites."

"I'm sorry I brought it up." I hated to see his beautiful face scowled up.

"No, I'm sorry for reacting that way. We have gotten way off topic. What about your father? Did you have a good relationship with him?"

"Not really. He was hardly ever around. He was always working. He had to pay for that house. I believe that is what killed him."

"Is that why you wanted your sister to sell the house?"

For a few seconds I didn't know what to say. "She told you about that? My sister can't hold water. When this mess is over, I'm going to have a long talk with her."

"Don't be mad at her. She was only trying to help you."

"How is she helping me by telling my business? Got me looking like a gold digger."

"She was assisting me. I wanted to know more about you before I agreed to come here and talk with you. The judge required me to submit a profile of you before he consented in letting me speak with you. Your sister was instrumental in that process."

"So, I should be thanking her?" I never thought I would see the day where I would be thanking my sister for anything.

"I think so. She loves you as well," Max said with confidence.

"If you say so." I wasn't feeling it. If she loved me, wouldn't she try to find me?

Max cleared his throat bringing me back to the conversation. "There is still something that is confusing me."

"What? I feel like I have told you everything except my bra size." I laughed nervously. I didn't mean to say that last part out loud.

"Typically, women chose mates with the same characteristics as their father. In your case, Wester seems like the complete opposite. Was that by your design?"

I nodded my head. "I guess it was. I didn't want a man that didn't have time for me. I wanted someone that was going to make me a priority. In the beginning, Wester did all that. Was I wrong for wanting that?"

"No, I don't think you were wrong for wanting to feel valued, but part of caring for a woman is providing for them. There needs to be a balance. I'm not saying that a woman should stay home barefoot and pregnant. Since Wester wasn't working, it is apparent to me he wanted you to take care of him."

"He did want that. He said I should want to do it to keep him happy. He would remind me on a regular basis that what I wouldn't do for him, another woman would. He said all those women at the casino wanted him."

"I strongly doubt that. The women I spoke to feared him. That's a damn shame that he lied to you about all of that. Relationships shouldn't be like that. I guess I'm old school. If you were my woman, I would show you how it's supposed to be done."

I was caught off guard. I didn't know what to say. Was he trying to trick me into making a fool of myself? "If I didn't know better, I would say that almost sounded like a proposition. I'm glad I'm not dumb enough to believe you would even consider spending time with someone in my situation."

"Why is that so hard for you to believe? You are a beautiful woman."

This had to be some kind of trick; one that I didn't appreciate at all. "You don't have to lie to me Max. I know I look a hot mess." I patted my hair self consciously.

"Apparently, you don't see what I see. We can table this discussion until you get out."

"Are you serious?" I felt my heart start to beat a little faster.

Max smiled brightly, "I can show you, better than I can tell you."

The bailiff came in before I could respond. Max left the room as I was being unchained from the table. A broad smile on my face illuminated the room, even as my hands were being cuffed, hopefully, for the last time. I was ready for anything.

CHAPTER TWENTY-EIGHT
LACY BATES

"Are you sure you want to do this? It's not too late to make a run for it," I said laughing as I put the final touches on Jordan's makeup.

"Girl, don't tempt me. I have knots the size of bowling balls in my stomach. If I jump up and down, I can even hear them."

"They ain't basketballs you are feeling Negro. Those are babies and I suggest you stop jumping around and mixing them up."

"The babies aren't that big yet. I'm telling you, these are knots."

"If I let you back out of this, Brody would hunt my ass down and I'm tired of running."

"I know that's right. We have done enough running for ten people."

"You ain't lying. In between going back and forth to Mississippi to visit my mother and my parole officer, a sister is tired. Once I marry you off, this lady is going on vacation."

"Vacation, huh? All by yourself? Or will a certain gentleman friend be joining you?" Jordan teased.

"Now you are trying to get all up in my business," I said laughing.

"You ain't got any business when it comes to me. We are sisters and we don't keep secrets. Right?"

"Yeah, if you say so." I turned away so Jordan could not see that I was about to get emotional. I didn't want to mar her special day with tears, but I couldn't help the way that I felt. It was different than when she was just dating Brody. Now that they were about to be married and have children of their own, I couldn't help but feel left out. Like she was moving forward and I was still standing still.

"Of course I say so. You are one of the most important people in the world to me." Jordan stood up and turned me around.

"You look beautiful Jordan. I still don't understand why you didn't go for the big church wedding instead of going to the courthouse. Didn't you want to walk down the aisle with all the pomp and circumstance?"

"No. Not really. As a child I might have dreamt of the big fantasy wedding. Now that I'm older, none of that means anything to me. I just want to spend my special day with the people I love."

"Well you have got a crowd out there waiting for you. The waiting room is packed. My aunt brought all the girls from her home too."

"Aww, really? She didn't have to do that."

"Are you kidding me? She really appreciates what you did for the home. Setting up that educational scholarship in her name was huge. Not to mention the renovations you had done on the home. She loves you like a daughter she never had."

"I love her too."

"Are you ready? I'm sure the natives are getting restless. Especially your husband to be."

"He will wait. I'm not going through that door until I know what is going on with you and Max. Every time I bring him up, you politely change the subject. It's obvious to me that he cares about you."

"Girl, why are we talking about that right now? You have a wedding to go to. We can talk about Max later."

"How much later? You know Brody and I leave for our honeymoon right after the ceremony. I don't know when we are going to get the chance to sit down and talk like we used to."

I didn't bother to hide my pouting lips. I wasn't a big proponent of change. Once we walked out the door, our lives would change. "We will talk boo. I'm going to insist on it. Even if that means I have to hijack you from your husband."

"Girl, please. Wild horses couldn't keep me away from your crazy butt. Don't forget you are the godmother so I'm going to need you around often."

"Are you still going to name one of the babies London if it's a girl?"

"I sure am and the other one will be Theresa. If it's a boy, I still think we can call him London but we will change the other one to Terry. Brody has already agreed to it."

"It's a shame we never found out what actually happened to my sister. Sometimes, it still wakes me up at night."

"I know babe. Not knowing is the hardest. I hate that we weren't able to find out anything else. But at least your mom will be okay in a couple of years."

"Yeah, she'll be straight. She gets out in a year or two. With the money Brody got us by selling our stories to Lifetime, she won't have to scramble for money, or be a sucker for the first dick that gets hard looking at her."

"Damn, Lacy, must you be so crude."

"It is what it is. Now, bitch, are you ready to get married?"

"Catch fire, bitch."

309

ABOUT THE AUTHOR

Tina Brooks McKinney is the author of several novels. All That Drama, Lawd, Mo' Drama, Fool, Stop Trippin', Dubious, Deep Deception, Snapped, Deep Deception 2, Snapped 2: The Redemption, Catch Fire. She has also participated in two anthologies, Around The Way Girls 8 and Don't Ask, Don't Tell. She is a wife, mother of two.

In 2014 look for some of those books to be republished through Taboo Publishing Company.

She began her writing career on a dare and continues to entertain us with stories from her vast imagination. She is currently working on the third installment of the book Snapped. For more information about Tina, visit her website www.tinamckinney.com. Or, shoot her an email at tybrooks2@yahoo.com. She would love to hear from you. Until next time happy reading.

www.ingramcontent.com/pod-product-compliance
Lightning Source LLC
Chambersburg PA
CBHW021458240626
47154CB00002B/429